Wilma's Outlaw

Agnes Alexander

A Wings ePress, Inc.
Western Romance

Wings Press, Inc.

Wings ePress, Inc.

Edited by: Jeanne Smith
Copy Edited by: Joan C. Powell
Executive Editor: Jeanne Smith
Cover Artist: Trisha FitzGerald-Jung

Wings ePress Books
www.wingsepress.com

Copyright © 2021 by: Agnes Alexander
ISBN-13: 978-1-61309-546-1

Published In the United States Of America

Wings ePress Inc.
3000 N. Rock Road
Newton, KS 67114

Dedication

To the sweet lady who won a drawing to have her name put in this
book, Cathy Chalfant, and her husband, Gaylord. Friends of mine
and all-around good people.
Hugs, Agnes aka Lynette

* * *

One

When he heard the rattle of a buggy and the clomp-clomp of a horse's hoofs on the dirt road that circled the graveyard, Clay Hunter paused on the way to his mother's grave. He hadn't expected to run into anyone as he visited the area this time of day. Grace was usually working or taking care of her husband and wouldn't come until later, though he knew she wouldn't fail to come, since it was their mother's birthday.

Knowing he couldn't yet be seen in Settlers Ridge, he turned his horse into the woods surrounding the hill-top graveyard where he would be out of sight. He hoped the people in the buggy wouldn't be the first of a group of people coming for a burial.

Looking around, he didn't see an open grave and decided it was probably someone coming to leave flowers, or visit the grave of a family member. He couldn't help sighing as he wondered how long this interruption would hold him up, because he knew he couldn't stay there for a long time. Not that it mattered unless someone happened to see him. He'd try to relax and wait until they were gone. Then as he always did, he'd give his mother one of the wildflowers growing nearby, say a quick prayer and be on his way.

It wasn't that Clay wouldn't like to see some of his old friends in Settlers Ridge, and he'd especially like to see his sister, Grace. But he knew that was impossible. Currently, anyway. He certainly didn't want to put anyone in jeopardy, especially his little sister. Of course, she wasn't little any longer.

By slipping in and out of town, he'd been able to sporadically keep up with her progression into adulthood. Because he'd been worried after the fire which claimed their parents' lives, he'd taken his first chance to find out if she was all right. He felt better to learn she'd been befriended by the Olsen family who owned the hotel in town. It pleased him when he found out they had not only given her a job and a place to live but treated her like family.

After that he had come as often as he could, and he always tried to slip in on or around his mother's birthday each year.

Then, last year Grace had married the town's popular sheriff, Lance Gentry. He remembered Lance, who was a couple of years older than he. That made him eight or nine years older than Grace. He also knew Lance was Nelda Gentry Barrington's older brother. He recalled Lance as a handsome man who many of the single ladies wanted to claim as their own. Though he was a little surprised Grace had accomplished what many other single women hadn't been able to do, he knew she deserved the best. He also knew she'd never have married Gentry if she wasn't in love with him. He hoped the man, who everyone thought of as a ladies-man and a confirmed bachelor, felt the same way about his sister. He didn't want to see Grace hurt. She was too special for that. Always had been.

The buggy came to a stop and the man got out. He hitched the horse to a nearby bush, then reached up, took the baby the woman held out and put it in the crook of his arm. He then held his hand out to help his wife to the ground.

Clay's breath caught in his throat as he recognized his sister and her husband. Did they have a baby? Of course they did, or they wouldn't have one with them. He couldn't help smiling as he wondered if he had a niece or a nephew.

He saw Grace's face as she turned and took a bouquet of flowers from the buggy, then joined her husband and baby. He was glad he'd seen her, because there was no way to describe the way she looked except everything about her showed she was a happy woman.

This pleased him and he had the urge to rush to them and tell her how much he had missed her through the years and how good it was to see her again. But no matter how badly he wanted to, he had to hold himself back. It wasn't yet the time, and he wasn't sure when or if it ever would be. Those in power still had some things to clear up with that foreign government before he could sever his involvement with them and get on with the rest of his life.

Long after he watched the little family at the grave, he stayed in the woods remembering the sight. He would go away today with the picture of his sister walking back to the buggy. Her husband had the baby in one arm and the other one around her shoulder as if he were comforting her. He helped her into the buggy, then handed her the baby before he walked around and got in. As they started to pull away, he saw Lance lean over and touch Grace's cheek, then kiss her the way a man kisses the woman he truly loves. When they rode off, she was smiling and had her head on his shoulder. He had his free arm around her. Clay knew they were a happy family, and this pleased him.

As the buggy pulled out of sight, Clay moved to his mother's grave. He wasn't about to toss Grace's flowers away. He simply moved them to the side, then knelt and placed the one wildflower beside her bouquet. For the first time, he wondered if, through the years, Grace had seen his offerings to their mother. If so, he hoped she found comfort in them. Maybe if she had, she'd realize he'd never forgotten her or their mother.

Standing, he said, "I love you, Mama, and I know Grace does, too. You would be so proud to know she's a happily married woman with a baby of her own. Someday soon, maybe I can tell her I saw your grandchild when it was tiny. God willing, maybe I can then become a part of their lives."

He said a silent prayer, then took up the reins and climbed on his horse. "I'll be back whenever I can, Mama. I think they will, but if the government doesn't release me before, I'll see you close to your next birthday."

Pulling his hat down, he turned his horse and rode in the direction of Cheyenne. At the moment, he was anxious to see how his assignment stood, and he knew he had to get back to headquarters as quickly as possible to find out.

~ * ~

Wilma Lawson stood behind the counter of Barrington's Mercantile, sorting the mail the stage had left during its midday stop. The bells over the door jangled and she looked up to see Grace. She had baby Kathrine in her arms.

"Hello, my friend. Come in and let me see that precious bundle." Wilma dropped the mail to the counter and smiled.

"You can take this bundle if you wish. She's getting heavy."

"Well, come here, sweetheart. Your Auntie Wilma will hold you. She doesn't think you're heavy at all."

"She's only heavy if you get stopped on the street by Juliette Cramer, and the woman insists on talking on and on and on."

Wilma laughed. "I didn't know you'd become good enough friends to have long conversations with her."

Grace smiled. "How could we become good friends? That woman still wants my husband."

"I thought she had given up trying to get Lance away from you."

"We thought so, too. After our marriage, she mainly left us alone. There would be a snide comment now and then, especially when I became pregnant. Lance says she has once again begun to pop into the office with the silliest of excuses every week or so. Since Kathrine's birth, her visits to him have become more frequent."

"She is persistent, isn't she?"

"That she is. She told me she'd been by the office today and Lance wasn't in. She said she was concerned he might be sick. I told her he was fine...then she wanted to know if the baby was keeping him awake and because of lack of sleep he was having trouble doing his job. She

8

kept on about how the job of sheriff would be hard on a man with a wife and child, and maybe he should rethink his decision to be married and have a baby."

Wilma shook her head. "What did you say to her?"

"After I'd listened as long as I could stand it, I told her our marriage was a solid happy one and she was wasting her time trying to take my husband. I even suggested that if she didn't want to end up an unhappy old spinster, she should stop acting the fool. Then maybe one of the single men in town might pay her some attention instead of laughing behind her back because she kept pining after a married man."

Wilma laughed out loud. "Then what did she say?"

"I'm not sure, but I think she called me a bitch as she slung her head around and walked away."

"I'm proud of you, Grace. Maybe you actually got through to her."

"I doubt it. I think after she walked off, she headed back to the jail. I was tired and Kathrine was getting heavy, so I came here to get what I needed for supper. Then I'm heading home."

"I'm sure you'll hear about her visit to him at supper."

"I'm sure of it, too. He keeps threatening to put her in jail if she doesn't leave him alone."

"He should do it." Wilma smiled down at the baby. "Kathrine sure is growing and she gets prettier every time I see her."

"Thank you. We kind of think she's pretty, too. In fact, no matter how many times I tell him not to, Lance is spoiling her."

"I don't doubt that." Wilma smiled at her friend. "Did you need something, or did you and Kathrine just come in here to get away from Miss Cramer?"

"I do need something. It's my mother's birthday and as you know, I always make a special dessert on her birthday like she did on ours when we were little. Tonight, I decided on one of Lance's favorite—cherry cobbler. I need to pick up some things including a couple of pounds of sugar. I'm running a little low."

Wilma handed her the baby and stooped to measure out two pounds of sugar. "I suppose you've been to the graveyard."

"Yes, and before you ask, there was no wildflower there. If Clay is in town, he hasn't been to the graveyard."

"I sure wish he'd get in touch with you, Grace. I know it breaks your heart to see those lone flowers on the grave and know he's been there."

"It does, but I'm trying to accept it. It has gotten easier as time passes. I know he's only coming to visit Mama's grave, and not me, though I wish it were different."

Before Wilma could answer, the bell over the door jangled and Luella Baldwin, the mayor's wife, walked in. Wilma knew her conversation with Grace was over. "Hello, Louella."

"Hello, ladies." She headed toward them. "Looks like I came in time to see that beautiful daughter of yours, Grace."

Grace nodded to Wilma, letting her know she understood they'd have to talk about Clay later. Turning to Luella, she said, "Kathrine is always happy to have the attention."

"I'm so glad, because I sure want to get my hands on her."

Grace handed Luella the baby. "Since you've been kind enough to babysit, Luella, I'll gather the other items I need to cook supper."

"I'll be more than happy to, and by all means, take your time." She looked down at the baby. "We don't care how much time she takes, do we, Kathrine?"

~ * ~

Late in the evening, two days later, Clay arrived at headquarters. It pleased him to see a light burning in the general's office. He hoped there would be some word about his fate, so instead of going to his quarters, he headed directly to the office.

Clay was not only surprised to find he'd been released from his duty to the government, but he was pleased to learn they had kept their word. His record had been wiped clean. Nobody would ever know he'd been a wanted man who had served time in prison. As long as he kept his word to never talk about his work with the army, he was free to go anywhere he desired without fear of his past following him.

At that time in his life, there was nowhere he wanted to go more than home to Settlers Ridge. His only problem was how would his hometown accept him? Most important of all, would his sister welcome him back, or would she prefer he settle somewhere else so she wouldn't have to deal with the fact he'd deserted her and their mother those many years ago?

He decided he'd never know unless he faced her. This time he wouldn't slip in and out as he had done in the past. He'd go in quietly, find a place to stay, get a feel for the situation, then make his presence known.

Decision made, he went to his quarters, gathered his few belongings, and lay down to sleep. At dawn, he climbed on his horse and spurred him through the fort's gate. He tried not to think about the fact it would take two days to reach Settlers Ridge to see if he could resume a normal life in his hometown.

Two

On the second day of Clay's journey home, he busied himself running various scenarios of what he would and should do, and who he'd see first when he reached Settlers Ridge. Not paying attention to what was happening around him, he was almost on top of the wreck before he saw it. Frowning, he jerked the reins and stopped his horse, Whisper.

"What the in the world is going on here?" he muttered, as he jumped from the saddle and moved to the small wagon turned on its side.

He swallowed bile when he moved to the back side and saw the woman. In his years of outlawing, then working for the government, he'd seen all manners of death and torture, but this was one of the most horrendous sights he'd ever encountered.

A middle-aged woman's graying hair was caked with blood from obvious severe blows to her face and head. Her arms had been broken and in one the bone stuck through the skin. The heavy wagon was turned over and her legs just above her knees were pinned under it. It was obvious she had been purposely placed in this position and was left to suffer and die.

Clay moved to check, though he was almost positive she was dead. The instant he touched her, her eyes flew open.

"Get...the...Bible...Save...my...children..."

Stunned, Clay asked, "What did you say?"

"Save...them. Alice...Phoebe...will...help...you."

Knowing the woman was suffering, Clay said, "I need to get this wagon off you, ma'am."

"Too...late. You...a good man...I trust...you." She grabbed his arm. "You're their...only chance. Promise me...you'll take care of them."

Thinking it didn't matter what he agreed to at that point, without hesitation Clay nodded and muttered, "I promise."

"Thank...you." With a smile on her lips, she closed her eyes and her life ebbed away.

Stunned and confused by not only her words, but also his agreement, Clay stared at the lifeless form. Why had he made such a foolish promise?

At the moment, Clay wasn't sure what to do. He knew he couldn't leave her there for the vultures. And what in the world did she mean about the Bible and children and two women named Alice and Phoebe? Why did the dying woman mention him being their only chance? Had she and her family been traveling in this small wagon? If so, where were they?

Knowing there was nothing he could do about any youngsters or the unknown Alice and Phoebe at the moment, he made a quick decision to try to get her from under the wagon so he could bury her, or at least cover her so the animals couldn't get at her before the undertaker picked her up. When he got to Settlers Ridge, he would report what had happened and the sheriff could take over.

The wagon was heavier than he expected, though the contents had mostly been thrown and scattered on the ground. After trying several times to turn it upright by using his shoulder, he knew it wasn't going to happen. Turning to his horse, he said, "I hate to ask you to do this to you, Whisper, but I need your help."

He tied a rope around the top board of the wagon bed, climbed into the saddle, wrapped the rope around the saddle horn and then around his gloved hand, and said, "Here we go."

Whisper backed up on Clay's demand. At first nothing happened. Then the wagon began to rock. The next minute it made a loud creaking sound and with a little more urging, the horse gave one last tug. In another minute, the vehicle was on its four wheels.

"Good girl." Clay relaxed the rope and patted the horse's neck. "I knew you could do it." He jumped from the saddle and grabbed the reins. "You've done your part. I'm going to lead you over there and let you graze near those bushes while I take care of this lady."

As he ground-hitched Whisper, he heard a strange noise, a noise he shouldn't be hearing out in this deserted area. It sounded like a child's whimper. He frowned. It had to be an animal of some kind. After all, he wasn't all that familiar with children or the sounds they made, and he could have mistaken the sound as one from a human.

Then he heard it again. This time he realized it was no animal he'd ever heard. It originated behind the bushes a few feet away. Before he could move to the end of the shrubs to check, a little girl of no more than three, with tears running down her face, darted out and toddled toward him.

Almost instantly, a little boy maybe a couple of years or so older came running behind her. "Come back, Mary. He'll kill you."

The child ignored him, and the next thing Clay knew, the little girl grabbed him around the calf of his left leg and clung tightly as she continued to sob, though no sound came from her.

In a panic-filled voice, the boy screamed, "Please don't kill her, mister. She's just a little girl. She don't know no better."

Clay frowned. "I'm not going to kill her."

The boy stared at him. "You're not?"

"No. I don't kill children."

"Are you sure?"

"Yes, I'm sure." He leaned down and pried the little girl off his leg. "Let go, honey. I need to try to find out what happened here."

As soon as she was free, she looked up at him, shook her head and grabbed his leg again.

"She's just scared, mister."

Clay looked at the little boy, and noticed he held a Bible hugged against his chest. He wondered if this was the Bible the woman had mentioned but he didn't think it was the right time to ask. Instead, he lifted an eyebrow. "Can you tell me what happened here, young man?"

"Don't you know?"

"I know you've had some trouble, but it's kind of hard to figure out. Your mother is...uh...hurt and your horse is gone and, well...I just happened by and found all this." When the boy only stared at him, he added, "If you can tell me what happened, maybe I can help you."

The boy continued to stare at him. "Miss Lucy ain't my real mama."

"Oh? Who is she, then, and why are you with her?"

He shrugged. "I don't know who she is. But she's nice. She took us away from the bad people and said we didn't have to ever see them again."

"Do you have a name?"

"Miss Lucy called me David." A shy grin spread across his lips. "She said I was little but I was strong like David in the Bible. He killed a giant, you know."

"David is a good name." Bending down, Clay took hold of the little girl. "Come up here, sweetheart. You can't hang on my leg all day."

When she was in his arms, she looked at him through her tears, then threw her arms around him and buried her head in his neck. She didn't speak.

"What's your name, mister?" David's voice showed he was almost too scared to ask.

"It's Clay."

He nodded. "She likes you, Mr. Clay."

"Is she your sister?"

"No. I never seen her 'til we found her. Miss Lucy said she was an innocent little girl like Mary in the Bible, so we was to call her Mary. I don't know why she said that, but I think it was because she liked Bible names. We've all got one."

Clay frowned. "Was there someone else with you and Mary and Miss Lucy?"

"Yeah. The mean men knocked Miss Lucy down and took them away."

"Mean men?"

"Uh-uh. They didn't want me and Mary."

"Why not?"

David shrugged and looked around. "Where's Miss Lucy?"

Clay had wanted to avoid that question. But now he knew he couldn't. "I'm sorry, David. Miss Lucy isn't with us any longer."

He gave Clay a hard look. "What do you mean? Is she dead?"

"Yes."

He shrugged again. "I figured she was, or she'd be fussing at us for letting you see us. She was afraid somebody would hurt us." Before Clay could react, David added, "Are we gonna bury Miss Lucy?"

"I was thinking about it when you and Mary ran out of the bushes."

"Mary probably won't be no help, but I'll help you." This time his voice sounded timid.

Clay wanted to put him at ease. "The best way you can help me is to take care of Mary while I see what I need to do."

David gave him a grin. "I can do that, all right."

It took a few minutes to get Mary to turn loose of him and sit with David. With that accomplished, Clay wrapped the dead woman in a blanket he found where it had fallen on the ground. He then decided to put her in the wagon and report the death.

Through the process, Clay wondered what he could do with these children? He finally decided there was only one answer. He had to take them to Settlers Ridge. He almost laughed when he realized that by reporting the death and showing up with two orphans, he had lost his intention of slipping into town and hiding until he found out if he could make amends with his sister.

~ * ~

Wilma straightened the material Marjorie Cramer had pushed around, looking for just the right piece to make a new frock. "I like to sew, and I want to make a new frock to wear to Elizabeth Donahue's wedding, though Juliette says I should go to Miss Purdy's shop and have a new dress made," she'd said.

Wilma smiled. She knew it was hard for the lawyer's wife to decide. Since she'd returned from boarding school, Juliette had continually tried to make her mother become something the sweet woman would never be. Everyone liked Marjorie and enjoyed her company, but many of the women in town had shied away from inviting her to their functions. Wilma knew it was because they didn't want Marjorie showing up with her daughter. Of course, nobody in the area would mention this to the woman because they didn't want to hurt her feelings.

The bells over the door interrupted her and two cowboys walked in. Wilma eyed them. Something about their bedraggled looks made her feel uneasy. She hurried behind the counter. "How may I help you?"

"Need to get a few supplies and some information, if you happen to have what we need," the one with a long beard said as he looked her up and down.

"I'll try to help you if I can."

He looked around the store. "Since we're alone..."

"Shut up, Merve," the other one pushed him aside and said, "We're on the trail of three friends of ours. One's over six feet, tough build, with brown hair, unless he's changed it. You'd know him by his grey eyes, which he couldn't have changed. He was clean shaven, last we saw 'em."

Wilma shook her head. "That could describe a lot of men around here, and I don't think I can help unless you have a better description."

"The other fellows are kind of average. Nothing special, 'crept one don't have much hair on his head. He has a way of making people think he's just a regular guy, then he'll surprise you and do something foolish."

"Like what?"

"Maybe burst out singing for no reason at all, or draw his gun and shoot out a winder just to hear the glass break."

"I don't know anyone like that. Maybe you should check with the sheriff. He might be able to help you."

"I was hoping we wouldn't have to deal with him."

Wilma raised an eyebrow and wondered why they didn't want to involve the sheriff. She felt compelled to ask. "Why wouldn't you want to go to the law? I'm sure he'd know if your friends have been around."

The man with the long beard butted in. "You, married, pretty lady?"

"I told you to shut up, Merve."

"I jest wanted to..."

The curtains to the back room parted and Spencer Barrington, the mercantile owner, stepped into the room. "Need any help, Wilma?"

"I don't think so. You could check the supplies the stage dropped off. I put them in the stock room.

The one called Merve got quiet; he never spoke again.

The other one said, "Since you ain't seen our friends, we'll get our supplies and be on our way." He rattled off what they needed, paid for the items, and they hurried from the store.

Spencer came back into the store. "Who in the world was that, Wilma?"

"I have no idea, Spencer. They said they were on the trail of some friends. The way they described them made me wonder if they were outlaws."

"Maybe they were bounty hunters."

"Could have been." She changed the subject. "How's Nelda feeling today?"

"Better. Doc said she should be giving birth in a few weeks. I hope my sister gets here before she does have the baby." He grinned. "I don't like seeing Nelda feeling so bad and I hate to leave her alone."

"You're a good husband, Spencer, and I know Nelda appreciates it."

"I hope so." He smiled at her. "Since I'm here, why don't you take a little time off? I know you've been putting in a lot of extra time since Nelda's been under the weather."

"You know I don't mind."

"I do know, and I appreciate it. But I insist. Take a little time for yourself this afternoon. You can come back and close up if you like."

"Thank you, Spencer." She took off her apron. "You're not only a good husband, you're a good boss, too."

As she headed to her apartment upstairs, she heard him chuckle.

Three

With Mary in his arms and David by his side, Clay took a deep breath, opened the jailhouse door and stepped inside. "Got a minute, Sheriff?"

Lance looked up from the poster he was studying. A surprised look crossed his face. "Sure thing. How can I help you?"

"I have a story to tell you, and I hope you can give me some advice."

"Then, have a seat and I'll get chairs for your children."

Clay took the chair in front of the desk. Mary clung to his neck and refused to move to the stool the sheriff dragged up. David sat on the other stool.

Clay knew he was a stranger to Lance Gentry, but that didn't surprise him. After all, he was about to enter his teenage years when he'd left Settlers Ridge. He wished he could continue to be a stranger but knew he couldn't.

Rejecting this idea, he said, "I know you don't recognize me, Lance. I was still a boy the last time you saw me."

Lance frowned. "I admit you look vaguely familiar."

"Name's Clay Hunter. I'm pretty sure I'm your brother-in-law."

For a minute Lance stared at him. Then a slow grin spread across his lips and he muttered, "You are?"

"I am."

When Clay said nothing more, Lance added, "Where in the world have you been all these years? I can see you've been busy having kids." He nodded at the children.

"That's what I need to tell you. These aren't my kids. I found them."

Lance's grin faded and a frown appeared. "What do you mean, found them?"

"I was on my way to town when I came upon a turned over wagon with a woman pinned under it, dying. These two were hiding in the nearby bushes. The one hugging the Bible is David. The one hugging me is Mary. According to David, there were three other children the men who attacked them took away."

Lance looked at David. "Why didn't they take you two?"

David dropped his eyes. "They said we was too little."

"Too little?"

"Yes, Mr. Sheriff. He said I wouldn't be able to do much work and I'd hold them up. He said Mary was too little for them...ah...to enjoy." He dropped his head. "I don't know what he meant, 'I wasn't big enough', cause I'm almost eight years old and I can work. I did some for Miss Lucy. She said I was strong like David in the Bible."

Lance raised an eyebrow and glanced at Clay. "Who is Miss Lucy?"

"The woman they were with."

The jail door opened, and Deputy Bryce Langston walked in. "Didn't know you were busy, Lance."

"Come on in. You need to be in on this."

David leaned over and whispered something to Clay.

Clay nodded. "You fellows wouldn't happen to have anything to eat around here, would you? David just told me they haven't eaten all day and they're hungry."

"We don't have anything here, but I'm sure Bryce won't mind going to get something for them before he sits down." Lance turned to his deputy. "Go to Olsen's Hotel and ask Effie Vaughn to send something for them. She's been the cook there for a long time and I'm sure she'll know what kids like to eat."

Looking puzzled, Bryce nodded and went out the door.

Lance chuckled. "I think he's like me, totally confused."

"I admit, I'm not clear on what happened either." Clay glanced at the little boy. "David told me Miss Lucy was taking the children to a new home because none of them had one. Three men attacked them and demanded money. Miss Lucy argued with them and that's when they knocked her down. The children scattered and before he ran, Miss Lucy grabbed David, shoved the Bible in his hands and told him to hide and not to let the men find it. As you can see, he's still clinging to it."

"She told me to watch out for Mary, too."

The sheriff winked at him. "Looks like you did a good job of that, son. Now, could you tell me a little more about what happened when the men attacked you?"

"Miss Lucy wouldn't give them any money and they got mad. They pulled her out of the wagon and knocked her down and beat on her. When Luke and Thomas tried to fight them, they knocked them down, too. Sarah jumped out of the wagon and tried to help Miss Lucy and one of the men grabbed her and said she was pretty. When they was looking at Sarah, I run to Miss Lucy. She told me to take the Bible and Mary and go hide. I did."

"Did they say anything to you?"

"One man said not to worry about me and Mary, 'cause I was too little to work and she was too little to have fun with. When one of them said they ought to kill us, another one said not to bother because we'd starve soon enough. They run off the horse and turned over the wagon and all our stuff fell out. Then they left." He looked down and mumbled.

"What did you say, David?"

"I said, I don't know what we would've done if Mr. Clay hadn't come."

"I'm glad he found you." Lance bit his lip. "Will you let me look at that Bible, David?"

"Miss Lucy said not to let nobody know I have it."

Bryce came through the door with a tray in his hand. "Miss Effie said there wasn't a child alive who didn't like her fried chicken and she just happened to have a couple of drumsticks."

David's eyes got big. "Real fried chicken?"

Bryce grinned. "Real fried chicken. Do you want to give me that Bible so you can pull up to the desk and eat?"

David shook his head as he eyed the plates Bryce uncovered. "I don't know you, but I know Mr. Clay. I'll let him hold Miss Lucy's Bible while I eat."

"I'm glad you trust me, David. Do you mind if I look in the Bible while you're eating?"

"I guess not. Miss Lucy said it's good to read the Bible. She read it to us every day." He handed Clay the Bible and allowed Bryce to push his stool close to the desk. "She give us all Bible names. All but Luke. She said he already had a Bible name. I'm not sure about Sarah. She might have one, too. I know she give Thomas his name."

Lance lifted an eyebrow. "She did?"

"Yeah. She said since he didn't trust her when we first got him, she would call him Thomas. She said something about him doubting, but I don't know what that means."

"Well, now that the food is here, are you ready to eat?" Lance asked.

"Yes, sir."

In a minute, they were able to coax Mary to move up to the desk, too.

Lance looked at Clay. "What happened to this Miss Lucy?"

"The outlaws messed her up good. She died before I could get the details of what was going on. I thought about burying her but changed my mind. I put her in the wagon to wait for the undertaker. Then their horse came walking up. I changed my mind again and tied her to it. I dropped her at the undertaker's before coming here. The kids rode on my horse with me."

"Did she say anything to you before she died?"

"She said to get the Bible and look after the children. She also said something about a couple of women named Alice and Phoebe, but I didn't know what she meant. There were no other adults around."

"Why don't you see if there's anything in the Bible that'll give us a clue as to what's going on?"

Clay opened the Bible and was surprised to find an envelope tucked inside. Opening it, he couldn't hide his surprise. "Lance, this is a letter from a lawyer named Hal Cramer. Looks like Lucy Baker had plans to or has already purchased the Anderson ranch. Isn't it a couple of miles out of town?"

Lance nodded and Clay went on. "According to the note, she planned to make a home there for these children."

"It's sure big enough for a large family. I've heard the house has at least ten rooms, maybe more. The place has always intrigued me." Bryce said.

"Old man Anderson had loads of money and he built the house for his wife. I heard they wanted to have a lot of children, but unfortunately they never had any." Lance looked at Clay. "It would be a good place for a big family, but right now, I figure we better come up with some immediate arrangements for these two little ones. Then I need to head out and see if I can track down the men who took the other three."

Bryce looked at Clay. "When I was getting the food, Henrietta Olsen said to bring the children to the hotel since you're new in town. I'm sure she meant it."

"Good. I'll take the children there, but since I'm involved in this situation, I'm going with Lance to find the other three. I've had some experience tracking and I know where we need to start the search."

"Maybe I should go along, too."

"No, Bryce," Lance said. "I need you to look after things here. Go to the livery and make arrangements to get the kids' wagon into town. Also, you might better keep an eye on the children while we're gone."

~ * ~

Mary sat close to David on the blue sofa in the Olsen family's private quarters of the hotel. She had stopped crying, but she looked as if she might break into tears again at any moment.

Henrietta smiled at her and said, "I sure wish you'd tell me what I could do to make you feel better, honey."

David spoke up. "She can't tell you 'cause she can't talk. But I know what's the matter. She wants Mr. Clay to come back."

Henrietta glanced at her seventeen-year-old daughter, Sophie, then looked back at David. "What do you mean, she can't talk?"

"I mean she can't say words. Miss Lucy said it was cause she's a mule."

"A mule?"

"Yes, but she's not deef. Miss Lucy said sometimes deef and mule go together. Mary is lucky. She's just a mule."

Sophie interrupted. "I think what David is telling us is that Mary is mute, but she isn't deaf."

"Is that right, David? Is Mary unable to talk at all?"

"Yes, ma'am. Miss Lucy said she was born that way or else somebody hurt her when she was a baby and that is why she can't talk."

Henrietta thought for a minute. "David, how long were you and Mary with Miss Lucy?"

He shrugged. "I'm not sure. I sort of remember being cold and she put a blanket around me."

"What about Mary? How did she come to be with Miss Lucy?"

"I don't know. Her and Luke and Sarah was already there." He gave her a quick smile. "I do remember when we got Thomas."

"When was that?"

"We was on our trip and we stopped in a town to get some things. When we left the store, we saw a mean old man beating Thomas with a leather strap. Miss Lucy stopped the wagon and got her gun from under the seat. She told the man to leave Thomas alone. He didn't want to, but he did, and Miss Lucy told Luke and Sarah to put Thomas in the wagon with us. They did and we left. We didn't see the mean man no more."

Henrietta had to turn her head away to keep them from seeing she was tearing up. "Miss Lucy must have been a very special woman."

He grinned. "She was. We all loved her."

Four

Riding side-by-side for some distance, Lance glanced at Clay and broke the silence. "Your sister has worried about you more than you can ever know."

"That's the thing that has haunted me the most, Lance. I realize how much she must have suffered, and it bears on me that I was a cause of that suffering."

"You could have relieved her if you'd have sent her a note now and then or contacted her when you came home and left flowers on your mother's grave."

"So, she saw the flowers?"

"She did."

"I hoped she'd think I was saying hello when she saw them."

"She only knew you'd been here and hadn't gotten in touch with her."

"That's just it, Lance. I wasn't allowed to contact her in any way."

"Not allowed?"

"That's right."

"Maybe you better start explaining."

"All I can say is that I was doing a job for the government and as I said, I wasn't allowed to contact anyone from my past in any manner. I only hoped she knew I was checking up on her if or when she found the flowers on Mama's grave."

"They confused her, Clay."

"I'm sorry about that. It was the best I could do."

"Why did you come back now and let your presence be known?"

"I was finally released from the government and could come home. I didn't intend to tell anyone for a while I was in town. I wanted to ease in and let her know I was here a little at a time."

"But you came straight to me." Lance frowned. "You also called me your brother-in-law. How did you know Grace and I were married?"

"I attended your wedding."

"You what?"

Clay chuckled. "I've been taught the art of disguise. I dressed myself up as an old man down on his luck. When everyone got inside the church, I slipped in the back and watched through a crack in the door. Of course, I was gone by the time you and she came out."

"It'll mean a lot to her to know you were there. But she'll be hurt that you didn't let her know."

"I couldn't, Lance."

"So you said."

"There's a lot I want to tell her. But she must accept that I can't tell her everything. There are things I want to know about her, too." When Lance didn't reply, Clay went on. "For instance, do I have a niece or a nephew?"

Lance grinned. "The most beautiful niece in the world. Kathrine is her name."

"That's a pretty name." He grinned back. "I hope she likes me."

"Not much chance she won't. Look how Mary took to you."

"I don't understand why, but I must say that little girl did come right to me." Clay nodded down the road toward the wagon. "We're getting close to where I found the children."

They stopped their horses and dismounted beside the wagon. Looking at all the blood, Clay muttered, "I didn't know the woman, but nobody deserves to die in the inhumane way Miss Lucy Baker did."

"Looks like those outlaws seem to want to torture the woman." Lance glanced around. "Maybe we should have gathered more people for a posse."

Clay shook his head, "According to David, there were only three of them. I think we can handle it." He walked several feet down the road. "I see their tracks. It seems they headed toward Swanson. Since it's a two-day ride, they'll probably make camp tonight."

"That'd be lucky for us." Lance headed to his horse. "Let's get going. It'll be dark shortly and we need to catch up to them before they harm those children."

Clay headed to his horse and mounted without speaking, then they headed out in a gallop. Nothing needed to be said. Just as he had, Clay figured Lance had the young Sarah on his mind, and what could happen to her if they didn't catch up to them in time.

The sun had slipped behind the orange and purple clouds, and darkness was fast falling when Clay sensed a change. He pulled back on the reins and motioned for Lance to join him.

"What is it, Clay?" Lance asked.

"I got a whiff of smoke. I can't say for sure, but it could be their camp. How do you suggest we approach them?"

"We'll keep going, but when we get closer, we'll decide what the smartest move should be."

~ * ~

Wilma got ready to close the mercantile as Bryce rushed through the door. "Glad I caught you, Wilma."

"You just made it, my friend. I was on my way to lock the door."

"I need to pick up a pack of needles and some thread. I was supposed to bring them home at dinner and forgot. Lettie got so upset with me she cried, and I sure didn't want to go home without them tonight."

"Then I'm glad you caught me in time. What color thread did she want?"

He looked lost. "I think she told me, but now I'm not sure. Maybe blue and some other color."

Wilma shook her head. "You men. You have no idea how important little things like color are. I bet you don't know what she needs the thread for either."

"She showed me some things she's making for the coming baby. But I don't know if that's what she's sewing now."

"I'll take a chance she's still making the blankets she was working on the other day. But she could be mending your clothes, so I'll have to take that into consideration." She sighed.

"She sure is having a good time getting ready for our baby."

"How about you, Bryce? How do you feel about the coming event?"

"I'm happy about it, of course. But it's still just something that'll be happening in the future." He gave her a big grin. "Lance says I won't understand how much you care about the little rascal until it gets here."

"He's probably right about that." She turned toward the sewing notions counter. "Tell you what. I remember she was trimming the blankets in pink and blue, so I'll give you a spool of each. I'll also throw in one of white since women use a lot of that, and in case she's mending, I'll add a spool of black. You can bring back what she doesn't need."

"You're a good woman, Wilma."

"Thank you, Bryce."

He followed her to get the thread. "Speaking of good women. A man brought a couple of kids into town today. He'd found them on the road where they'd been attacked. The woman had planned to move into the old Anderson place."

"What do you mean, he brought them in? Where was the woman?"

"Dead. He took her to the undertaker and the little ones to Lance."

"Did he work for the woman?"

"Nope. He came along after they were attacked and found the children. I don't suppose he knew where else to take them."

"Did you know him?"

"No. I may have seen him before, but I can't remember when or where. Lance seemed to know him. I think he said his name was Clay. In fact, he and Lance headed out to track the outlaws and see if they could rescue the children they took with them."

Startled when she heard the name Clay, Wilma asked, "Was the man Clay Hunter?"

"I wasn't told a last name."

"I see." She sighed. "I hope they catch the outlaws before they do something bad to those children."

"I do, too. According to the little boy the man brought to us, the outlaws left him and the little girl to starve to death."

"Oh, my heavens." She frowned. "How horrible."

"It sure is."

"I hope they get to the others before something awful happens to them."

"Me, too."

"Where are the children the man brought to town?"

"At Olsen's Hotel. Henrietta and Sophie are looking after them." He glanced at the supplies Wilma handed him. "How much do I owe you?"

"I'll put it on your bill until we make sure what Lettie wants. Then we'll settle up."

"Thanks, Wilma. Now I better get on home and let you lock up. I don't want Lettie to get mad at me again."

"You're right. You should hurry home, Bryce. I'll see you to the door and turn the lock behind you."

As soon as Bryce left, the door locked, the shades pulled and the money box in its hiding place in the stock room, Wilma climbed the stairs to her apartment. She made sure the fire was out in the kitchen stove, and decided she'd eat later. She headed out the back door and locked it behind her. She wanted to see for herself these children some strange man had brought to town. Maybe they'd know his last name.

Agnes Alexander

If not, maybe she could help with them. Besides, with all the children being born in Settlers Ridge, she knew helping with someone else's children was the only way she'd ever be able to express her motherly instincts.

31

Five

Stopping their mounts and dismounting before they were close enough to the campsite for the outlaws to hear their approach, Lance turned to Clay. "We'll leave the horses here and proceed on foot."

"How about we split up when we get to the edge of their camp so we can go at them from different angles? It'll probably surprise them that way, and make it easier for us."

Lance nodded. "I smell coffee and if they've cooked something, they could be eating. That'd also give us an advantage. See if you can get the kids out of their reach, then I'll try to take them without anyone getting hurt. But if you have to shoot to protect the kids or yourself, don't hesitate."

"Sounds like a good plan. I'll stay where you can see me and when you're ready to move in, signal me, then we'll move in at the same time."

"That'll work. Let's go."

Lance had no idea how much experience Clay had in helping the law in this type of situation. He hoped Clay would be able to get the children, but he had no way of knowing if his brother-in-law had done such a thing. He had said he had worked for the government, but had he? He almost wished he'd insisted that Bryce come with them because he could always count on his deputy. But someone had to watch out for the town.

Pushing those thoughts from his mind, Lance moved to the head-high shrubs which surrounded the area where the men had camped. Peeping through the limbs, his blood ran cold.

A boy of about ten or eleven was tied to a tree. His shirt had been removed and there were bloody strips across his chest. Another boy, about the same age, poured coffee for the three men sitting around the campfire. A girl, also probably around eleven or twelve, sat beside one of the men. Her tear-stained face testified to her fear.

A gruff voice said, "Hurry up, boy. Warm up my coffee. After I drink it, me and this young lady are going to take a little walk and have us some fun."

The man across the fire said, "Who said you got to be first with her?"

"Both of you shut up. I may decide to be the first, myself," a third voice boomed out.

Lance knew he couldn't wait any longer. He glanced to the other side of the camp. Seeing Clay, he took a breath and lifted his hand.

Clay returned the gesture, and they burst into the opening with their guns drawn.

"Stand up and put your hands above your heads. You're under arrest," Lance yelled.

The man beside the girl shoved her backward and stood as he grappled for his gun. He was too late. Lance fired and the man fell over the log where he'd sat.

Other shots rang out and the boy and girl screamed at the same time. Clay rushed up and grabbed them by their arms. "Get over there and hide behind that bush," he demanded.

"What about Thomas?"

"I'll get him. Now, go."

The boy took the girl's hand and they started to run.

One of the men started after them shouting, "Get back here, you dumb young'uns. You belong to us."

He stopped when the cold barrel of a pistol rested on the side of his head. When he heard the hammer click back, he froze. His gun tumbled out of his hand and fell at his feet.

Lance walked up with the third man, who was already in handcuffs. "I had to shoot one of them. Figure he won't give us any more trouble. Let me cuff the one you have so you can take care of the children."

"Good. I know they'll be anxious to get back to David and Mary."

~ * ~

The boy eased out of his hiding place. "You know David and Mary?"

"I do."

"Are they all right?" The girl's voice came out in a raspy whisper.

Clay wanted to reach out and comfort her, but he knew better. "Yeah, Sarah. They're fine."

She frowned. "How'd you know my name?"

"David told me." He looked at the boy. "And you're either Luke or Thomas."

"I'm Luke."

Clay headed to the tree where the other boy was tied. "Then this must be Thomas. Looks like he needs a doctor. In the meantime, I'm going to see if I can do something to help him until we get to town."

"While you take care of the boy, I'll work out the riding arrangements back to town," Lance said.

"Ain't you gonna bury Neely?" The bearded outlaw blurted.

Lance chuckled. "Nope. I'll strap him to a horse and let the town take care of burying him. You want to ride with him?"

"Hell, no."

Clay ignored them and moved to the unconscious boy strapped to the tree. His stomach almost lost the only food he'd had earlier today. He swallowed and, being as gentle as he could, he cut the ropes around the child.

Luke walked up, still holding Sarah's hand. Clay looked at them. "Why did they do this to him?"

"They said since he had Indian blood in him, he didn't feel pain like a white person does," Sarah explained.

"They also said that made him something they could torture for fun," Luke muttered.

Clay shook his head. "I wish my conscience would let me do to them what they deserve. I'd see they got as good as they gave this boy."

"At least Neely is dead. He was the meanest," Sarah whispered.

"Then good riddance to him." Clay eased Thomas away from the tree. "Luke, I'm going to whistle for my horse and when she comes over, I want you to get a blanket out of the bedroll. I don't want to put Thomas on the ground."

Luke nodded.

Clay whistled and Whisper came directly to him.

As Luke got the blanket, Sarah looked at him. Her eyes were full of questions, but she only asked one. "Why are you being so nice to us?"

At first, Clay didn't know what to say. Then it occurred to him that explaining the unfairness of their plight would not be the answer. He gave her a smile and said, "Because Miss Lucy asked me to."

Though it faded quickly, he was sure the girl gave him a little grin.

By the time he had done what he could for Thomas, and Lance had said he had everything arranged, the group headed for Settlers Ridge.

The outlaws cursed, fussed, and threatened as they rode off, but they soon saw it did no good. Things stayed arranged the way Lance wanted them. The dead man was wrapped in a tarp and strapped across a horse. Luke and Sarah rode on one of the outlaw's horses, and Clay carried an unconscious Thomas in his lap. He couldn't help smiling as he watched Lance lead the dead man's horse and the horse carrying the two grumbling outlaws.

"Let them fuss. Serves the fools right," he heard Lance mutter. He fully agreed. He also knew he was going to like this brother-in-law of his.

They had almost reached Settlers Ridge when Clay looked down and saw the boy in his arms staring at him. He was surprised but felt he should say something. "Are you riding all right, Thomas?"

Thomas frowned, but didn't answer.

Clay went on. "It won't be much longer before we'll reach town, and the doctor will be able to help you."

Still frowning, Thomas muttered, "You ain't going to bury me alive?"

It was Clay's turn to frown. "Of course not. Why would you think that?"

"That's what Neely said he'd do whenever they moved on. I figured you'd do the same thing."

"Well, you figured wrong. I'm taking you to the doctor in Settlers Ridge, and when you're better, you'll be able to join your friends again."

"I don't believe you."

After what the kid had been through, Clay could understand why he didn't believe him. Yet, he wanted the boy to know he was safe. He slowed his horse and yelled, "Hold up, Luke. I want you to come back here beside me so Thomas can see you're all three away from those men."

By the time Luke joined him, Thomas had passed out again.

Six

Clay stepped into Olsen's Hotel lobby with Thomas in his arms, although when they left the doctor's office, the boy had said he could walk. Clay had his doubts but didn't argue with him. Instead, he walked behind Thomas leading his horse because he wanted to be prepared if anything unexpected happened. He knew it had been Thomas's pride talking when the boy started stumbling and was about to collapse on the street. Tossing Whisper's reins to Luke, he grabbed Thomas before he hit the ground. He then carried the unconscious boy the rest of the way to the hotel.

Luke followed, leading Whisper. Sarah walked beside Luke. Neither said anything, though Clay could tell they were watching him closely. He knew that was why they'd insisted on going to the doctor with them.

Frank Olsen came from around the counter as they entered the hotel. "Hello, Mr. Hunter. The sheriff said you'd be coming in, and we have a couple of rooms ready for you and the kids. My wife is up there with the young ones because the little girl wouldn't stop crying and the little boy says it's because she misses you."

"I appreciate the arrangements, and I have another question. My horse is tied out front. Would it be possible to get someone to take her to the livery stable?"

"No problem at all. My son, Teddy. will do it. And before you ask, he'll make sure the animal is well cared for."

"Thank you, Mr. Olsen."

"Now, if you'll please follow me."

They went up the stairs and stopped in front of room eight. Frank knocked on the door, then opened it and said, "Mr. Hunter and the children are here, honey."

He held the door open for Clay and the kids, then nodded and headed back down the hall.

Before his wife could speak, David shouted, "Mr. Clay, you come back! I just knew you would come and bring Thomas and Sarah and Luke." He then grew serious as he stared at the boy in Clay's arms. "Is Thomas dead?"

"No, David, he's not dead, but he's hurt pretty bad, and I need to get him into a bed."

Henrietta laid a sleeping Mary on one of the three cots in the room and moved to another one. "Here you go, Mr. Hunter. I'll turn it down for you."

"Thank you."

"Lance said you'd taken him to the doctor. I'm surprised Doctor Wagner didn't keep him at the office."

He laid Thomas on the bed and covered him with a sheet. "He wanted him to stay, but these two wouldn't leave without him. Then Thomas became aware of where he was and refused to stay there."

"I see." She looked at the two children waiting, without talking. "I hope none of you objects. We set up three cots in here with the bed. We thought you and the boys would sleep here. I knew a cot would be too short for you to sleep on, but I didn't think the boys would mind sleeping on them." She pointed to a door. "There's a small adjoining room through there. It has a big bed. I hope the girls don't mind sleeping together."

"Can we leave the door open?" Sarah asked.

Henrietta raised an eyebrow. "I don't see why you can't. That is, unless the boys or Mr. Hunter snores."

"I don't snore, and I bet Mr. Clay don't snore neither." David looked at Clay. "Do you snore, Mr. Clay?"

"I might snore a little when I'm tired. But maybe I won't snore tonight."

"Then why don't I get out of here and let you all get to bed? Do you need anything else before I go?"

Clay noticed that Luke started to say something, but Sarah punched him with her elbow. A thought crossed his mind. He remembered how hungry David and Mary had been, and figured the others were, too. "I hate to bother you, Mrs. Olsen, but we've had a rough day and there hasn't been any time to eat. Would there be something left in the dining room that we could get?"

"My heavens, why didn't I think of that? You all get settled and I'll bring something right up. I might even find some hot coffee for you, and maybe there'll be enough milk left for all the children."

As she went out the door, Mary woke up. As soon as she saw Clay, she jumped off the bed and ran to him.

"Don't bother the man, Mary," Luke said in a frightened voice.

She ignored him and held her arms up to Clay. He reached down and took her. "She's not bothering me, Luke. As a matter of fact, she and David and I are getting to be good friends, aren't we, David?"

"We shore are." David grinned. "Mr. Clay is the bestest man I know, and I bet if Mary could talk, she'd say the same thing, wouldn't you. Mary?"

Mary didn't answer or even nod. She'd gone back to sleep in Clay's arms.

~ * ~

Lance came into the bedroom, placed the lighted lamp on the bedside table and glanced at Grace cuddled down in the bed. "You still awake, honey?"

"I am." She turned over and smiled at him. "Kathrine had a hard time going to sleep, so I've only been in bed for a few minutes."

"I'm sorry I didn't get home in time to help you put her to bed."

"That's all right, Lance. I know duty keeps you away at times."

He sat on the side of the bed, leaned over and kissed her. "I have such a wonderful understanding wife."

"She'll be more understanding if you'll hurry and get into bed and blow out that light. Your daughter will want to eat in a few hours and her mother needs to get some sleep."

He chuckled, then bent over and removed his boots. Standing, it didn't take him long to shuck his clothes, blow out the light and slip into bed. Slipping his arm around his wife, he took a deep breath. "I'm sorry to keep you awake longer, but I need to tell you something."

She snuggled against him and kissed his chin. "I don't mind you keeping me awake a little longer, my love."

Tempted to accept her invitation and make love to his wife and forget telling her about Clay, Lance hesitated. But he knew he'd have to face the consequences later if he followed his more primal instinct.

Taking control of himself, Lance pulled her closer. "Stop distracting me. I have something important to tell you."

"Then tell me so we can get to more interesting things."

Before he could change his mind, he said, "A man came into the office this afternoon. He had two children with him. He'd found them on the trail into town."

"Found?"

"Yes. He came upon a dying woman. She was on her way to town with five children."

"I thought you said there were two children."

"I did. Please let me explain."

"It's confusing but go ahead."

Lance told her about the little girl and how she clung to the man and how the boy seemed to turn to him before saying anything. He told her about Lucy Baker's death and how the outlaws had taken the three older children with them and left the little ones to die on the prairie. How, after the man arrived in town with them, he had sent the children to the hotel and then left to track down the three older ones.

He finished telling his story with how they found the two unharmed ones and one that was nearly beaten to death because he was part Indian. He told her one of the men had tried to shoot him and how he'd had to kill him. He knew she accepted that was part of his job. He also knew she was glad when he told her he arrested the other two outlaws and brought them back to Settlers Ridge. He explained that the man who had helped him had taken the Indian boy to the doctor.

Pausing and taking a deep breath he closed with, "I assume they're all at the hotel getting a good night's sleep at this moment."

She held him close to her. "I certainly think you have a good reason for being late tonight. There's just one thing I want to ask?"

He figured he knew her question and braced himself for it. "What is that, honey?"

"Did you know this Good Samaritan?"

"I did."

"Well, don't keep me in suspense. Who was he?"

Lance swallowed. "It was your brother, Clay."

Grace sat straight up in bed. "What did you say?"

Realizing there would be very little sleep for them for the rest of the night, he said in a soft voice, "You heard me, sweetheart. It was your brother, Clay."

Seven

Thomas waited until the strange man closed the door and left the room the next morning. He didn't know who he was, or why he had all the boys in this room sleeping in cots, but he intended to find out as soon as he could.

When he was sure the man wasn't going to return, he spoke. "Luke, are you awake?"

Luke sat up. "I am now."

"What the hell is going on here?"

"Don't cuss, Thomas," David sat up and rubbed his eyes. "Mr. Clay don't like it any more than Miss Lucy did."

Thomas frowned. "Where is Miss Lucy?"

David looked sad. "She's dead. We're with Mr. Clay now."

"What's he talking about, Luke?"

"It seems Mr. Clay came along and found David and Mary after those awful men took us. They had killed Miss Lucy, and Mr. Clay brought her body and the kids to town."

David interrupted. "I helped. I watched Mary."

Luke looked at him. "Be quiet, David and let me finish." He turned back to Thomas. "After he brought David and Mary to town...then to this hotel, him and the sheriff came looking for us. When they caught up with the outlaws, they killed that awful Neely and rescued us. You had passed out from the beating you'd took, so Mr. Clay wrapped you in a blanket and carried you to the doctor. You wouldn't stay there, so we all came here, and the hotel owner put us in this room."

"Where's Mary and what happened to Sarah?"

"They're in that room over there." David pointed at the connecting door.

Thomas frowned. "Why is that man doing this for us?"

Luke shook his head. "I don't know why. I just know if he hadn't come along, you'd probably be dead, and I don't know what would have happened to the kids or Sarah and me."

"I know why he helped us."

"How do you know, David?"

"He's nice and he likes me and Mary, and we like him."

"How do you know Mary likes him? She can't talk."

"I think David's right about Mary, Thomas. As soon as we got here last night, she ran and grabbed his leg and wouldn't let go until he picked her up."

Thomas frowned again. "I still don't trust him."

David looked puzzled. "Why not?"

"One, because a strange man wouldn't help five orphaned kids unless he had a good reason, and another because he's white. White people don't help Indians like me."

"Miss Lucy was white."

"Miss Lucy was different."

The adjoining door to the girls' room eased open. Sarah came in with Mary in her arms. "What's all this arguing going on in here?"

"Thomas said Mr. Clay is not helping us," David blurted.

"I did not. I said he had a reason for helping us. I just don't know what it is."

Sarah nodded. "Whatever it is, I'm glad he got us away from those outlaws."

"That was a good thing. I guess we'll just have to wait and see what happens when he gets back," Luke said.

"If he comes back," Thomas added.

"What makes you think he won't?" Sarah eyed him.

"Because..."

The rattling of the door interrupted him, and Clay stepped inside. He had a cup of coffee in his hand, but this didn't deter Mary. She wiggled free of Sarah's arms and ran straight for Clay's leg.

"Careful, little darlin'. I don't want to spill hot coffee on you." He sat the coffee on the washstand, picked her up, and looked around at the others. "I'm glad to see you're all awake. Miss Effie is the cook here and she has a big breakfast ready. All you need to do is wash your hands and face to go down to eat." He looked at Thomas. "If you don't feel up to it, I can bring you a tray."

Not sure of Clay's motive, he said, "I'll be fine to go with everyone else."

"Good. Now see how fast you boys can get ready."

"Come on, Mary," Sarah said. "We'll go to our room and wash."

Mary hesitated until Clay said, "Go ahead, honey. I'll wait right here for you."

Nodding, she let him put her down and she toddled off behind Sarah.

Thomas noticed but didn't say anything. He only promised himself he'd watch Clay to make sure he wasn't going to hurt the girls.

~ * ~

Gathered around the food laden table in the hotel dining room, Clay noticed the children, except for David, all held back from putting a lot of the food offerings on their plates. Filling his plate, he nodded to them. "Better eat up. It might be some time before we get a chance to eat again today."

Thomas gave him a suspicious look. "Why?"

After all he'd done to help them, Clay couldn't help but be a little irritated the boy didn't trust him. But somewhere inside him, he realized Thomas probably had had nothing except harsh words and bad treatment from white men. He didn't want to be one who added to that mistreatment. He took a breath. "The sheriff sent a man from the livery to bring in your wagon and I thought I could take all of you to the graveyard where they plan to bury Miss Lucy Baker today. That is, if you want to go to her funeral."

"Of course we do," Sarah said.

"Sarah's right. We all want to go." Luke nodded.

Sarah smiled, but Thomas raised his chin. "I suppose you'll make me stay here."

"No, Thomas. If you feel up to it, I think you should come along. If you get too tired, we'll make you a bed in the wagon."

Before Thomas could answer, a woman walked in with a baby in her arms. Coming straight to their table, she said, "Clay! Is it really you?"

~ * ~

Grace watched as he scrambled to his feet. It was hard to believe this grown man was her brother. Of course, she knew she hadn't seen him since he was a boy. At the time, he'd been tall and lanky, just as the man before her. But this Clay was taller, though somewhat lanky, he had muscles that stretched in the sleeves of his blue shirt. His brown hair looked familiar, but the heavy moustache was new, and his eyes told her he was full of hidden secrets.

He looked startled, but managed to mutter, "It's me, Grace, and you look wonderful."

"Where have you been all these years?"

Mary jumped from her chair, ran up to him and grabbed his leg. David followed her, though the others only stared at them and said nothing.

"Is that another baby for us, Mr. Clay?" David asked.

Clay shook his head. "No, David. This lady is my sister and that's her baby. Now why don't you get back in your chair and finish your breakfast while I move over to that table and talk with her?"

"What about Mary?"

"Don't worry. I'll take care of Mary." Picking up the little girl, he said, "Honey, I need to talk to this lady."

Sarah walked up to them. "I'll look after her, Mr. Clay."

He handed her the child. "Thank you, Sarah. I won't be long."

David nodded at them and returned to his chair. But he continued to watch Clay closely, as all the children did.

"Could we move to that table over there, Grace?"

Though Grace wanted to grab her brother and hug him tightly and simultaneously wanted to pick up something and hit him over the head, she did neither. Swallowing, she nodded and moved to a nearby table.

"Would you like some coffee or tea or something?"

She could tell from his voice he was nervous. "No, Clay. All I want is to know why you've been gone all these years and why you've chosen this particular time to return with all these children in tow."

He sighed. "I know I owe you an explanation. It's long overdue, and I will tell you more later. Right now, just let me say that I was released from my government job and allowed to return to Settlers Ridge. On the way, I found these children..."

She interrupted. "Lance told me you were a present-day Pied Piper, but that still doesn't explain anything."

He raised an eyebrow. "Pied Piper?"

"It's a poem by Robert Browning, telling of a piper who children followed out of town. But that isn't important now. What I want to know is why you're here now and what you plan to do with all those children."

Clay tried again to explain. "I was on my way into town when I found two of the children."

"I know all of that. Lance told me. He also told me how you went with him to rescue the others. I understand all that and it was noble of you to do it for these children. But the main thing I want to know is why you haven't got in touch with me...for all of these years."

"I wish I could tell you everything, but I can't."

"Why not?"

He sighed. "It's not that I don't want to tell you, Grace. I just can't. I did a job for the government and I was sworn to secrecy." When she only stared at him, he added, "I've longed to see you

46

through the years, but all I could do was slip into town and make sure you were safe. Then, when you and Lance married, I knew he'd protect you for the rest of your life."

"You're right about that. We're a happy family."

"I know. He told me." He nodded toward the baby. "Would you mind if I saw my niece?"

Pleased he was interested, she held the baby toward him. "I named her Kathrine after our mother."

"Lance told me and I'm glad you did." A smile crossed his lips when he looked at the sleeping baby. "She's beautiful, Grace."

"Thank you." She eyed her brother. "You like children, don't you, Clay?"

He kind of shrugged. "I like them well enough."

"Since you've taken on the responsibility of the five of them, I thought you might like them a little."

He kind of grinned. "In this case, I had no choice. Their leader was killed, and they didn't have anyone else."

"What's your next move?"

"I hoped somebody would help me decide what to do next."

"Lance said the woman they were with was planning on moving into the Anderson place."

"That's right."

"Why don't you ride out there and see it? There's the possibility it could be set up as the orphanage. That may even be what she envisioned. If it's suitable, the town might be in favor of supporting it. If not, I figure the church probably would help out."

"That's not a bad idea." He took a deep breath. "I would like to get with you sometime today, if possible. There's a lot we need to talk about. But first, I plan to take the children to their leader's funeral this morning."

"I'm glad you want to talk with me, Clay. I hoped you would."

Sarah walked up with Mary in her arms. "I'm sorry to bother you, Mr. Clay, but Mary is having a fit to get back to you."

He held out his arms and Mary jumped into them.

"You need to take care of the children now, so I'm going to go." She stood. "I just had to come and see with my own eyes that it was really you."

Clay stood, too. "After the children get settled tonight, could I come to your house so we can talk?"

She nodded. "I'd like that. Our house is on the street behind the jail."

"Then, I'll see you tonight." He paused, then reached for her hand. "It really is good to see you, Grace. You look wonderful."

"Thank you." She returned the squeeze he'd given her hand. "Though I'm still in shock, I'm glad to see you looking so well. I look forward to talking with you tonight."

David came running up. "Mr. Clay, Thomas won't say he hurts, but he keeps frowning, and we know he hurts."

"Go take care of the children, Clay. They need you now. We'll talk tonight." Grace turned and headed out of the dining room.

Eight

Clay watched his sister walk out, then turned back to the children. He took his seat, picked up his coffee and glanced around the table. "Looks like you guys are about through. I guess I better eat fast."

"We've about finished." Sarah smiled at him. "It was a wonderful meal. What do you want us to do to pay for it?"

"The meal is all paid for. What I thought we'd do when you finish is to let the doctor come and check Thomas—"

Thomas interrupted. "I don't need no doctor. I'm fine."

"I'm sure you are, but you were hurt pretty seriously. I'd feel better if the doctor looked you over. If we get his approval, I thought that after we go to the funeral, we'd ride out to see the house Lucy Baker was buying for you."

Luke raised an eyebrow. "How'd you know about that house?"

"I was able to have a few words with the lady before she died. She told me about the Bible. That's where I found the letter explaining about the property."

An hour later, the doctor did give Thomas permission to go with the group to the funeral and if he still felt up to it, to go to the Anderson ranch. That was how Clay found himself driving the wagon the group had traveled in with David on the front bench beside him and Sarah, who had Mary in her lap. They sat on the other side of David. Thomas and Luke sat in the back on a blanket Clay had insisted they bring with them.

~ * ~

Standing in the graveyard with Mary in his arms, David at his left side and the other three at his right, Clay tried to keep a close eye on Thomas. The boy had insisted he was fine, but Clay wasn't too sure. The young man's normal bronze skin looked somewhat ashen. Adding to that, he kept wiping away beads of sweat that were popping out on his forehead.

Clay's attention was diverted when David reached up and took hold of his arm. "Why are all these people here, Mr. Clay?"

"They came to say goodbye to Miss Lucy."

"Why? Did they know her?"

"I don't know whether they did or not. But most of them thought she was a special lady."

He nodded. "She was."

Sarah leaned around Thomas and whispered, "Hush, David."

He nodded and got quiet.

Clay glanced around. Like David, he was surprised to see the number of people who had gathered to attend the burial. Of course, he recognized a few of them. Lance was there, as was Grace with little Kathrine. Deputy Bryce and Henrietta Olsen and her daughter stood with them. Also with them was a pretty woman with shiny auburn hair. She looked a little familiar, but for the life of him, he couldn't remember who she was. Doctor Wagner stood beside a man Clay didn't know.

The preacher, who Lance had told him was named Ellsworth, arrived with an older woman. Clay knew the man was too young to have been the preacher in Settlers Ridge when he'd lived there.

There were some other couples, a few cowboys, some younger and older men, and women and one group of businessmen. He didn't recognize any of them except the auburn-haired woman who seemed to be alone intrigued him. Of course, he realized some of them might well recognize him. He wondered if the pretty woman did.

The preacher conducted a reverent ceremony, and Clay could tell he was a caring person. He hoped the man's words helped the children accept that the one person who tried to help them was gone.

After the final prayer, Clay turned to the group. "I know you don't know many of these people, but some of them want to speak to you."

"Why?" Thomas asked.

"It may be hard for you to believe, but they care about what happened to Miss Baker, and they care about you."

"I doubt that."

Clay didn't have time to respond because the preacher came over to speak to them. He said the right words and the children nodded to him and Clay said, "Thank you for such a good service for someone you didn't know, Preacher."

"She must have been a caring person. These children are a testimony to that."

"They sure are," the elderly woman with him said. "I'm the preacher's mama. Gertrude Ellsworth is my name and I want you to know I'll be more than glad to help you out with these dear children if and when you need me."

Clay didn't know what to say, so he muttered, "Thank you, Mrs. Ellsworth."

Others came to say a few words of condolence and he got the feeling some of them were there only to look the children over. He wondered why.

The crowd thinned out, and Lance and Grace approached him. Grace gave him a warm smile. "Little Miss Mary sure does like you, brother."

"I like Mr. Clay, too," David said.

She patted his head. "I'm sure you do, and it looks like he likes you also."

"What do you plan to do now, Clay?" Lance asked.

"I brought the kids in their wagon and as soon as I speak to the doctor to make sure Thomas is able to go, we're going to ride out to the

Anderson place. I want to see what if anything needs to be done before they can move in."

"We're going to live there," Sarah said.

"Yeah," Luke added. "Miss Lucy said so."

Lance reached in his pocket and took out a key. "I talked with Hal Cramer, the lawyer. He said he couldn't make the funeral but wanted me to give you the key to Anderson's house. He figured you'd want to go look it over."

"Thanks, Lance."

The doctor walked up to Thomas. "Well, young man, you look a mite worse than you did when I checked you earlier. How are you feeling?"

"I'm fine," Thomas snapped.

"I know Mr. Hunter plans to take you all out to the Anderson place, but I think it might be a good idea if you stayed behind and rested. You were beat up pretty good, you know."

"I'm going with them."

Doctor Wagner reached in his pocket and turned to Clay. "In that case, take this with you. He may need it."

Clay took the medicine and slipped it in his pocket. "I'm sorry he insists on going with us, Doctor. I'd rather leave him here, but he won't stay, and the others refuse to go to the house without him."

"I'm surprised they're so close, since you said they all came from different backgrounds."

"I guess Miss Lucy instilled a sense of family into them. Now that she's gone, it looks as if they think it's them against the world."

"Or they feel all they have is each other." The doctor gave him a grin. "That is, until you came along."

Clay didn't know what to reply but inside he was thinking, *I'll do what I can to get them settled. But I can't always be there for them. I have a life of my own to lead and it sure doesn't include taking care of a bunch of orphans.*

The graveyard cleared and after promising Grace he'd try to come to her house in the evening so they could talk, Clay moved toward the wagon he'd parked in the dirt road that surrounded the cemetery. The children followed in silence.

What they'd find when they reached Anderson's spread, he wasn't sure. He only hoped it would be somewhere these children could call home. Maybe with the help of the persons named Alice and Phoebe, who might or might not show up, it could be.

~ * ~

As Clay pulled the wagon onto the overgrown road leading to the Anderson house, he noticed the whispered chatter among the children had stopped. He didn't say anything either. He was busy wondering what would become of these unlucky kids if Miss Lucy Baker's plan for this to become their home didn't work out the way she had envisioned it. His mind drifted to the women named Alice and Phoebe. Maybe they would be the answer for them, or maybe they could pull off whatever it was Miss Lucy had planned. He sure hoped so.

The house came into view and Sarah let out a gasp. The boys stared openly, and little Mary left Sarah's lap and latched onto Clay's neck. He managed to get the wagon stopped and the brake set before putting his arm around her.

"Well kids," he said. "This is it. Shall we go check it out?"

Still silent, they jumped out of the wagon, but waited for him to climb down and lead the way.

On the wrap-around porch, he reached into his pocket and took out the key Lance had given him. He slipped it into the lock and turned it. The huge wooden door with the stained-glass windows on each side swung open after a gentle nudge.

Stepping into the entrance, he felt he'd entered another world. A world where only the rich and maybe famous lived. Before them, a curving staircase fanned off to the left and right from a platform above. There were two velvet chairs with a carved table between them against one of the entrance walls. On the other stood a huge grandfather clock. Clay realized the last time he'd seen anything as elaborate was when he'd served as a bodyguard for the princess.

"Are you sure we're in the right place, Mr. Clay?" Sarah whispered.

"Yes, Sarah. This is the place." He shifted Mary to his other arm. "Now that we're here, let's explore the downstairs first."

They found the kitchen with its two-bedroom adjoining apartment, informal eating area and large sitting area with rock fireplace. There were a formal dining room and living room which could be accessed from the entry or the kitchen.

Down the hall were four other rooms. Some had furniture and others didn't. Clay had no idea what the empty ones were used for, but figured they could be used for whatever purpose one liked.

Upstairs they went to the right and found three bedrooms on each side of the hall. The space to the left at the top of the stairway was a surprise. There was a large bedroom with a smaller room that he supposed was a nursery off to the side. Through another door, they found a small sitting room with a hall leading to a large office. The entire apartment was furnished in elaborate cherry wood furniture.

Clay decided that Cleve Anderson might not have had the biggest ranch in the area, but he sure must have had the most extravagant house.

A loud female voice sounded up the stairs and interrupted their tour. "Hello! Is there anyone here?'

Nine

When Spencer told Wilma Nelda wasn't feeling well, she insisted he go home and take care of her. "It's only a couple of hours until closing time and I'll close the store and lock up. You need to be with Nelda."

"I appreciate it, Wilma. The closer it gets to the baby's arrival, she feels worse and worse."

"I know you both will be glad when it finally decides to show up."

"We sure will." He hung up his apron. "By the way, did I tell you I got a letter from my half-sister, Kathy Chalfant today? She is excited about coming west to help us out for a while."

Wilma had almost expected this to happen. But she didn't let him know she was worried. To keep Spencer from knowing she was concerned, she forced a smile. "I'm guessing Nelda is excited about her visit, too."

"She sure is." He smiled. "Now, don't you stay too late. I know how responsible you are, but you need to take your time off."

She laughed. "I'll leave on time tonight, Spencer. I need to go to Miss Purdy's shop and pick up my dress to wear to Elizabeth Donahue's wedding."

"Nelda was talking about that. I sure hope she feels up to going."

"I hope so, too."

"Then I'll leave, and I'll see you tomorrow."

"Sure thing," she said as he went out the door."

Sighing, she turned to the shelf behind the counter and began rearranging the cans there. She knew this would keep her busy and she wouldn't think her job might be in jeopardy. But if this weren't the case, why was his sister coming to help out when Nelda had the baby? Though Spencer hadn't said a word, she knew by the way he treated Nelda, family came first with him, and she believed it should be that way.

The bell over the door jangled and she looked around. Surprise crossed her face when she saw Clay Hunter headed toward her. She remembered how she'd looked at him with the little girl in his arms at the funeral. At the time she'd thought he was a handsome man, and one who would someday make a great father. Then she'd silently berated herself for having such thoughts. But they flitted through her mind again. He was even more handsome this afternoon.

Forcing her eyes from his face she muttered, "Can I help you?"

He gave her a smile. "I sure hope so. Miss Alice gave me a list of what she said she had to have tonight." He handed it to her and smiled again. "I hope you don't think I'm being too bold, but I have a feeling I should know you."

"It's been a long time, but we did know each other when we were younger. I'm Wilma Lawson and I know you're Grace's brother, Clay."

He nodded. "I knew you looked familiar. Please, don't think I'm trying to be forward, but I have to say, you sure grew up beautifully."

Wilma couldn't help it. She blushed. "Thank you."

"And I want to thank you for coming to the funeral this morning. It was thoughtful of you to do so."

"I wanted to be there." To avoid his deep grey eyes, she looked at the list. "If the lady is in a hurry for these items, we better gather them."

"You're right. She wanted me to get it back so she could cook supper for the children before it got too late." He chuckled. "She also told me to buy a milk cow and some chickens because the children needed milk and eggs. I told her she'd just have to wait on those because you didn't sell them at the mercantile."

She kind of frowned. "Lance said the children were alone. Except for you, of course."

"The children were traveling with Miss Lucy Baker, but Alice and Phoebe Baker didn't want to come by wagon. They came in on the stage to meet her here. They got into town this afternoon and found out Miss Lucy had been killed and had already been buried. They asked around and learned I had taken the children out to the Anderson ranch to look around, so they hired a man at the livery to take them out there. They arrived while the children and I were still looking around at the house." He shook his head. "I intended to bring the kids back to the hotel tonight, but Miss Alice wouldn't hear of it. She said Lucy told her the house was going to be their home and they might as well spend the night there."

"Sounds like a strong woman."

He chuckled. "It didn't take me long to learn I shouldn't argue with her."

Wilma smiled. "Then I guess we better start gathering her supplies. You don't want to keep her waiting too long."

"Can I help?"

"Sure. You can start gathering the canned food while I measure out the dry ingredients."

The bell jangled and a tall cowboy with a little boy in his arms walked in.

Wilma rose up from the barrel she was bending over. "Hello, Jed. Don't tell me you and Aaron are shopping without Amelia."

"She stopped in at Miss Purdy's Dress Shop. Something about the dress for her mother's wedding. My son and I didn't want to get involved, so we told her to meet us here."

"I can understand that. I'm going there to check on my dress after work." She reached out her arms to Aaron. "What have you been up to, big boy?"

Jed set his son down and the little boy toddled to Wilma with outstretched arms. "Candy?"

"My goodness, son. At least say hello to Miss Wilma before you start asking her for candy."

"He knows I'll not let him out of here without a peppermint stick."

"I know. You have him spoiled."

"I sure do." She picked Aaron up and walked to the candy jars. "I'm glad you and your daddy came in. Jed, let me introduce you to Clay Hunter. He's Grace's brother, but he had left town before you showed up here." She turned to Clay. "Do you remember Amelia Donahue?"

When Clay nodded, Wilma continued, "This is her husband, Jed Wainwright, and this handsome little fellow is their son, Aaron."

"I do remember Amelia. I recall how much Grace cried when her friend left for school in the east. I see she must have come back to Settlers Ridge." He set the cans in his arms on the counter and reached out his hand to Jed. "It's nice to meet her husband and son."

Jed shook his hand. "Good to meet you, too, Clay. Have you returned to Settlers Ridge for a visit or are you moving back?"

"I've been released from my government job and plan to settle here."

"In that case, welcome home."

Wilma looked down at the little boy in her arms, "Sweetheart, let's get your candy so Auntie Wilma can help Clay gather the rest of his supplies. He needs to get them back to Miss Alice because he doesn't want to make her mad." Her voice fell to a whisper. "I think he's afraid of the woman."

Clay laughed. "I might be. A little bit, anyway."

Jed raised an eyebrow but didn't say anything.

Clay went on. "I don't know if you've heard or not, but I was on my way to town when I came upon a wrecked wagon. The woman driving was penned under it and dying, and I discovered two little kids there alone."

"I did hear about the rescuing of those children and how you went with the sheriff to rescue the other three from outlaws. I'm glad to meet the Good Samaritan. Lucky for all those kids you came along when you did."

"I guess I did show up at the right time."

"I also heard the woman had or was going to purchase the Anderson ranch. Is that still the plan?"

"I sure hope it can be worked out. The woman's two sisters, Alice and Phoebe, showed up there this afternoon. I'd taken the children out there to look the place over. I intended to bring them back to town, but Miss Alice wouldn't hear of it. She demanded I come get some supplies while she and her sister began setting up housekeeping. She said they were going to stay there tonight."

"Sounds like a tough woman. I admit, I'd probably be afraid of her, too."

Wilma walked back with Aaron. He was sucking on a peppermint stick as she plopped him in his daddy's arms. "Now, Jed. You have to admit, if you can handle Amelia, you can handle any woman who comes along."

"You're probably right." Turning back to Clay, he said, "If there's anything I can do to help you out getting the place up and running, I'd be glad to."

"Clay said she wants a milk cow and some laying chickens. He told her he couldn't get them today and she'd have to make do for a day or two. Maybe you know where he can find some for sale."

"I'm sure I can." He looked back at Clay. "As a matter of fact, the other day, my partner, Curt Allison said something about extra cows on his section of the ranch. If he still has them, I'd be happy for you to have one or two of them. We have plenty of beef and I'd rather see them being used for milk instead of being slaughtered."

"I'd appreciate it if you'd let me know if he wants to sell them. I'm willing to pay the going price."

"We can discuss the price after I find out if they're available."

Wilma finished gathering the things on Alice's list. She held Aaron while Jed helped Clay load the wagon.

When the wagon pulled away, Jed came back into the mercantile. "Clay seems like a nice guy."

"Yes, he does. But I can't help wondering why after all the years he's been gone he suddenly decided to come back to Settlers Ridge."

He smiled. "I can understand him rescuing the children and bringing them to town, but he has gone the extra mile. I don't know many men who would do that."

"I agree." She shrugged. "I remember Clay when he was a young boy, but I still wonder where he was and what he has been doing all those years while Grace kept hoping he'd come home one day."

"Well, he's here now. Maybe he'll explain to her and eventually to us why he didn't get in touch."

"Maybe so."

~ * ~

As soon as Clay returned with the supplies, Alice shooed him and the children out of the kitchen. They gathered in the parlor. He took a seat on the sofa and Mary immediately jumped into his lap. The others gathered close to him and kept looking as if they had a secret they needed to share.

He took a deep breath, "It looks like you all have something you want to tell me, so why don't you come out with it?"

For a minute, nobody said anything, then David blurted, "I'm scared of Miss Alice. I always have been."

Clay chuckled. "She's not going to hurt you. It's just her way."

"But..."

"Hush, David," Luke said, then looked at Sarah. "You said you'd tell him."

"Tell me what?"

Sarah swallowed, then in a soft voice she said, "We had a meeting after you left and picked out our bedrooms. Mary and I will sleep in a room together until she's older. The boys said they wanted to stay in one of the rooms across the hall from us."

"We're all going to sleep in the same room together like in the hotel." David grinned.

"For a while, anyway," Luke added.

"Miss Phoebe is going to sleep upstairs because she said we might need something. Miss Alice is going to sleep in one of the rooms near the kitchen."

"It sounds like you have it all worked out."

"We do."

"Hush, David," Luke said again.

Sarah took another breath. "Miss Alice said it wouldn't be proper for you to sleep with the boys since they're across the hall from the girls, so..."

He interrupted. "I thought I'd go back to town to sleep."

"No," several voices said at one time.

He raised an eyebrow. "Why not?"

"Miss Phoebe made up the room at the other end of the house for you. Miss Alice said it was probably where the owners slept, and it would be the right place for you, since you'd need the office there to run this place."

"I don't think..."

"You will stay with us, won't you, Mr. Clay?"

He looked into Sarah's pleading eyes, then at all the faces before him. Though he hadn't said a word, even Thomas had that look in his eyes. He needed someone he could count on, too. How could he say no to these trusting faces?

"All right. I'll stay." He didn't add, 'for tonight anyway' because there were several expressions of relief and happiness from them. Mary jumped up from her sitting position on his lap, threw her arms around his neck and placed a kiss on his cheek. It occurred to him that Mary was more aware of what was going on than anyone suspected.

Ten

When the children went in to eat supper, Clay went to the barn and saddled his horse. "Well, Whisper, I'm glad I picked you up at the livery and tied you to the back of the wagon, so I'd have a ride back to town. I didn't fancy riding that work horse that belonged to Miss Lucy."

Whisper slung her head and snorted.

"Good thing I made you a place in the barn when we got here. I figured we'd go back to town and stay, but it looks like those kids had other plans." He chuckled. "David made me promise twice that I'd come back and sleep here tonight. I wonder if he's not getting a little too attached to me."

Mounting, he added, "Now, I better start thinking about what I'm going to tell my sister when we get back to Settlers Ridge. I know I can't tell her everything, but I want to tell her enough to explain why I haven't been in touch with her for all these years."

Over and over he ran the scenarios in his head as they headed to town. But he was pulling up to the neat little house on the street behind the jail, and he still wasn't sure what he was going to say to her.

Throwing the reins around the hitching post, he dismounted, stepped onto the porch, then knocked on the door.

Lance, with the baby in his arms, opened it. "Glad you could make it, Clay. Come in."

He followed him into the cozy room, which was connected to the eat-in kitchen. "I see you're taking care of my niece."

Lance chuckled. "Grace lets me hold her while she's cooking."

Grace turned from the stove. "Don't bother to sit down over there. Put Kathrine in her cradle and come on to the table. I'm getting ready to dish up supper."

Clay watched as Lance put the baby in the cradle beside the wall near the fireplace. He smiled as he looked at her. "As I told Grace, Kathrine is a real beauty."

"She looks like her mother, thank the good Lord."

"I hope she grows up to be as beautiful as my sister."

Grace walked up to them. "If you two are through swooning over Kathrine, please come to the table. Supper is ready."

~ * ~

On his ride back to the ranch, Clay found himself deep in thought. He couldn't believe how easily and quickly his sister had welcomed him back into her life or how she'd accepted his explanation of why he hadn't contacted her earlier.

Maybe he should have told her about his stint in prison, but he didn't want to tell her that was the reason he couldn't come home. He'd only admitted the government officials had recruited him and his work with them had to be kept top secret, and that was the reason he slipped in and out of town without contacting her. He was pleased that she had figured out the flowers he'd left on their mother's grave had been from him.

~ * ~

Sitting around the campfire, the man took a sip of the black coffee that was laced with whiskey. "When you gonna get that gal in the general store off your mind, Merve?"

"I can't, Woody. She done somethn' to my heart the minute I looked at her."

"That's foolish. She's probably a nice woman who's married to that fellow who came into the store. He looked like he was tough enough to blow your head off if'en you touched his woman."

"I could handle him."

"Well, forget it. We ain't got time for you to pine for a woman. I've got to figure out how to get Buck and Slappy out of jail."

"I can't believe that sorry sheriff shot Neely."

"Don't worry. He'll pay for it as soon as I find out more about him."

"Maybe my pretty Wilma could probably tell us all about him."

"How do you know her name's Wilma?"

"That's what that fellow called her when he come in the store."

Woody chewed his lip. "You know what, Merve? You might of hit on somethin'."

"What?"

"We might be able to get her and make her tell us a lot of things about this town. She might even know the sheriff."

"Why do we need to know about the sheriff?"

"Don't you see? It could give us a idee on how to get our buddies out of jail."

Merve's eyes lit up. "I see what you mean. That way you can ask her questions and I can do somethin' else with her. When we gonna do it?"

"We've got to do it right. Let me think on it a bit."

"Think fast, Woody. I can't wait long." He lifted his coffee to his mouth and took a drink. His eyes had glazed over in anticipation.

~ * ~

The next morning it was still too early to open the store when Wilma, with a mug of coffee in her hand, came down the stairs and into the mercantile. She hadn't slept well, and though she knew she should try to sleep longer, she knew it was impossible. She had too much on her mind.

Though she thought she'd have more time to look for another job, Spencer had informed her last night that his half-sister Kathy Chalfant would arrive at the end of the month. He hadn't mentioned Wilma leaving her apartment or her job, but she knew she couldn't continue with either. It wouldn't be fair to the Barringtons or Spencer's sister, or to herself.

The Barringtons had been wonderful to her and she decided she'd help the woman get started in the store. But it wouldn't take long for her to grasp the requirements of the job. Especially since Spencer would be here to help her.

Though she knew she'd eventually have to find another job, Wilma wasn't as worried about that as she was about finding a place to live. She'd saved most of the income she'd been paid since working there and it amounted to enough to live on for a while. Though Spencer hadn't told her his sister would be moving into the apartment, she was sure she eventually would. After all, she was sure he and Nelda wouldn't want her living with them for a long period of time.

For a moment, she wondered if she should write her family in Texas and let them know her situation had changed. But she didn't want to do that. She'd write her mother, as she did every couple of months, but she'd tell her something else because if the woman knew the situation, she'd write back and demand Wilma head there immediately. Of course, Gladys Lawson did tell her daughter she should go there in every letter she wrote. But Wilma had always ignored the demand and wrote about other things. She knew unless something drastic happened, she'd never move to Texas. Leaving Settlers Ridge, Wyoming, was the last thing she wanted to do.

She loved it there and wanted to spend the rest of her life there. If she ever went to Texas, it would only be to visit her family. She had long ago decided that wouldn't happen until she was married. That way her mother couldn't demand she stay there with her.

Finishing her coffee, she sat the cup on the edge of the counter and donned her apron. Since the sun was up and there was enough light in the store, she decided she'd put out the rest of the stock that had arrived yesterday. After all, it might help take her mind off her troubles, and when she was through, it would be time to open up the store.

~ * ~

Surprised to see Thomas and Luke coming into the barn so early in the day, Clay muttered, "Good morning, fellows."

"You're still here," Thomas blurted.

Before Clay could answer, Luke said, "I told him you would be, but he didn't believe me."

"Why would you not think I'd be here, Thomas?"

Ignoring the question, Thomas asked, "How long are you going to stay?"

Clay took a deep breath. He knew Thomas didn't trust him, and the others were waiting to see what would happen next. Since they'd lost the person who had given them some hope for their future, the last thing he wanted to do was make these children worry about what was to happen to them when he did leave.

Finally, he said, "I'm not sure what's going to happen to any of us. I figure the best thing we can do is take it one day at a time."

Luke nodded. "Miss Lucy used to say things like that, and I think it makes sense to do it that way."

Thomas didn't look as agreeable. "What are you going to do today?"

Clay hadn't wanted to say anything about his doubts until he found out more about the situation, but he decided maybe it was best to let them know. That way, if they had to pull out, it wouldn't come as a shock. "When I got back last night, I went over some of the papers Miss Lucy Baker left and the ones her sisters brought. Things are not clear about the ownership of this ranch now that Miss Baker is no longer with us. I thought I'd go into Settlers Ridge and check with the lawyer. After that, we'll make plans of what should be done next."

Luke looked startled. "You mean we don't own this ranch?"

"As I said, there are some things that need clearing up. After I meet with the lawyer, we'll know more."

"Are you going to take this ranch away from us?" Thomas demanded.

"Of course not."

"I wouldn't bet on that." A furious Thomas whirled around, and Clay heard him mutter as he stalked out, "I knew from the start we couldn't trust him."

Luke shook his head. "Don't pay no attention to him, Mr. Clay. It took him a long time to trust Miss Lucy and he don't know you yet."

"I know, Luke. He probably has reasons not to trust strangers, and I'm still a stranger to him."

"I trust you, Mr. Clay."

"Thank you, son. I trust you, too."

Before either of them could say anything else, David came running into the barn. "Miss Alice told me to tell all of you to come eat breakfast before it gets cold."

"Sounds good. Let's go eat so I can get to town."

But it was two days later before Clay was able to go into town. On the first day he planned to go, two hands from Jed Wainwright's Circle Two Ranch showed up with two milk cows. Though they stayed to help, it took most of the day to repair the fence and the stalls for the cows.

On the second day, he, along with the boys, built a chicken coop for the fowl the men said would arrive late the next afternoon.

On the third day, he was able to get away before there was an interruption.

Eleven

Arriving in Settlers Ridge by midmorning, Clay found the office with the sign reading *Hal E. Cramer - Attorney at Law* located a little way down the street from Barrington's Mercantile. He tied his horse to the hitching post, hoping the lawyer wouldn't be too busy to meet with him. Opening the front door, he entered a small room with a desk, a couple of chairs and a table at the window with a lamp and a few books. The office was empty, but he noticed a door to the left stood ajar.

"Hello," he called. "Is there anyone in?"

A male voice answered. "Be right out."

The adjoining door opened wide and a slightly overweight man came out. He had thinning hair and a neat mustache. "How can I help you?"

"I'm Clay Hunter and if he's not too busy, I'd like to talk with Mr. Cramer about the Anderson ranch."

Hal frowned. "Do you have a reason to talk to me about it?"

Clay wondered why the man was so unfriendly but decided it must be his personality. "I need to make sure the place is still available for the children before they get settled in."

The man lifted an eyebrow. "Are you the man who found those children?"

"I am."

Cramer seemed to relax. "Good. I thought you were one of the fools trying to get hold of the kids."

"What do you mean?"

"Let me lock the front door and we'll go into my office where we won't be disturbed. I'll explain it to you then."

~ * ~

Alice looked up as Phoebe came into the dining room a little late. "Sorry," she muttered as she took her seat. "I wanted to finish upstairs before I came down."

"We will forgive you this time, sister," Alice said.

The children only looked at her but said nothing.

Alice was a little surprised because the young ones were usually vocal when an adult broke one of the rules. She glanced at the subdued children sitting around the dinner table. For some reason, they were unusually quiet and only picked at their food. She wondered what could have changed their mood between breakfast and noon. She recalled it had been a relaxed and joyful morning meal.

Sarah had said she planned to take Mary to see if there were any eggs in the chicken coop. Luke said he and Thomas were going to make sure things were still all right in the barn for the cows. David had asked what he could do. They all had laughed, and Luke told David he was to come with him and Thomas. After eating, they all rushed outside with their spirits high.

Now here they were acting as if their world had collapsed, and Alice felt it her duty to intervene. She decided not to ask them directly but try another tactic.

"I notice none of you are eating much. Is there something wrong with the food?"

The children glanced at each other, then Sarah said, "The food is fine, Miss Alice, I guess we're all just tired."

"What have you done to make you all so tired?"

Sarah shrugged, but didn't answer.

"What about you boys?"

Thomas and Luke also shrugged, but David blurted, "I'm worried."

Phoebe looked at him and frowned, and Alice looked concerned. "What in the world have you got to be worried about?"

"I'm afraid Mr. Clay won't come back."

"Why do you think he's not coming back?"

"Thomas said he won't."

She turned toward Thomas, "Why in the world would you tell him such a thing?"

Thomas looked smug. "Well, he's not here, is he?"

"You're right, He is not. He had business in town today. I'm sure he'll be back as soon as he is finished."

Thomas shrugged and looked down at his plate. "You'll see when he doesn't show up."

"Yes, we will." She looked around the table. "As for the rest of you, finish your dinner. I didn't spend all morning standing over a hot stove cooking for you not to eat."

"Yes, ma'am." Several voices muttered as they began to eat. Although it was without enthusiasm.

~ * ~

Clay stared across the desk at Hal Cramer. "I can't believe this is happening."

"I suppose they think they've been sent their own orphan train."

"Their what?"

"Orphan train."

"What's an orphan train?"

"I'm surprised you don't know about the trains filled with orphans being sent from the East and the South in hopes they will be adopted to good homes with families in the West who want children."

"The children I brought in are not looking for homes. They had planned to live with Lucy Baker and her sisters."

"I only wanted you to know what several families are doing."

"What I don't understand is why they would think these children could be adopted."

"I don't know for sure, but I think some of them really want to give one or two of them a good home. I suspect others think they can get their hands on some or all of the Anderson property through one of the kids."

"The possession of the ranch is what I came to check with you about, Mr. Cramer. I'm confused about the papers Miss Baker left and the ones Miss Alice gave me." He took the papers from his vest pocket and handed them across the desk. "I need someone who knows about such things to explain them to me."

"Let me have a minute to glance through these. I need to see if anything has changed."

"I also have a message for you. I'm not sure what she meant by it, and I don't even know if I should tell you, but Miss Alice sent you a message."

"Oh. What was it?"

"She said to tell you she and Phoebe agree with Lucy's choice. Does that make any sense to you?"

"Maybe, a little." Cramer gave him a half smile and went back to studying the papers in his hand.

Clay sat back and watched the lawyer. He felt there was something about the situation Cramer wasn't telling him. Something that could possibly affect the lives of the children, and he hoped he could ask the right questions to find out what it was before it was too late.

The attorney laid the papers aside. "Well, Mr. Hunter, I see the Baker women have agreed you're the right person to be responsible for these children."

"Wait a minute. I just rescued them and brought them to town. That's as far as my responsibility goes."

"I realize why you'd think that. Maybe I should make myself clear."

"Please do."

"There is nothing saying you have to raise these children. Nothing at all. It only means you will make the decisions concerning their future, whether it be with you or someone else."

Clay frowned. "Could you be a little clearer about that?"

"As I mentioned earlier, several people in town have said they'd like to adopt the children. For instance, Mr. and Mrs. Costas said they could give the older boy and girl a home. Seems Mr. Costas is developing rheumatism and it's hard for him to get around. He said another boy would be a big help to him and the two sons he has, and the girl would be a help to his wife."

"Are they a nice family?"

"Salt of the earth." He took a breath. "The Smithers are childless and said the little boy would be a blessing to them, and before you ask, as far as I know, they're good people, too. They live in Swanson. She's the circuit judge's niece and he has a good job."

When Clay said nothing, Hal went on. "Now, this one I can't vouch for. Her name's Matilda Hurley and everybody calls her Big Matilda because she's as big as any man around. She lives out in the hills and doesn't come to town often. But she was here the other day to sell the skins she'd trapped. Besides trapping, she does all sorts of strange healings and picks up a little money from superstitious people who swear she does have special powers. Some folks even say she's a witch. While she was here, she said she's sure she can make the child talk, and she felt led to come back later and get the little girl who couldn't talk."

Clay grew irritated. "She sounds touched to me."

"She may be. I'm only telling what I've heard people say about the children."

"So, the good citizens of Settlers Ridge have decided this is what should be done with the kids, though they've never met them?"

"I didn't mean to offend you, Mr. Hunter. I'm just giving you the facts."

"What will happen to the ranch the Baker sisters bought for them if the children don't live there?"

"It will have to be sold and the money divided among them." He sighed. "There is another alternative. If a suitable couple will agree to raise all five of the children, then the ranch will become theirs with the stipulation that the children all live there until they are grown, and when they do grow up, they will be given a parcel of land to build a home on or enough money to settle elsewhere."

"You mean by agreeing to raise the kids, someone will be given the ranch?"

"Yes. A portion of it, anyway. The children will still get their share."

Clay frowned. "This is a lot to try to understand. Is there anything else I need to know?"

"Nothing at this point. You need to make some decisions about the children's future before we go any further."

"Then I suppose I have a lot to think about."

"You certainly do, Mr. Hunter. Why don't you let this all settle in, then come back to see me in a week or so? We'll talk again then."

"I'll do that, Mr. Cramer." He stood and held out his hand. "Thank you."

~ * ~

Mulling over the things he'd learned at the lawyer's office, Clay opened the door to Barrington's Mercantile and stepped inside under the jingling bell.

Wilma turned from the shelves with a duster in her hand. "Hello, Clay."

"Hi, Wilma. I hope you're having a good day."

"I am." She placed the duster on the counter and smiled at him. "How can I help you?"

"I'm getting ready to go back to the ranch and I thought I'd get a treat for the children."

"How nice. I have a selection of candies, if that is what you were thinking about."

"It is."

"We have the usual peppermint sticks we always carry, and I just put out a new jar of lemon drops this morning."

"I'll take both. A couple of the peppermint sticks each and a sack of lemon drops. Add some extra lemon drops. Miss Alice and Miss Phoebe might like some of them."

"You're so thoughtful, Clay. I know the children will be excited, and I'm sure the ladies will appreciate you remembering them." She moved to the front counter and opened the big glass jars containing the candy.

"Wilma, Mr. Cramer told me there had been some talk in town about the children. Have you heard anything?"

"I've heard some, but I figured most of it was just talk. You know how people are."

He shook his head. "I guess I'd forgotten how gossip can spread in a small town."

"Well, when anything unusual happens, it gives folks something to think about except their dull routine." She laughed. "You should have been here last summer when Mr. Benson's cow had a calf with three legs. Some people actually thought it was a sign the end of time was at hand."

He chuckled. "I guess that did cause a stir."

"It did. But not as much as when you showed up in town after being away all these years, and on top of that, having five orphans with you. By the way, how are those children adjusting at the ranch, and is Miss Alice still keeping you straight?"

"The kids are doing all right. Jed Wainwright sent us a couple milk cows and some chickens. The boys helped me fix a stall for Minnie and Beulah, as they named the cows, then they helped build a chicken coop." He smiled. "As for Miss Alice, she's doing a good job. So is Miss Phoebe."

"They're good kids, Clay. I knew that as soon as I met the little ones." She smiled. "I went by to see them the first night at the hotel."

"They told me. Thank you for doing that."

"It was my pleasure."

The bell over the door jangled and Gertrude Ellsworth came in. "Hello, folks."

Wilma greeted her and Clay tipped his hat and gave her a big smile. He then paid for the candy and bid the ladies good-bye.

Twelve

As soon as the door closed behind him, Mrs. Ellsworth said, "Oh my. Did I interrupt?"

Wilma wished Gertrude weren't so intuitive. She decided to pretend she didn't know what the woman was talking about. "Whatever do you mean?"

"You know good and well what I mean. You watched the handsome Mr. Hunter go out the door and I could see in your eyes you wished you were going with him."

Wilma blushed. "Now, Mrs. Ellsworth…"

Mrs. Ellsworth interrupted. "Don't try to hide it, my dear. Some people might not notice, but I've lived long enough to know a young lady is having romantic ideas about a young man by the look in her eyes."

"Oh, Mrs. Ellsworth."

She reached out and patted Wilma's arm. "Now, now, dear. Don't you worry. I'm not going to say a thing. I fully remember the first time I laid eyes on Mr. Bernard Ellsworth. I instantly knew he was the man

I wanted to spend the rest of my life with. Of course, it didn't work out that way. He passed on nearly ten years ago and left me."

"I'm so sorry."

"Don't be, Wilma. It was meant to be. They say the good Lord leaves the stronger person behind. I've lived long enough to know that's true. Bernard could have never made it on his own. But thank you to the Man above, we had over thirty fantastic years together."

"What a wonderful story." Wilma gave her a big smile. "But in this case, I'm sure my attraction to Clay Hunter is all one sided."

"Don't think that way, Wilma. He's like all men. He just needs a little encouragement from the right woman."

"I'm afraid he'll never think I'm the right woman. He's shown no interest in me at all."

"I wouldn't say that. I'm sure he's more interested in you than you think."

"How can you say that?"

"Maybe I shouldn't say this, but I saw how interested he was the first time he laid eyes on you."

"When was that?"

"I probably should have been more focused on the solemn occasion, but I've lived long enough to know a funeral is for the living, not the dead. Their soul has already met its destiny. It is nowhere near the empty corpse."

"What do funerals have to do with it?"

"Everything. The day they buried poor Miss Baker's body, I watched Mr. Hunter and those precious children. His eyes were roving all over the crowd. Then he saw you and his eyes lit up just like when you strike a match and hold it to a wick that hasn't been trimmed short enough. You know how the flame shoots to the top of the lamp. That's the way his eyes became when his look rested on you."

Wilma's cheeks colored again. "Oh, Mrs. Ellsworth. If only I could believe you."

"You can, my dear. You can. In fact, I'll go so far as to say you'll be making wedding plans by the end of the year. That is, if you're not already married to the man."

"Mrs. Ellsworth!"

"As I said, just mark my words. Things will work out the way you hope." She patted Wilma's arm again. "Now, dear. Let's tend to business. Margo has decided to make my son a special pie for supper and she needs some sugar. I guess about two pounds. I tell you this second pregnancy of hers put all sorts of crazy notions in her head. She made a cake two days ago and we still have half of it. Yet she's determined to cook another sweet."

~ * ~

It was dusk when Clay started home. He hadn't meant to stay so long in town, but after the meeting with Hal Cramer, he needed time to think. To do that he had to stay away from the children.

He thought going to the mercantile would help. It helped, all right. It made him realize how much he'd missed female company in the last weeks he'd been on the government job and the few days it took him to transition back home. He might have known a woman as pretty as Wilma Lawson would make him feel that way.

But had this been wise? Maybe she had a special man in her life. Or maybe she was dedicated to working in the store and wasn't interested in any man, especially a man like him. A man with a checkered past.

To get pretty Wilma and what she might want out of his mind, he'd headed to the saloon. There, he found little to ease his troubled mind. Though the women were friendly and seemed agreeable, none of them could compare to the beautiful shopkeeper, and he was in no mood for a substitute.

The only productive thing he garnered in the Wildcat was gossip about the children and a little insight on the people wanting to adopt them. From what he'd learned, none of the homes being offered seemed promising. Especially the one offered by that woman, Matilda. After hearing the talk and remembering what the lawyer had said, he knew he had to make sure she didn't get her hands on Mary.

The closer he got to the ranch, the more he wanted to hurry. For some reason he had the need to make sure the kids were all right, and not just Mary. The words the burly man in the bar had said resonated in his mind: *"Don't give a damn what he says, with a few licks of*

my whip that Injun boy could do the work of two men at the mill."
Before Clay could react, the man was dragged away by one of his
buddies.

Now he had another child to watch out for, and the sooner he
got back home to do it, the better it would be.

After brushing down his horse and putting her in a stall, he
hurried to the house and went in through the back door. He hadn't
realized he was hungry until the smell of food that permeated the
room hit him. He wondered what Alice had served for supper, and if
there was any of it left.

"So, you did come back." Alice said on her way into the room
from the walk-in pantry.

"Of course, I did. Did you think I wouldn't?"

"I thought you might, but I may be only one of the few who
thought that. Thomas convinced most of the kids that you'd run
out on them. I think David still believes in you, and of course, Mary
had no doubts. I don't know what Phoebe thinks. As you may have
guessed, she doesn't talk a lot."

"Where are the kids, Alice?"

"Gone to bed. Thomas said they'd have to do all the work
tomorrow and they better turn in early so they could get enough rest.
Phoebe went to tuck the girls in."

"I brought them a little treat, but I guess I can give it to them in
the morning."

"They only went up a little while ago. Why don't you go upstairs
and let them see you? I know it'd make them sleep better to know
you did return."

"I'll do that." He swallowed, slung his saddlebags over his
shoulder and started for the stairs.

"I saw that hungry look on your face. I'll have a plate for you
when you come back."

He didn't turn around, but he smiled and nodded. Miss Alice
was one in a million. She acted tough but he was sure she was hiding
a tender heart. Too bad she didn't have children of her own. She
would have made a fabulous mother.

Clay opened the door to the boys' room and a light was still burning in the oil lamp on the table. "I see you're still up."

David broke into a wide grin and ran toward him. He threw his arms around his waist. "I knew Thomas was wrong. I knew you'd come home."

"What are you talking about?"

Luke said, "Thomas said you'd left, and you wouldn't come back."

Clay lifted an eyebrow. "Why in the world did you tell these boys such a thing, Thomas?"

He shrugged. "I thought you were gone."

"I told you I had things to do in town. I didn't intend to be gone for the day, but it took longer than I thought it would. I had no intention of not returning."

Luke gave Thomas a sharp look. "That's the last time I'm going to listen to you, cause you're just about always wrong."

"I am not!"

"How about you saying you didn't trust Miss Alice? You said she'd starve us, but she hasn't so far."

"She still might." Thomas let a stubborn look cross his face,

"No, she won't." David yelled. "I'm kind of scared of her, but I don't think she's going to hurt us."

"Of course, she won't," Clay said. "But Thomas has a right to his opinion. He may have good reason not to trust people."

"What reason?" David asked.

"If he wants you to know, I suppose he'll tell you. Now, why don't you guys all get in bed? We have things to do tomorrow."

"You will be here, won't you?" Luke asked.

"Yes. I'll be here."

"I'm glad," David said as he ran to his bed. "Good night, Mr. Clay."

As he went out the door, Clay heard Thomas say, "Maybe I was wrong about him this time."

"Yes, you were," Luke answered. "Remember, Miss Lucy always told us there were good people and bad people in the world. I'm beginning to think Mr. Clay is one of the good people."

"I know he is," David said.

"Time will tell," Thomas said. "I'll make up my mind later."

Clay smiled as he went across the hall to check on the girls. Mary was asleep, but Sara gave him a big smile. "Just wanted to say goodnight."

She continued to smile and whispered, "I'm glad you're back."

He figured Thomas's tale about him not returning had gotten to her, too. He decided not to mention it. Maybe he'd discuss it with them tomorrow. "Sorry I didn't get here in time to eat supper with you, but I'm glad to be back. I'll see you in the morning."

"Good night, Mr. Clay."

He nodded at Miss Phoebe, winked at Sarah, and slipped out the door. He headed to his side of the upstairs to deposit his saddlebags. On impulse, he'd decided he'd give the children the candy later. Right then, all he wanted to do was go downstairs and see what Miss Alice had put on a plate for him. If the smells had indicated right, it would be delicious.

Thirteen

It was midmorning two days later when Clay walked out to the wood pile where Thomas was splitting logs. "Looks like you've been busy. Maybe you should take a break."

Thomas picked up another log and put it on the stump. "Miss Alice uses a lot of wood and I didn't want her to run out."

"I don't think there's any danger of that. There's enough here to last her through a lot of meals."

"I don't want you to beat me because I don't do enough work."

Clay frowned. "What gave you the idea I would beat you?"

"They always do. It don't matter how nice people are at first. They change and beat me cause they say it makes me work harder. You'll probably do the same thing."

"That won't happen here, Thomas."

The boy shrugged and lifted the axe above his head, then brought it down on the log. It fell into two pieces of the same size. "See how even the pieces are? I hope I'm cutting them the way you want them done."

"They're fine. Now, put that axe down and come with me."

"Why?"

Clay saw the defiance as well as the fright in the boy's dark eyes. He knew he had to get things straight with this young man. "We need to talk."

"About what?"

"You'll see."

Thomas dropped the axe and muttered, "Let's get it over with."

"We'll go through the house and get something to drink, then we'll go sit on the front porch. Nobody will bother us there."

Clay was right. They were alone on the porch. He took a chair and sat with a cup of coffee in his hand.

Thomas set his glass of lemonade on the porch railing and took a chair facing Clay. "Well, let me have it."

"All right, Thomas. You're old enough and I feel I can tell you the truth." Thomas only stared at him, so Clay went on. "You might want to keep this to yourself until some things are cleared up."

There was still no remark from Thomas.

"As you know, I came upon your wagon sometime after it had been attacked. Miss Lucy was in no shape to tell me how much time had passed since it had happened and David couldn't tell me either. By the way Miss Lucy was suffering, it had been some time since the attack. She was only interested in making sure you children were taken care of. As she died, I promised her I'd do that."

"Why? You didn't know her."

"No, I didn't. But I believe when you make a promise to a dying person, you keep it."

"But she don't know whether you keep it or not."

"Maybe not. But I would know. In my way of thinking, if a man breaks his word, he's not much of a man."

"A lot of men have broken their word to me."

"I figured as much. I know you don't know me, and you have no idea if I'm trustworthy or not. I'm not asking you to take my word that I am what I say I am. All I want is for you to give me a chance to prove to you I'm only around to help you kids because of what I promised the lady."

"For how long will you be around?"

"Honestly, Thomas, I don't know. Let's just say I'll be here as long as it takes to settle things."

There was a minute of silence, then Thomas said, "What would make you beat me?"

Clay shook his head. "I have never beaten a child or anyone else, for that matter. I may have to reprimand you now and then, if you do something wrong. But there will be no beatings. I don't believe in them."

Thomas frowned. "Are you sure?"

"I'm positive."

Thomas sighed. "I suppose you expect me to work hard."

"We're all going to have to work hard at times. But I don't expect you to do more than your share."

"What's my share?"

"That's something we need to discuss, but so far, I think we're doing pretty good at sharing the chores. Maybe we should get the others together after we eat dinner. We can make plans of what needs to be done and then who is to do what."

~ * ~

Lance laid the wire he'd received from the circuit judge on his desk and shook his head. He felt he should get in touch with Clay, but it could wait until this afternoon. When his deputy arrived, he'd go home and see if Grace would like to take Kathrine and ride out to the Anderson ranch with him. She'd said at supper last night that she wondered how Clay and the children were getting along. It would be a good time for her to find out in person.

The jailhouse door opened, and he couldn't help groaning as Juliette Cramer came in. Before she could speak, in a not too friendly voice he asked, "What do you want now?"

She waltzed to the chair in front of his desk, spreading out her purple satin skirts as she sat. She then plopped a bag on his desk. "That's a fine way to greet someone who brought you a present."

"I don't want a present from you, Juliette."

"Oh, you'll want this one." She reached for the bag. "I went into Miss Carson's sweet shop and she'd just taken a pan of freshly baked apple fritters from the oven. I know how much you love apple fritters and I bought two so we could share them and have a nice conversation. I was sure you had coffee made because you always have a pot on the stove ready for any occasion."

"For heaven's sake, woman. What's the matter with you? I don't want your apple fritters, and I sure have no intention of sharing one with you. Pick up your bag and get out of here."

"Oh, Lance." She looked as if she couldn't believe he meant what he was saying. "I know it's hard for you to be faithful to your pitiful wife when you're around me. But I'm sure she'll get over it when she eventually accepts the fact that you and I have always been meant to be together."

He stared at her and it dawned on him Juliette had to be sick in the head. No matter what he said, she'd never accept that he was married to Grace and would be until the day he died. He was going to have to do something she couldn't put out of her mind. Something she'd never forget. Without her seeing, he eased open the desk drawer and took out a key.

Standing, he walked around the desk and took her arm. "Come with me, Juliette. I want to show you something I've been keeping for you."

She gave him a girlish grin and stood. "What is it, dear?"

"It's in here." He opened the door leading into the cell area.

She went in without protest. Looking around, she asked, "Where is my surprise, Lance?"

He nodded toward one of the empty cells. "It's in there at the foot of the bed. You're welcome to go get it."

She flashed him a smile. "I knew you cared as much for me as I do for you. You just didn't want to admit you'd made a mistake in your choice of a woman to marry."

"Are you going to step in and see what it is or not?"

"Of course I am." She entered the cell and headed toward the bed.

Lance slammed the cell door and turned the key in the lock. "Now maybe you'll learn to quit bothering me."

"What do you mean? I thought we loved each other."

He shook his head "I guess I was wrong when I thought you'd given up on that foolish notion. When are you going to get it through your head...I love Grace? I've never loved you, and I never will?"

She looked scared. "You can't mean that."

"I mean every word. You've hounded me enough and I'm tired of it. I've never wanted you in my life and I sure don't want you now. This foolishness has gone on way too long and it's time you stopped acting the fool."

Juliette screamed. "What are you saying? You've got to be wrong."

"It's the truth and you need to accept it."

"I won't accept it. I can't be wrong, so let me out of here."

"No, Juliette. You're going to stay in jail until you understand I'm a happily married man and I'm tired of your shenanigans. If you can't get that through your head, I'm going to inform the authorities you are touched in the head and need to be put in an insane asylum." He shook his head. "By the way, I'm sorry to tell you that you'll have to spend your time in here alone. The outlaws I arrested for kidnapping were picked up this morning by the prison wagon going to Cheyenne." He then went out of the cell area and slammed the door behind him.

She was still yelling when he entered the office area. He spied the fritters on his desk and was tempted to eat one because they did smell good, but changed his mind. If he wanted a fritter, he'd go to Miss Carson's and buy one. He wasn't going to touch one of hers.

Smiling at that idea, he wrote Bryce a note, donned his hat, walked out the front door, locked it, hung the sign saying *BE BACK SOON* on the door, then closed it behind him. He couldn't help the smile that crossed his face as he headed to the sweet shop.

Fourteen

Bryce removed the sign from the jailhouse door, unlocked it and stepped inside. Hanging his hat on the peg, he moved to the desk and picked up the note Lance had left. He laughed when he read it. "You've got more guts than me, my friend."

He had to see this for himself. Without taking the key with him, he went into the cell room, and was confronted with the words, "It's about time...You're not Lance!"

"No, ma'am, I'm not."

"Well, tell him to get in here."

"He's not here."

"Of course, he's here. He wouldn't leave me in this cell."

"He did and he left me a note about it."

"I don't believe you."

He held up the paper. "Want me to read the note to you?"

"You're lying."

"No, I'm not. Listen." He looked at the note and began to read, *"I've taken all I can from crazy Juliette Cramer. Arrested her and put her in a cell. Don't let her out until you charge her with interfering with a law officer's duty and then go get her father to come and pay her bail, then release her into his custody. Sorry to lay this on you. But you can handle it since you're not personally involved. I'm taking my wife and baby to the Anderson ranch to have a talk with Clay Hunter. See you tomorrow. By the way, don't eat the fritters. They're evidence. Lance.*

"You're making that up!"

"No, I'm not. It's right here in black and white."

"Let me see." She reached through the bars toward the paper.

He jerked it back. "Sorry. This is evidence. I read it to you because I thought you might be interested in why you're in jail."

"I shouldn't be in jail. I've done nothing wrong. Let me out of here."

"Can't do that. You heard what my boss said to do. I'll go get your father."

"I don't want my father involved."

"I'm afraid it's too late for that. Just relax, and I'm sure your father will be here to get you out soon."

"Don't you dare shut that door and leave me in here! I want out."

He ignored her and closed the door, though he could still hear her yelling through it. He chuckled. "No wonder Lance left. I'm not going to put up with that either. I just hope Hal Cramer is in his office because I can't stay in the office with her screaming at the top of her lungs."

~ * ~

Sitting on the buggy seat beside Lance, Grace looked down at sleeping Kathrine. "Baby girl, I don't know what we're going to do with your daddy. I'm sure there are going to be repercussions from his actions. Miss Cramer is not going to take his treatment of her lightly."

"I've had all I can take of that woman's ways. I think it's way past time I put my foot down. For all the aggravation she's caused us, a stint in jail is a small price for her to pay." He slid his free arm around her. "Now, let's forget silly Miss Cramer and enjoy this outing. You know we don't often get to visit friends in the middle of a working day."

"Often? I'd say never." She laughed. "Not that I'm complaining, but just why are we going to visit Clay today?"

"Can't get away with anything around you, can I?"

"I hope not."

"This morning, I got a wire from Judge Dickerson concerning those children Clay's taking care of and thought he should hear about it."

"What did the wire say?"

"Basically, it was concerned about them being in the care of a single man when there were families willing to give them homes."

"You mean someone is willing to adopt five children?"

"No. I gathered he meant different families were willing to take one or maybe two of them."

"But that would mean splitting them up."

"Yes. But they would have the advantage of a real home with a mother and father who want to be parents to them."

"I understand that, but don't you see, Lance? Those boys and girls consider themselves brothers and sisters. They would be losing the family they've created and are happy with, because of that lovely woman, Lucy Baker."

"Don't you think they'd like to be part of a real family?"

"Not unless their brothers and sisters were with them."

"I don't know..."

"It's true, honey. Please don't think I'm complaining, because I'm not. I had a good home with the Olsens after my parents died. But I would have lived in a tent if I could have been with my brother."

Lance thought a minute. Then he nodded. "Maybe you're right. Yet, I feel Clay and the kids have a right to know about this."

"I agree, but do me a favor."

"What's that?"

"Don't say anything to the children. After we visit for a while, I'll distract them, and you can talk to Clay alone. He knows them better than we do, and if he thinks they should be told, let him tell them after we leave."

"If you feel that's the right thing to do, I'll do it your way."

She smiled up at him. "You're such a good man, Lance Gentry. I almost feel sorry for Juliette Cramer."

He frowned. "What brought her into the discussion?"

"It's just that I know I'm going to get to spend the rest of my life with you and she's going to die an old maid still thinking she can have you."

He laughed out loud and pulled her closer to him. "Oh, Grace. I know there's not another person in the world who can surprise me like you do. You have a way of making everything in my life make sense."

"It's because I love you, Lance Gentry."

"I love you, too, and if you don't stop getting me stirred up, I'm going to have to pull over there in those bushes and show you how much."

Baby Kathrine let out a cry.

Grace laughed. "I guess that puts an end to that thought, doesn't it?"

He chuckled. "I suppose you're right. We'll just have to make up for it when we get home tonight."

~ * ~

The front door opened, and Hal Cramer yelled, "Marjorie, where are you?"

She came into the parlor with a dish towel in her hand. "I'm right here. What in the world is going on?"

"There's a lot going on."

Marjorie frowned. "Juliette, why are you crying?"

"Daddy's being mean to me."

"What's all this about, Hal? Why are you making Juliette cry?"

"You'd make her cry, too if you had any idea what this crazy daughter of ours has done."

"I haven't done anything wrong," Juliette wailed.

"Oh, no?" Hal gave her a sharp look. "Then, why did I have to go bail you out of jail?"

Marjorie looked shocked. "Jail?"

"Yes, my dear. Jail. Our silly child finally pushed Lance Gentry too far and he arrested her."

"I only brought him an apple fritter."

Marjorie still showed confusion. "Why would he arrest you over an apple fritter?"

"It wasn't just a fritter," Hal said. "According to the note the deputy showed me, she's been charged with interfering with his work as sheriff. When I questioned that, Bryce said he'd witnessed her coming into the office and bothering them on many occasions. He said he figured Lance had finally gotten his fill of it."

"I only went by to speak to Lance. I know he has to like me coming by and I'm sure he'll say so when you ask him."

"Juliette, why would you go to speak with Lance unless you need his help with something?"

Hal spoke before Juliette could answer. "The deputy also said Lance had told him that he'd learned Juliette had been saying things to Lance's wife upsetting her and that Lance didn't want it to happen again."

"What did you say to her, Juliette?"

"Nothing for him to get upset about, Mother. I only told her I thought she and her baby were wrong for Lance. I do think that, but of course, I only speak to her when I accidentally run into her."

"According to Bryce, Juliette's trying to break up their marriage because she thinks she wants him," Hal said. "He also said if I didn't believe him, I should ask around town because everyone is talking about it. I intend to check this out."

"Well, he shouldn't have married her. I know deep down she's not right for him. He needs somebody like me."

"From all I've heard, he's very happy, and their baby is wonderful."

In a hateful voice, Juliette snapped, "What would you know about it, Mother? I—"

"Shut up, Juliette. You don't have a right to take that tone with your mother." Her father turned to his wife. "That's not all Bryce told me."

"He couldn't know—"

"I told you to hush."

"Mother, don't let him talk to me like that."

"Your mama won't stop me from saying what has to be said. It's time I see that you put a stop to your foolishness."

Her voice came out like a little girl's. "But, Daddy..."

"None of that baby talk, Juliette. It won't work this time. I'm like Lance. I've reached my limit."

"What are you saying, Hal?"

"I don't think Juliette realizes the seriousness of what she's done. Today alone cost me almost a hundred dollars, but that doesn't matter to her." He shook his head. "Do you realize what she did? As soon as I bailed her out of jail, she wanted to go find Lance and ask him why he'd done this to her."

"Well, I want to know."

"It's easy to see and if you'll use your head, you'll figure it out."

She frowned but said nothing.

"Let me enlighten you, little girl. Lance has had a belly full of your silliness. He's told me on more than one occasion he hasn't wanted you from day one and he doesn't want you now. If you don't stop your foolish actions, he'll see you're punished for them. He'd even go as far as doing something more drastic than putting you in jail because he means for you to leave him and his family alone. If you don't, I know he can and will keep locking you up. It won't surprise me if he has you sent to prison for your actions."

"Don't you be silly, Daddy. He'd never do that to me."

Marjorie's voice was soft. "Isn't that what you said about him putting you in jail the first time he threatened to do it?"

"I didn't think he meant it. Besides..." She turned up her nose. "Just wait until my professor answers my letter. I wrote and told him how I was putting in practice the theory he taught us, but for some reason it was taking longer to work for me than I expected it to."

"What are you talking about?"

"I told you, Mother. Professor Smyth told us that if we wanted something bad enough and believed hard enough, we'd get it."

"I've never heard such malarkey in my life." Hal took hold of her arm and pointed to the stairs. "Go to your room and let your mother and me talk about what's going to change around here, because there must be some changes, and they're going to start today."

"I don't see why anything should change."

He pointed again. "Don't argue with me, Juliette. Go!"

She flipped her skirt around and ran toward the stairs.

"Don't you think you're being a little rough on her, Hal?"

"I wonder if I'm being rough enough." He took his wife's arm. "Now let's go have a cup of coffee and I'll clue you in on everything the deputy told me."

Fifteen

After supper, Clay gathered the children in the parlor. "I feel I need to tell you about the talk that is going around in town about us."

Subdued, they gathered around him and waited for him to explain.

He took a deep breath and hoped he'd use the right words to make them all feel comfortable with what he had to say. "When I was in town yesterday, the lawyer mentioned some things that were being said about us. I didn't pay it much mind because I knew all of you showing up would cause a commotion in a place like Settlers Ridge where nothing much exciting happens. But, while you were busy this afternoon, the sheriff had a talk with me, and I thought I should let you know what some of the wagging tongues are saying."

"I hope they don't plan to run us off," Luke said.

"There's no danger of that."

"Good," David said. "I like it here."

"Me, too," was muttered by the others.

"Before you get too excited, let me tell you what the sheriff said." They got quiet and he went on. "One of the circuit judge's relatives contacted him and told him about the five of you. I think it was a niece of his. He then turned around and sent Sheriff Lance a wire saying he wondered if each of you wouldn't be better off living with a real family instead of being out here on a ranch with a man and two older women."

"What's wrong with that?" Sarah asked.

"He told Lance that his niece and her husband wanted to adopt one of you and she was sure there were others in Settlers Ridge or surrounding towns that would want to give some of you homes, too."

"Would we all be together?"

"I'm afraid not, Sarah. You would probably go to different homes."

"I don't want to go to a different home," David blurted.

Mary jumped off the sofa and ran to Clay. He reached for her and she threw her arms around his neck.

"You can see where Mary wants to stay," Luke said.

"Who did that judge's niece want to adopt?" Thomas spoke for the first time.

Clay hadn't wanted to name names. But now that he was faced with the question, he decided not to lie to them. "She wanted David."

"No!" David yelled. "I ain't going nowhere."

"She can't take David. We have to look after him. Miss Lucy said so."

"I agree with Sarah." Luke looked defiant. "Miss Lucy said we had to stick together and look after each other. She said we are a family."

"And we are!" Sarah added.

"Yes, we are," Thomas said. "It's the only family that wants Mary and me to be a part of it."

"The lawyer told me a man wanted to adopt you, but he wasn't sure about his motives and I shouldn't trust him. He also told me there was a strange woman in the hills who considers herself capable of working miracles. He said she was sure she could make Mary talk. He told me not to trust her either." Clay sighed. "Now that I've started, I need to tell you there's a family who wants to take Sarah and Luke. It seems the woman is sickly, and Sarah could help in the house. The man has some health problems and needs help and he figured Luke could supply that help."

"Are you saying you're going to make us go live with these people?"

"No, Thomas. What I want you to do is decide for yourselves what you want to do. I'm going to go to my room to get something and while I'm gone, you children talk about it among yourselves, and let me know what you decide when I come back." He grinned down at Mary. "You stay with them, honey. I won't be gone long."

"Yes, Mary. Come sit with me. Mr. Clay said he'd come back, and he will."

Mary hesitated, but finally joined Sarah on the couch.

It didn't take long for Clay to get to his room. He wanted to give the children time to discuss what he'd told them, so he sat at his desk and thought a little while. Though he had a good idea of what they'd decide to do, he didn't want to rush them. After a few minutes at his desk, he figured he'd been gone long enough. He stood, picked up his saddlebags and went back downstairs.

As he walked into the parlor, he met a wall of silence. Moving to the chair he had vacated, he put the saddlebags on the floor. He'd already decided he wouldn't say anything. He'd wait for one of them to speak first.

Finally, Sarah said, "They asked me to talk for us all, Mr. Clay. I'm supposed to tell you that we've made a decision. We decided none of us want to be adopted by these people you told us about. We are already a family and we want to stay here on this ranch with you, not go live with strangers."

"You all wanted it that way?" He looked at Thomas.

"Yes," Sara said. "We all voted by raising our hand. Even Mary raised hers."

Clay grinned. "I thought you might decide that was what you wanted, so I want you to know I'll do everything I can to make sure you all stay together."

"So, you don't mind we voted that way?" Thomas asked.

"I don't mind at all. In fact, I think we should celebrate your decision. Yesterday, while I was in town, I bought something for you, and I haven't had a chance to give it to you. I think now would be a good time to hand it out so you can celebrate your decision." He reached in the saddle bags and pulled out a handful of peppermint sticks.

The room filled with excitement.

"Are they really for us?" David asked,

"Yes, David?"

"Do we get a whole one?"

"Of course."

"I can't believe we get a whole one."

"Why not?"

"When Miss Lucy bought us one, but we had to break it up and share. This is the first time we get a whole one all by ourselves."

Seeing the excitement and happiness on their faces, Clay decided he'd let them enjoy their peppermint sticks. He'd hold back the lemon drops and give them out later. He did think he'd slip Miss Alice and Miss Phoebe a few, though.

~ * ~

As the days passed, Clay and the children fell into a routine. While Sarah helped Alice and Phoebe around the house and took care of Mary, he and the boys worked on the ranch. They mended fences, plowed fields, and discovered there were stray horses and cows about. Clay made the decision to take a trip to the livery stable with Thomas and Luke in tow. "If we're going to run a ranch, you guys need horses, and we need to go buy you some," he explained. "That way we can round up some of this stray livestock and start our own herds."

The boys were thrilled. "I never dreamed we would ever own horses," Luke said.

"I can't believe he'd buy me a horse," Thomas said.

When they arrived at the livery stable, it took a while to choose the right horses. Clay pointed out six animals that were acceptable for their needs. Luke settled on a bay and Thomas chose a pinto. They also bought saddles and headgear.

"Now, fellows, let's go to the mercantile and get the supplies Alice wanted and pick up a couple of other pieces of gear you'll need."

"Like what?" Thomas asked.

"Rope, for one thing. Probably work gloves, maybe chaps if they have them to fit you, and who knows what else we'll see?"

As they stepped into the store, they found it busy with shoppers. "Go over there to the wall on the left and get a roll of rope for each of you. I'll go give Miss Wilma the list from Alice."

Wilma finished adding the bill for the pretty Mexican woman in front of him. "Thank you, Juanita. It's good to see you."

"Good to see you, too, Wilma."

"Let me introduce you to the man behind you. Clay Hunter, meet Juanita Allison. She and her husband Curt own a portion of the Circle Two ranch."

"Nice to meet you, Mrs. Allison. Jed Wainwright told me your husband sent us the milk cows, and please let me thank you again. They're working out well."

"You're welcome."

A commotion on the other side of the store distracted them. Luke shouted, "Help, Mr. Clay. This man is trying to kidnap Thomas."

Clay raced across the store in time to see the big burly man slap Luke across the face and continue trying to drag a fighting Thomas toward the door.

Clay didn't hesitate. He grabbed the man's arm with his left hand, whirled him around and hit him in the jaw with his right fist.

He fell to the floor, letting Thomas go in the process. "Why'd you do that? I was trying to keep that Injun from stealing the rope."

"He was not stealing."

"Of course he was. All Injuns steal. I was gonna take him out and teach him a lesson."

"You're a fool. What gives you the right to discipline someone else's child?"

"Well, he ain't yours."

"How do you know?"

"Cause you're white."

"What's that got to do with it? Maybe his mother was an Indian and maybe she was the love of my life."

"Well..." The man sputtered as he got to his feet.

Clay took hold of his arm and ushered him to the door. "If I see you in here again when my boys and I are in the store, I'll have you arrested."

"You can't do that."

"Oh, can't I? It just so happens the sheriff is my brother-in-law. Who do you think he'll believe?" He opened the door and shoved the stumbling man outside. He didn't bother to see if the man managed to stay on his feet when he hit the plank sidewalk.

Clay turned to face a round of applause from the customers in the store. He looked embarrassed. "I'm sorry for the uproar, folks. I can't abide people who are mean to kids."

"Don't be sorry, young man," An older lady in a dark blue cotton dress said. "It was wonderful seeing you defend your son in such a way."

The pretty woman with her said nothing, though she kept looking at Clay then glancing at Thomas as if she wondered what the relationship between the two of them might be.

"I'm not his son," Thomas said to the older woman. Then *almost* under his breath, he whispered, "But I wish I was."

~ * ~

Juliette hung her bonnet on the hat rack in the front entry and turned to her mother. "I'm glad we finally got home. I thought you'd stay in that store all day. You knew I wanted to get home so I could read my letter."

Marjorie hardly knew what to say to her daughter anymore, so she muttered, "We had to pick up a few things. You knew that when we left the house, Juliette."

"You shouldn't have let the cook I hired go. She would be going to the store for your supplies."

"I didn't like another woman in my house doing my job."

"You shouldn't be doing menial tasks like cooking, Mother. Since I've been home from school, I've tried hard to make you act like a real lady. You just don't understand how the world works, do you?"

"Sometimes I think you're the one who doesn't understand, Juliette. It seems the happy daughter we sent off to school has returned a different person."

"Of course, I'm different. I learned in St. Louis how a real lady should live."

"So, real ladies go around trying to take other women's husbands?"

Juliette stared at her. "I can't believe you said that to me."

"Maybe I should talk more plainly to you more often."

"I think Daddy has done that for you. I don't know why he said I have to go with you every time you go to town. I feel like a prisoner."

"I guess in a way you are. You know he said you were not to be alone until he decided he could trust you not to go running to the sheriff's office again."

Juliette shook her head. "I just don't understand you and Daddy. If you would just admit that Lance and I should be together, things would work out."

"Why? So, Lance can put you in jail again?" Her voice was sharper than she meant it to be.

Juliette didn't seem to notice. "Oh, Mother. I'm sure he was just having a bad day. Probably that silly wife of his said something to upset him. I still can't understand why he married Grace Hunter. She's not his type at all."

"From what I hear, he loves her very much."

Juliette shook her head. "I don't believe it. Now why don't you go do whatever it is you need to do in the kitchen? I'm going to the parlor and read my letter. I'm sure the professor will inform me what I am doing wrong since his theory is taking too long to work for me."

"Juliette, Juliette. I don't understand you at all."

"Don't try, Mother. I'm way too smart and sophisticated for you to try to figure me out." She flipped around and went to the plush parlor chair she always liked to sit in.

With tears forming in her eyes, Marjorie Cramer headed into the kitchen wondering what happened to the sweet young girl Juliette used to be.

Sixteen

After the mercantile cleared, Clay looked at Wilma. "Sorry about all the commotion. I may have caused you to lose a sale, but I couldn't let him get away with assaulting Thomas."

"Of course, you couldn't. Besides, I must admit, I'm glad you threw that man out of here. He's always hard to deal with when he comes in."

"Who is he, anyway?"

"I don't really know. He's not local. He and his partner came in a couple of weeks or so ago, bought some supplies and said they were looking for some friends of theirs. For some reason, I thought they might be bounty hunters, though I don't know why they're sticking around Settlers Ridge. You and Lance brought in the only outlaws that have been around here for some time and as far as I know, there aren't any other outlaws around to be caught."

"Lance told me the kidnappers had been picked up and sent to Cheyenne. He said he'd let me know when we had to go there to testify at their trial."

The boys walked up, and each laid a length of rope on the counter without speaking.

"Hello, young men," Wilma said.

"Hello, ma'am," they muttered.

"These are the two older boys of the ones who were with Miss Lucy. We came into town to buy horses so they could work on the ranch."

"I saw you at the funeral, but we didn't meet. I'm glad to meet you now."

Again, they muttered to her.

She smiled at them and went on. "I went to the hotel and visited David and Mary while Clay and the sheriff were out searching for you. I hope they're doing well."

"They are and I'm glad Mr. Clay found us. Those men had almost killed Thomas and I don't know what they would have done to me and Sarah if they hadn't got there."

"I'm glad they did get there in time to save you, too."

Clay changed the subject. "The boys and I are going to round up some of the stray cattle and maybe some horses running loose on the ranch. We're here to get the items we'll need as well as to pick up Miss Alice's supplies."

"I suppose you'll want to get chaps and other protective gear for the boys, so why don't you go over there to the right side of the store and see what we have while I gather the things Miss Alice wants?" She glanced at the boys. "I hear she gives Clay a hard time if he doesn't do things to her liking."

The boys laughed and Clay said, "You're right, Wilma. Sometimes, I feel like David. He says he's a little afraid of Miss Alice and so am I." Clay chuckled. "Miss Wilma's suggestion sounds like a good one. You guys go on over there and start looking and I'll be along in a minute. I want to talk to her about something."

When they were alone, Wilma asked, "What's going on, Clay?"

"First, I want to ask you, who was that attractive woman who was with an older one? I assume the older one was her mother?"

He didn't understand the dark look that crossed Wilma's face, but her voice was pleasing enough. "I'm sure you're talking about Juliette Cramer. Yes, that was her mother, and her father is the only lawyer here in town."

"I thought that might be her. I wanted to make sure she was the woman who is a thorn in my sister's side before I said anything."

"She is certainly that, though she seems to have calmed down a little since Lance put her in jail."

He grinned. "He told me about that. I hope it worked. I don't like the idea of anyone upsetting Grace."

She returned his grin and her demeanor changed. "I agree with you on that issue."

"The second thing I wanted is to ask you for a favor. I know there's some talk going around town about different families who want to adopt the children and I've discussed the possibility with them. They don't want to be split up to go to different homes, so if you hear anyone talking about it, would you please tell them I intend to see the children stay together?"

"I'll be happy to do that, Clay."

"Thank you, Wilma. I appreciate it more than you know." He gave her another grin. "Now, I better get over there and see what they've picked out."

~ * ~

Juliette stared at the words of the missive in disbelief. "How can Professor Smyth say this? I didn't get it wrong. I couldn't have. I know the professor said it just the way I recall. Not the way he says in this letter."

Reading the letter again, she became frustrated. "No! It can't be!" She wadded the page and screamed.

Marjorie ran into the parlor. "Juliette, what's wrong?"

"This." She shook the crumpled letter in the air. "That stupid professor says I got it wrong."

"Honey..."

"No, I didn't. I couldn't have. I remember well what he said." Juliette's voice was still several octaves higher than usual.

At that moment Hal Cramer walked into the room. "What in the world is going on?"

"Juliette got a letter..."

Still shaking the paper, Juliette interrupted. "He said I got it wrong. But I didn't. I know I didn't."

Frowning, Hal said, "Let me see that letter."

"No...I..."

Hal raised his voice. "I've had a rough day, so don't try my patience, Juliette. Give me that letter."

"But..."

He snatched the paper and smoothed it out. After a quick read, he looked at his daughter. "So, this is what it's all about. You misconstrued what the professor actually said."

"I did not! He said it. I know he did."

"He admits he said it, but his explanation here sounds reasonable to me. Your teacher said what we've been telling you all along."

"But I know he said if you want something bad enough, believe you'll get it and you will."

"He still says that, my dear, though you have ignored the perimeters. He adds that for your dream to come true, you can't infringe on anyone else's rights and you certainly can't make a person think what you want them to think, if they have no inclination to do so."

"But—"

"No buts, Juliette. He says right here, if you want a man, you're to set your heart on getting true love, not a particular man who doesn't want you."

"But—"

"It's time you accepted the facts, Juliette," Marjorie said. "You'll never get a husband if you don't."

"I want Lance!"

"Well, daughter," her father said. "You're not going to get him! Now, go to your room and let the facts settle in your head. I told you, I've had a rough day and I don't want to hear any more of your silly foolishness."

Juliette jumped up and ran out of the room shouting, "You don't want me to be happy because you don't love me any longer. Maybe you never have."

"Hal, maybe you..."

"Don't you start, Marjorie. She needs to face up to the truth and if we keep catering to her, she never will."

"I suppose you're right." Marjorie sighed. "What happened at work to make you have such a bad day?"

"That crazy mountain woman, Matilda, came in and demanded I get that little girl who can't talk for her. When I told her I didn't have a right to do that, she wouldn't give up. It took me two hours to get her out of my office."

"Come into the kitchen and I'll pour you a cup of coffee. Maybe it'll help you to relax and you can tell me all about it."

"Sounds good, Marjorie. Let's go."

Seventeen

The next day, Wilma wondered why Spencer was late coming to the store. She was getting hungry and it was past her lunch time. She'd almost decided to lock the door and slip upstairs to eat a bite when she heard someone coming in the back door and through the stockroom. She was about to remove her apron when Spencer and a lovely blonde-haired woman walked in.

"Sorry I'm late, Wilma. I was getting her settled." He smiled at the pretty woman. "I'd like you to meet my sister, Kathy Chalfant. Kathy, this is Wilma Lawson."

Kathy smiled. "I'm delighted to meet you, Wilma. Spencer told me how invaluable you've been to him and Nelda since he bought this store."

"Hello, Kathy. Welcome to Settlers Ridge."

"Thank you. I'm looking forward to settling down here."

"Wilma, I know you're hungry," Spencer said. "Why don't you go eat your dinner while I familiarize Kathy with the mercantile?"

"Thank you, Spencer. I'll do that." She removed her apron and headed upstairs. Inside she was thinking, *Well, this is it. I'm on my way out and Miss Kathy Chalfant will be taking my job in the store. She'll probably take my apartment, too. I guess I better start seriously looking for another job and a place to live.*

Twenty minutes later, she returned to the store to find Spencer adding up Luella Baldwin's order. The mayor's wife was talking to Kathy. "I'm so glad you've come to Settlers Ridge. I know you'll soon feel at home here."

"Thank you, Mrs. Baldwin. I'm sure I will."

"Will you be working in the mercantile with Spencer and Wilma?"

"I hope to be of help to him and Nelda any way I can."

Wilma plastered on a smile. "Hello, Mrs. Baldwin. I see you've met Spencer's sister."

"Yes, I've had the pleasure. She's delightful and I know you'll enjoy working with her."

Wilma didn't have to answer. The door opened and the Carlson family walked in. She knew she'd be busy watching their eight children to make sure they didn't break or damage too much of the reachable merchandise.

~ * ~

Alice looked at David as he plopped down in the chair at the kitchen table. "Young man, you've been out of sorts ever since Mr. Clay and the boys got back from town."

"I don't mean to make you mad, Miss Alice."

"I'm not mad, David. I simply want to know what's wrong."

"Nothing."

"Don't tell me that. You were fine until the others returned. What happened when they got home with the horses yesterday?"

He hung his head but said nothing.

"Miss Alice is right, David," Sarah said. "You've moped around ever since they went out on the range to look for cows today."

"Nothing's wrong," he muttered, then hung his head.

Phoebe put a spoonful of potatoes on Mary's plate. "I heard you muttering about not getting a horse while I was straightening your room,"

"No, you didn't."

"Yes, I did. You said something about Mary would get a horse before you did."

He stuck out his mouth. "She probably will."

Mary smiled.

"Look at Mary," Sarah said. "She's laughing at you."

"Well, now we know the problem. You're upset because Luke and Thomas got a horse and you didn't. Don't worry about it. Your time will come to get one. Go on and eat your dinner before it gets cold. I've already had to heat it up one time."

Phoebe looked at her. "Why, sister?"

"Because I fed Mr. Clay and the boys before they went out to work. It was too early for you to eat, so it got cold. It's time to eat now, so start filling your plates. I want to get the kitchen cleaned up before I have to start cooking supper."

The sound of an approaching horse filtered through the open window. Alice frowned. "What now?" Phoebe stood. "I'll see who it is."

"We're never going to get finished with this meal," Alice said under her breath.

Phoebe backed away from the open door as a tall muscular woman wearing a black dress and man's black hat stomped across the back porch.

"I come to get the girl." Her voice was loud and rough as she pushed Phoebe aside and walked into the kitchen.

Alice jumped up. "Who are you, and what do you mean, you came to get the girl?"

David slipped out of his chair and went to stand beside Sarah. Mary had already thrown her arms around Sarah's neck.

"I'm Big Matilda Hurley and I intend to make her talk. Is that little one her?" She moved toward the children.

"Leave her be," Alice demanded. "She's afraid of you."

"Don't matter. She'll get over that. I said I could make her talk and I mean to do it." She grabbed Mary out of Sarah's arms.

"Leave her alone," David shouted, and lunged at the woman.

Matilda reached out and knocked David down. "Get away, brat. You've got nothing to do with this."

Sarah screamed, "Give her back to me."

"You shut up." Matilda started to slap her, but Sarah backed away with tears in her eyes.

Mary began wiggling and kicking. Matilda slapped her on her behind. "Hold still. I'm going to make you talk again, you stupid girl."

Alice moved toward them, but Matilda took a gun from her skirt pocket and held it toward her. "Now, I intend to take this child and ain't nobody gonna stop me. So, step back."

With a pan she'd grabbed, Phoebe was easing up behind the woman. But she was too loud.

Matilda whirled around and hit her across the face with the gun. Phoebe crumpled to the floor.

"Now, if anybody else has any bright idea of trying to stop me, see what'll happen to you." She turned around and carried Mary out of the house. The child still kicked and wiggled and had silent tears running down her cheeks.

As soon as they were out the door, Alice moved into action. "Sarah, check Phoebe," she said as she ran toward the pantry.

Returning with a rifle in her hand, she ran to the back porch. She fired two shots into the air.

Through tears, David asked, "Did you shoot the woman who got Mary?"

"No, David. I signaled to Mr. Clay to let him know we need his help." She moved to Phoebe. "Is she all right?"

"She's coming around." Sarah looked up at her. "Did she get away with Mary?"

"I'm afraid so."

Sarah burst into tears and Alice felt like crying with her.

~ * ~

Clay pulled back on the reins and frowned as Luke and Thomas reined up beside him.

"Why did you stop, Mr. Clay?" Luke asked.

"I heard two shots, and I'm waiting to see if there are any more."

"Why?" Thomas looked at him.

"Because when there are two shots and no more it means somebody needs help." Before they could ask any more questions, he went on. "I don't hear any more shooting. That means there's trouble at the house. Let's go."

They rode fast and hard and it didn't take long to reach the back yard of the ranch house. Clay dismounted, ground hitched Whisper, and ran to the porch and through the backdoor. The boys followed.

David ran to him and grabbed his arm and between tears babbled, "She pushed me...and got Mary and...and...hit Miss Phoebe and..."

"Calm down, David. I don't understand what you're trying to tell me." He looked at Alice, who was patting Phoebe's head with a wet cloth.

Alice handed the cloth to Sarah and turned to him. "A woman who called herself Big Matilda came in here and grabbed Mary. When Phoebe tried to stop her, she hit her in the face with a gun and knocked her down. She said she was going to make Mary talk."

Clay was shocked. "Which way did she go?"

"I think I saw her headed toward the east when I went out on the porch to signal for you."

Clay nodded. "All right." He turned to the boys. "Luke, get on your horse and head to town and tell the sheriff what happened. Tell him I'm going after the woman and to meet me at the foot of Clayton Mountain. I've heard that's where this woman lives. Alice, keep your gun handy and keep David and Sarah in the house. David, I want you and Sarah to help Miss Alice. Thomas, come with me and we'll see if we can pick up her tracks."

Luke went out the door and David asked, "Why can't I go with you and Thomas?"

Clay took a deep breath. He didn't want to be gruff with the boy, so he said. "Don't argue with me, David. We have to work together when things happen. Miss Alice needs a guy here to help her and Sara take care of Miss Phoebe and that's your job this time. She'll tell you what to do."

David didn't look happy but he nodded.

"Come on, Thomas. If we're lucky, we might catch up with them."

Eighteen

It was almost time for her father to come home for lunch when Juliette told her mother she was sleepy and wanted to take a nap. Instead, she had stood at her window and watched until Hal came up the walk.

She waited until she was sure he was eating, then she slipped down the stairs and out the front door. She knew she could get away without being seen if she could get around the house on the corner.

Juliette felt her parents were being unreasonable. She was twenty years old and had a good head on her shoulders. Why did they think they had to watch her every move? She wasn't a criminal. Well, not a hardened one. Just because she'd been in jail didn't make her a bad person.

Yet, ever since her father had bailed her out, he'd insisted she not go out of the house without one of her parents being with her. But today she'd planned her escape carefully. By the time they realized she was gone, she'd have worked out things about their future with Lance.

As she rounded the corner, she took a deep breath. She'd made it and was safe from detection. Now, all she had to do was get to the jail and clear up things with Lance.

No matter what her professor said, she knew she'd been doing the right thing. She had to be. It would be too hard to accept the fact that she'd been wrong about the theory. She was right, and one day soon, Lance would realize it, too. He'd leave that awful crippled Grace, then the two of them would marry and move away from this terrible town. Maybe their destination would be St. Louis. It would make her feel wonderful to walk into the professor's office holding Lance's arm. She couldn't wait to tell him she hadn't done anything wrong. She'd tell him she'd set her heart on being Lance's woman and it had worked out just the way she'd wanted it to.

Once she reached the main street, she hastened her steps. She was full of excitement as she reached the jail. Plastering on a smile, she opened the door and stepped inside. Lance was leaned back in his chair with his feet propped on the desk. In a gay voice she said, "Hello, Lance."

He lowered his feet and frowned at her. In an irritated voice, he asked, "What are you doing here?"

"Oh, my sweet Lance." She cocked her head to the side and continued smiling. "You should have known I'd forgive you for your little outburst the other day. I do hope you're in a better mood today."

"Though I hoped it would, your little stint in jail didn't teach you a thing, did it?"

"Oh, my dear. Let's put that behind us and move forward."

"We're going to move forward, all right." He stood, took her arm, and ushered her toward the cell area.

"Oh, no." She pulled back. "You're not going to lock me up again, are you?"

"I'm going to lock you up every time you come into my office spouting your foolishness."

She couldn't believe he was doing this again and tried to prevent him from taking her into the cell room, but he was stronger. In a matter of minutes, he shoved her in the cell and slammed the door.

"What are you doing, Lance? I told you I came to forgive you... and I..."

"It doesn't matter why you came, Juliette. I'm telling you again, anytime you come through the jail door, you'll be locked up."

"You can't mean..."

He nodded to her. "Have a nice rest. I'm sure your father will be by later to bail you out."

Juliette couldn't believe he'd done that to her again. "Let me out of here this minute, Lance Gentry. We need to talk about our future."

"Your future is to sit here in jail until you come to your senses. Mine is to go home and have dinner with my wife. Yell all you want to. There won't be anybody in the building to hear you." He went through the door to the front office without looking back.

A stunned Juliette dropped to sit on the side of the cot. What had just happened? Was the professor right? Did she get it wrong?

No! She couldn't have. If she did, everything she'd done since she'd been back in Settlers Ridge could be wrong, too.

~ * ~

As he went into the office, the front door flew open and a young boy ran in. "What's the matter, son?"

Almost out of breath, he said, "A woman kidnapped Mary, and Mr. Clay sent me to get you. We need to go get her cause she might hurt Mary."

"Slow down and tell me again what's going on."

It took a few minutes, but Lance decided he had a grip on what the boy was trying to tell him. He moved to the desk. "Let me leave my deputy a note and we'll head out."

"Why is that woman yelling, Mr. Sheriff?"

"She doesn't like being in jail."

"Is she an outlaw?"

"Something like that."

The door opened and Bryce walked in. "I hear you've arrested the Cramer dame again."

"Yep." He dropped the pencil. "You know the routine with her.

"I do," He looked at Luke. "What's your problem, young man?"

"Somebody grabbed Mary and I came to get the sheriff."

"Clay Hunter sent Luke to get me. Big Matilda forced her way into their place and kidnapped the little girl who can't talk. I'm heading out to help him get her back."

"Need my help?"

"I might. Put a note on the door and let's go."

"Thank you. Anything will be better than listening to your prisoner."

~ * ~

Settling behind a grove of berry bushes, Clay glanced at Thomas. "You doing all right?"

He nodded. "Do you believe this is her cabin?"

"It has to be. The Hurley family only has two. The one she lives in and her brother's. The first one we saw had a woman hanging her wash on the line and a child playing in the yard. I figured that belonged to the brother."

"It looks like there ain't nobody at home here."

"There's an old horse in the shed behind the cabin, so if this is her place, it means she's inside."

"Why don't we go in and get Mary?"

"We will when we're sure she won't hurt her."

"Do you think she'd hurt her?"

"Alice said she slapped Mary because she tried to get away when the woman picked her up. You never know what a woman like that will do if you get her cornered. Our main concern is to make sure Mary's safe."

"How do we do that?"

"First of all, I'm going to slip up to the cabin and see if I can see what's going on inside."

"What am I going to do?"

"You're to stay here and watch for the sheriff and Luke. I expect they'll be along soon."

"Why did you want him to come?"

"I wanted him here because as soon as we get Mary, I want us to head home. The sheriff will arrest the woman and take her to jail, and we won't have to see her again until the trial."

"I thought maybe you'd kill her."

"I wouldn't do that unless I had to, Thomas. The law will take care of punishing her." Clay lifted an eyebrow. "Now, you stay out of sight and I'll signal when it's safe for you to come to the cabin."

~ * ~

There was a knock on the door. Grace turned from the stove and hurried to open it. She smiled when she saw Teddy Olsen and Joel Wagner standing there. "Hello, boys. What's up?"

Teddy said, "We were on our way to the fishing hole when we passed the sheriff's office. He stopped us and gave us a nickel to come tell you he couldn't come home to eat dinner. He's gone to find somebody and didn't know how long it will take."

"The deputy and some boy we didn't know went with him," Joel added.

"I appreciate you coming to tell me. Would you like to come in?"

"No, ma'am." Teddy smiled at her. "We plan to take our nickel and go by the store and get us a couple of peppermint sticks to take fishing with us."

"Then I won't hold you up. I hope you boys have a good time and are able to catch a lot of fish."

They started down the walk, then turned around. Joel said, "There was something else we wanted to ask you."

"Oh. What was that?"

"Before the sheriff shut the door and left, we heard a woman yelling all kinds of things. Do you know who he had put in jail?"

A smile crept across Grace's face. "No, Joel. I don't know who it could have been."

"We just thought you might," Teddy said. "She was making an awful noise."

"Yeah," Joel added. "She sure was loud and we didn't know who it was."

"I'm sorry. I can't help you. You'll have to check with the sheriff when he gets back."

They nodded, turned around without saying anything else, and headed out of the yard.

Grace turned back into the house smiling and muttering to herself. "No, boys. I don't know who the woman in jail could be, but I sure know who I hope she is."

Nineteen

Clay heard a rustling behind him and glanced around. Lance walked up closer and whispered, "What's the plan?"

"Trying to figure out one."

"I know Matilda Hurley can be as tough as any man when she's cornered. I've got Bryce waiting back there with the boys."

"What do you think we should do?"

"Let's get to the porch. You hang out at the side of the building and I'll see if she'll come out."

Clay nodded and they crept forward. As Lance had suggested, Clay placed himself beside the corner of the house.

Lance knocked on the door.

A gruff voice from inside yelled, "Go away. I'm busy."

"It's Sheriff Gentry, Miss Hurley. I need to talk to you."

"Ain't got no time to talk."

"I won't keep you long. Just open the door."

"I ain't opening the door and I'm going to tell you this one time, Sheriff. If'en you don't go away and leave me be, I'm a gonna come out there with my shotgun."

"You don't want to do that."

She seemed to ignore him as she yelled, "Quit wiggling, young'un or I'm gonna slap you again."

Clay tensed when he heard those words, and it was all he could do not to force himself into the house and confront her.

Before he could react, Lance said, "All right, Matilda Hurley. I've tried to be civil, but you leave me no choice. I'm coming through the door."

"A bullet will meet you when you enter that door, lawman."

"Maybe so. But if you shoot me, there's enough men out here to take you down."

There was a moment of silence, then she said, "What do you want to talk to me about?"

"Open the door and I'll tell you."

The door began to ease open.

"That's better."

"I ain't gonna ask you again. What'd you want?"

"There's a little girl missing. Somebody told me you were seen with her."

"Ain't none of your business."

"Her folks want her to come home."

"I ain't lettin' her go nowhere 'til I make her talk. Now go away."

Clay jumped on the porch when Lance motioned for him. He started in the door behind Lance. He was stopped when Lance, with blood streaming from his nose, fell against him.

"I told you to get out!" The woman screamed at them, then tried to close the door.

Clay managed to get to the door to put his foot inside before she could close it. His heart began to pound when he saw little Mary inside. She was tied in a chair and tears ran down her cheeks as she reached out her arms toward him.

The next thing he knew, a pain shot down his leg as Big Matilda slammed his knees with a fireplace iron she'd grabbed. He tried to ignore it. At the moment, the only thing that mattered to him was getting to Mary.

Lance had managed to get to his feet and was trying to wrestle the iron out of the big woman's hand.

Bryce and the boys came rushing into the cabin.

Big Matilda still screamed at all of them, and swung, not only her fists, but any piece of furniture she could reach.

Seeing they were going to be able to hold her back, Clay rushed to Mary and released the little girl from her bondage. As soon as she was free, her arms flew around his neck.

He held her close and whispered in her ear. "It's all right, little darling. I'm here now and you're going to be fine. Let's get out of here."

He managed to get around the commotion and stepped onto the porch. He still whispered to Mary and she seemed to be settling a little.

It took a while until things began to ebb. But when it did, the boys joined them on the porch.

"Is Mary all right, Mr. Clay?" Luke asked.

"She's scared, but she'll be fine."

"I'm glad we found you, Mary," Thomas said as he reached out and patted her back. "Mr. Clay said we would, and we did."

Lance came out to join them. He wiped his nose with a handkerchief. "We finally got her subdued. Bryce is handcuffing her now."

"Are you sure?" Luke asked.

"I'm sure. But it wasn't easy. I do appreciate all the help you guys gave us."

"We just wanted to get Mary back," Luke said.

"And we did," Clay said. "I'm sorry you got hurt, but I'm glad you showed up when you did, Lance. I don't think I could have handled that lady alone."

"Neither could I." He chuckled. "You see what happened to me. Grace is going to be upset when I walk in with all this blood on me."

"Did she break your nose?" Thomas asked.

"It's sore, but I don't think it's broken."

"I don't think I've ever seen a woman as big and as strong as her."

Clay nodded. "Neither have I, Luke."

"I came out here to tell you that Bryce and I will see to getting her to jail, Clay. Why don't you and your kids head home? I'm sure Miss Alice is waiting to see all of you."

"Sounds good to me." Clay nodded to them. "How about you boys?"

"I'm ready," Luke said,

"Let's go," Thomas added.

Though she hadn't let go of Clay's neck, Mary nodded her head under his chin. He hoped that meant she wouldn't be traumatized by the events of today.

~ * ~

It took both Lance and Bryce to get Big Matilda into the jail and through the door to the cells.

Juliette jumped off the cot and ran to the front of her cell. "It's about time. Who in the world is that?"

They ignored her as they put the protesting prisoner into the adjoining cell.

When they stepped out of the cell and locked it, Lance glanced at Juliette. "We brought you some company."

"I don't want company. I want to go home." She stared at him. "Why is there blood all over you?"

Lance ignored her. "I'm going home to clean up, Bryce. Sorry to leave you with these two."

"I don't mind. I'll go over to Hal's office and let him know Juliette's been arrested again."

"Thanks." Lance turned toward the door.

"You better not walk out of here without letting me out!" Juliette screamed at him.

Matilda's loud voice made them all jump. "Shut up, fancy lady!"

"Are you going to let this person talk to me like that, Lance?"

Lance didn't answer. He'd already gone out the door.

"Come back here and let me out!"

"Hey! Didn't I tell you to shut up?" Matilda grabbed the bars separating the two cells.

Though she knew the woman couldn't reach her, Juliette backed up. Her voice was almost a whisper. "I shouldn't be in here. I haven't done anything wrong."

"I ain't done nothing wrong neither. But do you think that matters to that hard-headed sheriff?"

"I don't think he's hard-headed. He's just not happy. He married the wrong woman. He used to be the most wonderful man in town."

Matilda frowned. "So, you want him yourself?"

Juliette was taken aback. "How did you know?"

The big woman chuckled. "'Cause I know things other people don't."

Juliette plopped down on the cot. "That's impossible."

Big Matilda gave her a toothy grin. "You don't know who I am, do you?"

"No."

"I'm the woman everbody says is a mountain witch." A strange cackle came out as a crooked smile crossed her lips. "I think it's funny that they jist don't know how right they is. They soon learn 'cause I cast a spell on them who makes fun of me. It works, too."

Juliette stared at her for a minute, then she moved to the front of the cell and yelled, "Let me out of here! I want to get away from this woman."

"No need to do that. Ain't nobody except me to hear you."

Ignoring her, Juliette called again. "Lance. Let me out."

"I told you. He ain't out there. He went home to get a clean shirt."

"How do you know?"

"Use your head, woman. You seen him. Do you think he's gonna wear that bloody shirt all day?"

"Bryce!" She called.

"He ain't there neither."

"For heaven's sake. Will you please be quiet?"

"Don't like to hear the truth, does ye?"

"Leave me alone."

Matilda didn't answer. Instead, she began to hum a mantra as she slowly turned in a circle.

"What are you doing now?" When Matilda didn't answer, Juliette added. "Stop it. You're making me nervous."

In a moment, she did stop. Staring at Juliette, she said in a sinister voice, "You should be nervous. I jist might put a spell on you 'cause you thinks you is some important person. But you ain't. I conjured up your past, your present, and your future. It don't look too good fer you, girl."

Fright filled Juliette's eyes. "You can't do such a thing."

Ignoring her, Matilda went on. "I's gonna tell you about it and I ain't gonna charge you a cent."

"I don't want to hear it."

Matilda ignored her. "When you was young, you was what people called a sweet young girl. Shy, but nice and everbody liked you. Then you went to that school and all your goodness and sweetness left you. You come back an empty shell of the nice woman you used to be. You was stuck-up and selfish and nobody liked you or wanted to be around you. They still don't."

"That's not so! I believe Lance loves me. He just doesn't realize it yet."

"That proves my point. You think people look at you as something special. They don't. The sheriff don't love you. Never has, and never will. He don't even like you. Fact is, he almost hates you and if'en you don't stop pestering him, he'll end up hating you for sure. While you live your life in a dream world about him, he goes home and lives his life with the woman he loves, and always will."

"You can't know…"

"Oh, yes. I does know. As fer your future, if'en you don't change your ways, when your ma and pa are dead and gone, you'll end up a dried-up old maid living alone. You won't have a friend in this world. If'en you get sick, nobody in town will come to help you. Then when you die there won't be nobody at your funeral 'crept the undertaker and maybe a preacher. You'll just be a dead old spinster nobody will remember ever lived in this town."

"No!" Juliette covered her ears. "I don't want to hear any more."

"Only way to change it is to change your ways. If'en you don't, you'll see all I predict come to pass."

"Please, stop talking."

"Maybe I should put a spell on you that you can't break, even if you do change your ways."

Before Juliette could answer, Hal Cramer walked through the door with Bryce.

Big Matilda yelled as they left with Juliette, "Don't forget what I told you. It'll happen and this world will be better off without you in it."

The big woman's cackle sounded like clanging symbols in Juliette's ears as the door closed and she faced her furious father.

Twenty

When Wilma put the honey jars Mr. Carson had brought in on the shelf, one slipped out of her hand and hit the corner of the counter, dripping the sticky liquid on the shirts there, plus the front of her dress.

Fussing at herself for not putting on her apron before shelving the jars, she knew there was nothing she could do except hurry upstairs and change clothes before anyone came into the store.

Holding up her skirt so she wouldn't drip honey on the floor, she rushed to the door, turned the latch and hung up the sign saying *BE BACK SOON.* She then rushed upstairs to change.

It didn't take long to get out of the soiled dress and into the blue checked one she'd finished sewing yesterday and planned to wear for supper with Nelda and Spencer on Saturday. But there was no time to worry about it now.

Pinning back a loose strand of hair, she didn't bother to check herself in the mirror. Hurrying, she turned to go back downstairs to the store. Maybe it was because she felt rushed or maybe because she wasn't paying enough attention, but as she reached the third step from the bottom, she slipped.

The next thing she knew, she sat at the bottom of the stairs crying out in pain. Her right leg was folded under her and it took a minute for her to realize she'd fallen. Instinct made her try to get up. It was impossible. She couldn't put any weight on her right leg.

"Oh, no! I can't have broken it." But as she muttered these words, she knew she could have very well done just that.

~ * ~

After supper and the kids had gone to their rooms for the night, Clay walked out to the barn. Picking up a curry brush, he moved into Whisper's stall and began giving the horse her second brushing of the evening. He knew she liked being brushed and it always helped him relax and clear his mind when he groomed her. Tonight, his mind needed clearing. He had a lot to think about.

Today had been grueling and it had taken most of the evening to get Mary to leave his arms and go to bed. He understood the little girl's fear, and he knew she depended on him for her security. But, in the long run, wouldn't it be better if she leaned more on Alice or Phoebe? He wouldn't always be there to reassure her when she needed it. Would he?

He kept asking himself this question over and over, and he kept getting the same answer. He had either to get out of these kids' lives soon or take on the responsibility of them until they could take care of themselves.

"The problem is, I don't know what the right answer is, Whisper," he muttered to the horse. "Don't I have a right to a life of my own now that I'm a free man? Why should I care about these children anyway? I don't really know them. I'm sure my promise to look after them to the dying Miss Lucy didn't mean I was to take them on forever."

The horse turned her head, slung her mane, snorted, then settled down.

Clay laughed "I know you were reacting to the brushing, Whisper, ole girl. But it's almost as if you were telling me I know the answer to my dilemma and I just don't want to face it." He patted Whisper's neck. "I'm going to get a good night's sleep and see if things are clearer in the tomorrow when you and I go into town."

~ * ~

When Wilma opened her eyes, it was dark. She wasn't in pain. But she wasn't comfortable either. She didn't know why she felt this way until she realized she couldn't tell where she was. The last thing she remembered she had fallen down the stairs in the mercantile. But she wasn't there now. She was in a bed, though it didn't seem to be her bed. The mattress didn't feel like her feather one and the bed seemed to be too narrow. Where was she and how did she get there?

Knowing there was only one way to find out, she called, "Hello."

The door opened and Doctor Sheldon Wagner stepped in. "So, you decided to wake up."

"What's going on, Doc, and why am I here?"

"You have a serious sprain and I've got you in bed here in my office."

She frowned. "How did I get here?"

"When you didn't show up for supper at the Barringtons, Spencer went to the store to see what had happened to you. He found you passed out at the bottom of the steps."

"I remember I fell. But I don't remember passing out."

"We figured you passed out from the pain."

"How did I get here?"

"Spencer was afraid to move you, so he came to get me. I showed him how to carry you so he wouldn't injure your leg further."

"Why am I not in that awful pain now? I remember hurting after the fall."

"I gave you something to ease the pain. Don't worry. You'll hurt again as soon as it wears off."

"That's reassuring."

He chuckled.

"Why did you put me to bed here? Why am I not at home?"

"It seemed the logical thing to do. I figured it would be kind of hard for you to get up and down the stairs at the store. Besides, as I said, you have a bad sprain and won't be able to walk for a few days.

You have injured some tendons and you're going to need somebody to look after you. Esther and I decided we'd do it."

"But what about the store? I need to get back to work."

"Not so fast, Wilma. You won't be able to work for a while."

"But..."

"Don't worry. Spencer said he had the store covered and for you to concentrate on getting well." He picked up a bottle. "Now, that's enough questions. It's getting late and I'm going to give you a dose of this medicine. It won't be long until you won't have a worry in the world."

"But I'm not sleepy."

"You will be. Now, open your mouth."

"I don't want..."

"Stop arguing with the doctor, Wilma. It's getting late and Esther is waiting for me to come to bed. Open your mouth and take the medicine."

Knowing it was useless to protest any further, she opened her mouth and swallowed the liquid. In her mind she vowed she wouldn't let it put her to sleep.

She was unable to keep her promise. By the time Sheldon reached his upstairs bedroom, she had gone back to sleep."

~ * ~

Sitting at a table in the Wildcat Saloon, Woody leaned over the table and said, "Now that we know the boys have been sent to Cheyenne, how much longer are we gonna hang around here, Merve?"

"Till I get pretty Wilma."

"It don't look like we're ever going to get her. Ever time we try go in the store to grab her, somebody comes in."

"We'll get her."

"When I went in there today, there was a yeller-haired woman working. Maybe your Wilma has left town."

"She wouldn't do that."

"How do you know? You don't know her."

Merve let out a drunken chuckle. "No, but I'm going to."

Twenty-one

The next day, Clay left Hal Cramer's office confused. He could tell the man was upset about something. Though he didn't say what his problem was, he was able to give Clay some helpful information. The lawyer told him one of the complaints about him taking care of the children was that he hadn't bothered to see they attended school. Another was that he was single, and shouldn't be looking after them, especially the girls, without the help of a woman who would act as a mother. Alice and her sister, Phoebe, didn't count.

He knew he couldn't do anything about being single at the moment, but he sure could remedy the school situation. He'd hire somebody to come to the ranch and teach them at home. They could even live at the ranch if they desired. There were certainly plenty of rooms and the teacher could have all those downstairs bedrooms if he or she wanted or needed them.

He decided to go talk to Grace about the situation. He was sure his sister would have a good idea as to what he should do. He'd already learned that Grace had grown into not only a beautiful woman, she was smart.

He was disappointed when he got to her house and found she wasn't home. Having no idea where she might be, he headed to the sheriff's office. Surely Lance would know where she was and when she'd be back.

At the lawman's office, Deputy Bryce informed him Lance and Grace had gone to the Circle 2 ranch because he had business with Jed Wainwright. He had taken Grace with him because she wanted to visit with Amelia.

A little frustrated, he went over to Barrington's Mercantile. Wilma was the only other person he felt he could search out for advice. Besides, he had the list of supplies Alice asked him to pick up while he was in town.

Going through the door, he was surprised to see a strange woman standing behind the counter beside Spencer. He did notice she was pretty. But, to his way of thinking, not as pretty as Wilma.

"Hello, Clay," Spencer greeted him.

"Howdy."

"Come on in and let me introduce you to my sister, Kathy Chalfant. Kathy, this is Clay Hunter. He's Grace Gentry's brother."

Clay tipped his hat to her. "Hello, ma'am."

"Hello, Mr. Hunter."

He smiled at her. "Clay, please."

She returned his smile but said nothing else.

"How can we help you today, Clay?" Spencer asked.

"Got a little list from Miss Alice. No matter when I come to town, she always needs something."

Spencer chuckled. "Wilma says she makes you step around."

"She does that. Nobody in the house bucks her."

"I've got to meet this woman."

"You will, I'm sure." He glanced around. "While you're filling this order, put in a handful of peppermint sticks for the kids. Might as well put in some of those lemon drops. Alice hinted she and Phoebe liked them."

Spencer grinned. "Got them spoiled, haven't you?"

"Guess so." He looked around. "Is Wilma not working today?"

"Of course, you'd have no way of knowing. Wilma fell yesterday, sprained her ankle and hurt her leg. She's at the doc's office."

Clay felt his heart lurch. "Doc's office? Is she that bad?"

"She'll be fine. It's just that he has a couple of rooms for patients, and since she lives alone, he decided she should stay there for a few days. I also thought it was a good idea. It'd be too hard on her trying to live upstairs until her foot and leg get better."

Clay handed Spencer the list. "Do you think it'd be all right if I went over there to check on her? I'll come back and pick this up."

"I think she'd like that, and I'm sure Doc would like it. Knowing Wilma, I'm sure she's giving him a hard time."

"Probably so."

"We'll have your order ready when you get back. Do you know where Doc lives, Clay?"

"I do. I had to take Thomas there when we got him away from the outlaws."

"Good. Tell Wilma we miss her and will be glad when she's better."

"Thanks, Spencer. I'll do that." He tipped his hat again. "It was nice to meet you, Miss Chalfant."

She smiled at him. "Likewise."

As Clay went out the door, Spencer handed the list to Kathy, and Clay heard him say, "See how many of these items you can find. I'm here if you have trouble finding anything."

Clay climbed on his horse and rode toward the doctor's house.

~ * ~

Marjorie walked into the parlor and noticed how sad Juliette looked as she sat on the plush chair in the corner of the room. She had the letter from her professor in her hand and there were dried tears on her cheeks.

As any mother would, Marjorie wanted to comfort her daughter, but she wasn't sure how to go about it. Juliette had become someone Marjorie didn't know or understand.

Taking a deep breath, Marjorie moved to Juliette and put her hand on her daughter's shoulder. "Honey, is there anything I can do for you?"

Juliette looked up at her mother with puffy eyes and shook her head.

"How about a cup of tea? Wouldn't that make you feel better?"

She nodded and whispered, "Maybe."

"I'll be right back with it."

When she returned with the tea and handed it to Juliette, she said, "Here you go. It has a dollop of honey, just the way you like it." She then sat in a chair close to Juliette.

Juliette took a sip of the tea. "Mama, do you think Daddy meant what he said before he went back to work?"

Marjorie bit her lip. She wasn't sure what to say, but after the talk she had with Hal, she realized the time had come for Juliette to face the truth. Taking a quick breath for courage, she said, "Yes, honey. I'm sure he meant every word."

"You mean he'd actually let me sit in jail instead of bailing me out again?"

"I know he's tired of your actions, and I have to agree with him. You shouldn't have been in jail again, Juliette, and you certainly don't need to go back."

"But I thought you and Daddy loved me."

"We love you with all our hearts, but you've got to understand how we feel. Not only are your actions costing your daddy money, they're embarrassing for the family as well."

"Well, Lance shouldn't have put me in jail again."

Marjorie sighed. "If you're going to talk about *shouldn't*, then you must realize you shouldn't have gone to the jail the first time he arrested you. Much less the second."

"Doesn't anyone understand I just wanted to talk to Lance? I wanted him to know how I feel because I thought he'd realize he had the same feelings for me."

"Juliette, when are you going to accept the fact the man has no romantic feelings for you?"

"But..."

"Please listen to me, dear." Marjorie took a deep breath. "You've got to face it. Lance Gentry is a happily married man and there's no place for you in his life. He's told you time and time again he has no interest in you, and when you continued to badger him, he put you in jail. Not once, but twice. It's time to accept the fact he's not the man for you."

Juliette burst into tears. "Why not, Mama? I'm young, I'm single and I'm the prettiest woman in town. I don't understand why he doesn't want me."

"Yes. You're pretty, and you're at the right age to fall in love. But that's not enough to make a man care."

"What do you mean?"

"You must admit that you're not...Well, you haven't taken an active part in the community as we hoped you would when you came home from school. You haven't connected with any of your old friends and the only time you're around other people is when I insist you go somewhere with me or when you attend church."

"Maybe I don't need other people."

"We all need other people in our lives. People who don't have friends end up as lonely old people who eventually die alone, and nobody cares."

Juliette shuddered. "Don't say that."

"Why not, dear? It's the truth."

"That crazy woman in the jail told me I'd end up like that."

"Your father said there was another woman there. But he didn't say who she was. Do you know?"

"She was a huge woman who said she came from the mountains and people called her a witch."

"Big Matilda Hurley."

"Do you know her?"

"Not personally. But everyone knows the Hurley family has lived on Clayton Mountain for generations. In fact, I think she and her brother's family are the only ones left. They don't bother nobody when they come to town for supplies. But I have heard about some of the strange things Big Matilda does."

Juliette's eyes narrowed. "Is she really a witch?"

Marjorie shrugged. "Some say she is. I don't know myself. I only know they say some of her predictions come true. I've also heard she can cast a spell on people. But as I said, I don't know anything personally. I've never met her. I've only heard the tales people tell about her."

Marjorie was sure she saw a flash of fear in her daughter's eyes. She couldn't help wondering why. She didn't get a chance to ask because Juliette set her tea aside and rushed out of the room in silence.

Twenty-two

The door to the bedroom in the doctor's office opened and Esther Wagner stuck her head in, "You have company, Wilma."

For some reason, this irritated Wilma. Her voice showed it when she said, "I hope they came to take me home."

Clay walked into the room. "I'd be more than happy to take you home if the doctor says you're ready to go."

Wilma looked startled as her face turned crimson. "Oh, my," she stuttered. "I didn't expect it to be you."

Esther smiled. "Maybe I should leave you two alone."

Wilma turned even redder. "I'm sorry, Clay. I didn't mean to be rude. Please come in."

Esther shook her head. "I'll leave her to you, Mr. Hunter." She slipped out and closed the door.

He moved to the chair beside the bed. "Do you mind if I sit?"

"Of course not." Though she wanted to cover her head, she forced a smile. "I really am sorry about what I said. I thought you would maybe be Spencer coming to get me."

"I went by the store to talk to you, and Spencer and his sister were working. He told me about your accident, and I decided to check on you. I'm so sorry you were hurt, but I'm glad to hear it wasn't worse."

"Thank you, Clay. You're right. I should stop complaining and be thankful I didn't break my leg or my neck. I guess it's just that I don't like having to lie around in bed." She couldn't help wondering what he wanted to talk to her about, but she decided she shouldn't ask. She'd wait and let him tell her.

"Spencer did tell me to tell you he hoped you were feeling better."

"That was nice of him." Now she had an idea of why he was here. Not that she minded he wanted to talk to her. In fact, she was thrilled. Any reason to see him was good. She only wished she'd known he was coming. She could have at least combed her hair in a more flattering way than simply pulled back and tied with a ribbon. That would have made her more presentable. In her present condition, she felt she must be a terrible sight.

"Since I've been back in Settlers Ridge, I haven't had time to make many friends with people who I felt comfortable enough with to ask their opinion of a situation. All I can list are Grace and Lance, Deputy Bryce, the lawyer, Hal Cramer and you."

Wilma looked surprised but pleased. "I'm honored you included me."

"Of course, I'd include you. You've been helpful when I come into the mercantile, and you always have a friendly smile the minute I walk in the door. On top of that, you're easy to talk to."

"You flatter me."

He chuckled. "I don't mean to do that."

"That's fine. A woman likes a little flattery now and then." She grinned, and before she could change her mind, she asked, "What did you want to talk to me about, Clay?"

"I met with Mr. Cramer about the children today and he told me why the people want to adopt them."

"Do you want to tell me why?"

"I do. One reason they gave him was that I hadn't bothered to make sure the children went to school."

"That's not a good reason. You've only been in town about three weeks. What do they expect?"

"I don't think they need a reason, Wilma. They just want the children. Problem is, different families want only one or two of them. When I told the kids about it, they let me know right off they wanted to stay together. I promised I'd do everything I could to see they weren't split up."

"You're a good man, Clay Hunter."

He looked a little embarrassed. "No, Wilma. I'm just a man."

"I think you're a good man. I also think I'll do anything I can to help you keep those youngsters together."

"Thank you, Wilma. I don't like the idea of them coming into town every day to attend school, and I know you know a lot of people. I hoped you might give me the name of somebody I could hire to come out to the ranch to teach them."

"What a good idea. Give me a day or two to ponder it and I'll see if I can't think of someone."

He grinned. "I thought I could count on you."

"Did the lawyer tell any other reasons people had for wanting to adopt the children?"

Before he could answer, there was a tap on the door and Esther stuck her head inside. "You're popular today, Wilma. Mrs. Ellsworth is here to see you."

Clay stood. "I'll go, since you have company."

"I'm sure she won't mind you being here."

"I'd feel like I was intruding. We'll talk later." He smiled at her. "I hope you feel better soon."

Gertrude Ellsworth came through the door. "Hello there, Clay It's good to see you again. You sure don't have to leave on my account."

"Good to see you, too, but I was getting ready to go, ma'am. Enjoy your visit." He turned and winked at Wilma, then went out the door.

~ * ~

Juliette had been in her room most of the day. She'd been thinking about everything that had happened since she'd returned from the school in St. Louis. It had taken all this time, but she thought she'd finally found the answers she'd been seeking.

She washed her face, combed her hair, put on a clean dress, and went downstairs. She found her mother in the kitchen preparing to cook supper. "I'm sorry I stayed in my room so long, Mother, but could I get a cup of tea?"

Marjorie turned to stare at her daughter with a questioning look on her face. "I'll get it for you, dear. Want me to bring it to you in the parlor?"

"I'll drink it here, then I want to go to Daddy's office. I need to talk to him, but I know you're not supposed to let me go out of the house alone. Will you go with me?"

"It won't be that long until he comes home. Can your talk with him wait until then?"

"I really want to go see him now."

"I was getting ready to cook."

"I bet Daddy will agree to take us to Olsen's Hotel for supper when we go see him. I know he likes to eat there occasionally, and it's been a while."

"Then if it's what you want, while you drink your tea, I'll go freshen up a bit."

"Thank you, Mother."

~ * ~

The older mountain man looked at his son. "I's still trying ta figure out how they was able to take Big Matilda to jail without her killing them."

"Must have took a bunch of 'em, Pa."

"You's right 'bout that, Beetle." He wrinkled his brow.

"Why you frownin'? I thought you'd be glad she was in jail."

"Oh, I is. I was jist wondering why I hear somebody close by."

"Who, Pa?"

"I don't know. Hush up and we'll creep up on 'em and see what they's doing here on my land where they don't belong."

In a minute, the boy whispered, "I see 'em, Pa. They's over there in the clearing around that group of pines."

"Get ye gun and try not to make no noise," he whispered back.

They burst into the clearing and the old man raised his shotgun. In a voice that seemed to growl, he yelled, "What is you doing here on my land?"

Merve and Woody jumped up.

"Git them hands in the air and away from your guns."

They raised their hands above their heads. Sputtering, Merve said, "We don't mean no harm, mister."

"Then why is you here?"

"We needed to get out of town."

"Why?"

Merve said nothing, so his partner spoke. "I'm Woody and this is my friend, Merve. We come here 'cause there was some cowboys working on the land where we most often go."

"Didn't want you there, huh?"

"We figured they didn't." Merve took a breath. "How about lettin' us put our hands down?"

"Can they, Pa?"

"Not yet." He waved the shotgun toward them. "You go get their guns, son, then they can put 'em down."

When they were unarmed, the old man said, "Now put your arms down and tell me, why'd you have to git out of town?"

"Merve here wants to get somethin' going with the shopkeeper, and he's afraid nobody will want him to do that."

"Why not? Nothing wrong with a man wantin' a woman and takin' her. Otherways, not many of us would get a woman."

"I don't know for shore about that, but I heard in town that they put a big ole crazy woman in jail for grabbing a little girl. If they'd do it to somebody for takin' a young'un, no telling what they'd do if'en you grabbed a grown woman."

The son looked up at his father. "Weren't that why they arrested Big Matilda and put her in jail?"

"That's what we heard."

"Is they gonna let Big Matilda out of jail?" the boy asked.

"I don't know. We just pick up things when we hear 'em in the saloon."

He lowered his gun. "Maybe we should have a little talk. Set down."

"Don't you want us to leave, Mr....uh..."

"Hurley. Ezra Hurley. Yeah. I want you to leave and you's going to. They's just one thing."

Merve rolled his eyes. "What thing?"

"You's gonna help us get Matilda out of jail."

"Why would we wanta do that?"

"'Cause if'en you don't, we's gonna kill you."

Twenty-three

Grace put her hands on her hips and stared at her friend. "Will you please stop whining and finish peeling those potatoes, Wilma? Just because you're in a wheelchair doesn't get you out of helping me cook. Lance will be coming home soon, and he always wants to eat shortly after he gets here."

"I'm sorry. I don't mean to whine, but I don't like the idea of my friends putting themselves out for me."

"Would you have rather stayed at the doctor's office?"

"Of course not, but I don't want to be a bother to my friends either."

"I told you...Amelia, Nelda and I had a meeting, and we decided you'd probably had your fill of being in Doc's office. We also understood since your apartment is on the second floor of the mercantile, you needed to stay with one of us until you can get up and down the stairs again."

"But..."

"No buts. Since Spencer's sister is with the Barringtons, and Amelia lives out on their ranch, it was logical for you to stay with me first. We have the extra bedroom and frankly, I'll enjoy the company." She grinned. "That is, if you'll stop whining."

Wilma laughed. "I'll try."

"Good. Let's talk about something else. Did you know Lance arrested Juliette again?"

"Did he really?"

"Yes, he sure did. Said he was going to keep doing it until she got it through her head he was fed up with her pestering him."

"Good for him." Wilma dropped a peeled potato into the pot of cold water. "Guess who came to see me at Doc's yesterday morning."

"I have no idea. Who was it?"

"Your brother."

Grace looked surprised. "Clay?"

"Unless you have another brother I don't know about, yes, Clay."

"Not that I care, but I didn't know you and Clay were friends."

"Neither did I. But he explained it."

"Oh?"

"He said he hadn't been in town long enough to make many friends, and he thought you and Lance, Hal Cramer, Bryce and I were the only people he felt he could talk to."

"Then why didn't he come to me?"

"He did. You weren't home, so he went to see Lance. It happens you and Lance had gone out to the Circle Two. I was his third choice." She looked into the pan. "Have I peeled enough potatoes?"

"Yes, I think so."

"Good." She pushed her wheelchair away from the worktable. "I hear Miss Kathrine moving around in her cradle. I think I'd like to look after her while you continue to cook."

"Good idea." Grace walked over to the cradle, plucked up the child and moved to plop her in Wilma's lap.

As she hurried back to her cooking, she noticed how happy Wilma looked holding the baby in her arms. She couldn't help thinking, *I hope Wilma will meet a man, get married one of these days soon, and have a child of her own. She'll make a wonderful mother.*

~ * ~

Clay walked into the jail office, followed by Thomas.

Lance dropped the wanted-poster he was studying. "Howdy, fellows. What are you up to?"

"We came by to see if we could get a little information."

"Glad to help you out, if I can."

"I thought you might." Clay took the chair in front of the sheriff's desk and Thomas took the other one. "We need to hire someone to help out at the ranch and since you've lived here all your life, we thought you might have an idea of who you could recommend."

"I guess you're looking for someone who has ranching experience?"

"That's right. I admit my ranching skills are limited and, though they're working hard, Thomas and Luke have no more experience than me."

"So you need somebody to tell you what you should do?"

Thomas muttered, but it wasn't clear.

Lance looked at him. "What did you say, young man?"

"We want somebody who won't mind working with an Indian."

"I'm sure somebody like that won't be hard to find."

"I don't know, Lance. Thomas hasn't had the best of experiences with the men he's come into contact with. That's why he insisted on coming with me, to let whoever we hire understand he's to treat him as well as he does Luke, or me."

"I see. But after you've been around here a while, Thomas, you'll realize one of the most respected men in the area is Jed Wainwright, who makes no apologies for being half Lakota."

"I think I'm Cheyenne."

"You think?"

"Yeah. One of the men who owned me, used to call me ... 'that stupid Cheyenne Injun boy.'"

Lance grinned. "I wouldn't be afraid to bet you won't be hearing that expression from the man you're with now."

Thomas kind of grinned, too. "I don't think I will either. I trust Mr. Clay."

Clay nodded. "Thomas knows I don't own him. He's with me because he chose to be. Now, to get back to my question."

"If you don't need someone to run the ranch, I think I might know someone you could talk to."

"Who?"

"Red Castlebaum. He's the livery man's brother. Was hurt a couple of years ago while working on a ranch and lost part of his foot. He limps some but is strong as an ox."

"Think he'd be interested?" Clay asked.

Before Lance could answer, the door opened, and Juliette Cramer stepped inside.

Lance frowned at her and started to stand. But before he could say anything, she blurted, "Don't worry, Lance. I didn't come to see you. I want to see Big Matilda Hurley."

~ * ~

"What you looking at, Merve?"

"That blasted man, who acts like he's the daddy of that Injun boy I tried to tame in the store. He jest come out of the sheriff's office."

"Looks like that Injun is with him."

"He is. 'Course when I get him, he won't be with him fer long."

"Why do you want to get your hands on that boy so bad, Merve?"

"I hate Injuns, Woody."

"I don't like 'em neither, but he's jest a boy. He ain't gonna do much harm."

"He could do more than you think. Don't matter how old he is now. He's gonna grow up into a buck, if I don't stop him." Merve sneered. "I decided the day I first seen him in the store I couldn't let him do that."

"Why not, Merve?"

"I got my reasons." He whirled around. "Let's foller them. We might get a chance to grab the Injun. If'en we don't, we'll learn where they stay and we can get him later."

"We've gotta figure a way to get that witch out of jail, Merve."

"We'll do that later. Now come on. Looks like they's headed in the direction of the livery stable."

Woody frowned. "Wonder why they're going there. They both got horses."

"I guess you can't trust an Injun boy or a Injun lover like that man." Merve slapped him on the back. "If'n we's lucky, we might get the Injun and then git that ole witch back to the mountain tonight."

~ * ~

"Well Lordy mercy, look who's a'coming here. If it ain't the fancy lady," Matilda said.

Juliette turned to Lance. "I want to speak with Miss Hurley alone. Please leave us."

"You sure?"

"Yes, Lance."

"If you say so." He turned and left the cell area, closing the door behind him.

Matilda laughed. "Why you here, fancy lady? You startin' to feel that spell I put on ye?"

Juliette didn't answer. Though her heart was pounding, she walked up to the cell. "I don't care about that. I need something else."

"I done give you all the free information I intend to give."

"That's all right. I have some money."

Matilda's eyebrow went up. "It'll cost you five dollars."

"Fine."

"You got that much on you?" There was doubt in Matilda's voice.

"I have more than that on me. In fact, if I like what you say, I might give you ten dollars."

"I need to see the money."

Juliette opened her reticule and pulled out some bills.

Matilda grinned. "All right, fancy lady. What do you want to know?"

Twenty-four

Leaving the livery, Clay turned to Thomas. "That went better than I expected. I think Red will work out well on the ranch."

"Maybe."

"If you weren't sure, you should have said something."

"I just appreciate the fact he didn't seem to mind working with me."

Clay shook his head and changed the subject. "There's one more place I need to stop before we head home."

"Can I ask where?"

"Sure. I want to drop in on my sister for a few minutes. You don't mind stopping there, do you?"

"No. Not as long as she doesn't mind me coming to her house."

"You've met Grace, Thomas. Do you think she'll mind?"

"She was nice when she and her husband came to the ranch."

"Then, let's go to her house and see if she's still nice."

Thomas shook his head and climbed on his horse.

Clay heard a baby's cry when they stepped on the porch of the sheriff's house.

"Sounds like the baby's hungry." Thomas said.

"Sure does." He knocked on the door and called out, "It's Clay, Grace. May I come in?"

"Come on in."

He didn't think it sounded like Grace's voice, but who else could it be? He went inside and Thomas followed.

He stopped when he spied Wilma sitting in the room in a wheelchair.

She laughed and nodded at them. "As you can see, I'm not Grace. She's gone into the bedroom to feed Kathrine. But I'm sure she'll be glad you both came."

Clay grinned. "In the meantime, I'm glad to see you."

Wilma blushed. "Likewise." She turned to Thomas. "It's good to see you again, too, young man."

"We came to town to hire a hand for the ranch."

"Did you find someone to hire?"

"Yes, ma'am. Red Castlebaum, the livery man's brother."

"Oh, he's a good man. I'm glad you hired him. He's had a hard time since his accident."

"I don't mean to butt in, but I've got to ask, what are you doing here, Wilma?"

"It seems my friends don't think I'm capable of taking care of myself in my little apartment, so they've decided I'll stay with them until I'm better. Grace is my first hostess."

Grace walked into the room with Kathrine in her arms. "Well, hello. I'm delighted to see you. I hope you came for supper."

"I wish we could stay, but we can't. Alice expects us to come home."

Thomas grinned. "Mr. Clay doesn't like to upset Miss Alice."

"I need to get to know this woman better. She seems to have good control over my brother."

Thomas nodded. "We're all a little afraid of her. But we don't let her know."

"Thomas is right. She has a way about her." Clay frowned. "I just had a bright idea."

"What?" Grace turned her head.

"I know Nelda is about to have a baby and Amelia lives a good distance out of town."

"So?"

"I'm sure you enjoy having Wilma here, but she seems to think she should be at home."

"But she can't. There's no way she can get up and down the steps."

"That's true. That's why she should come out to our ranch."

"What?" Wilma stammered.

"Think about it. We're not that far from town and she could answer a big question for me. Mr. Cramer says I need to have the children in school. I know Wilma is smart enough to teach them. She reads and writes, she's good with figures from working in the mercantile. I think this is a good answer for all of us."

"I don't think…"

"Wait a minute, Grace. This might not be a bad idea. Since Kathy Chalfant came to town, I've been wondering how long it would be before I had to find another job. Maybe…"

"So, let's call it settled. I'll bring a wagon to town tomorrow around noon and help you move to the ranch." Pleased with himself, Clay grinned. "Now, let me see my beautiful niece before she goes to sleep."

~ * ~

Beetle turned up his nose. "Ma, these here beans taste funny."

"Eat 'em and shut up. They's the best I could find. I had to open six cans afore I found one fit to cook."

"What was wrong with 'em, Vergie Mae?"

"They was soured almost to the point of being rotten. I ain't never had nothing like that happen to my canned beans." She shook her head. "Then when I got the lard to season 'em, it smelled bad, too. I think ever thing I put up last summer is going bad. Maybe I done my preserving under the wrong sign."

"Tweren't that, wife. It was that damn curse Big Matilda put on us."

"Does you think them men will get her out of jail, Pa?"

"Probably not, son. But they will cause sich a stir that I can break her out and they will be blamed."

Virgie Mae looked at them. "What men you talkin' bout, Ezra?"

"Set down and eat your supper, woman. Then we'll tell you all about 'em."

~ * ~

Wilma felt both excitement and fright as she wondered if she was doing the right thing. Excitement because she would be seeing Clay every day, plus the opportunity to do something she'd always wanted to do. Teach school.

Fright filled her mind for almost the same reasons. Could she be an effective teacher for those children? Would being close to Clay every day let her secret feelings for him slip out? She couldn't let that happen.

To get those thoughts off her mind, after she gathered the few belongings she had there, she rolled her chair to the front porch. It was a pretty day and it would be a good place to wait for Grace to return.

She smiled as she remembered how insistent Grace had been about going to the mercantile and packing some clothes for her. Then when Wilma had offered to keep Kathrine, Grace said the baby might have to eat before she got back. So, she took Kathrine with her.

To get her mind off being alone, she looked up and down the street...there was nobody in sight. For some reason, she thought it a little lonely. Maybe because she was used to seeing people in the store daily, or maybe because she lived in the apartment that looked out on Settler Ridge's main street where things happened day and night. She just wasn't used to all this quiet.

A noise on the right side of the porch made her jump. She whirled her head around as a fuzzy grey cat jumped up and ambled toward her. She laughed as it eased up to her and rubbed on her good leg.

She reached down and patted its head. "What are you doing around here, little fellow? You usually show up on the back porch where Grace feeds you."

The cat mewed and continued to rub. She laughed. But her merriment was cut short when a man leaped onto the porch. She started to scream, but his rough hand covered her mouth as he kicked the cat from the porch. It let out a howl, and she wondered if it was hurt as she tried to wiggle free of his grip.

"Got ye, jest like I knowed I would." His voice was rough and deep.

Wilma's heart began to pound as he pulled her out of the chair. She lost her balance and started falling.

He grabbed her. "You got to stand up."

"I don't think she can stand, Merve." A second man joined them on the porch. "Look at that leg. It's got a bandage on it."

Merve looked down at her. "Can't you walk at all?"

He still had his hand on her mouth, so she shook her head.

"You gonna have to carry her, Merve."

"You may be right." He dropped her back in the wheelchair.

When she started to scream, he grabbed his bandana, twisted it, and tied it around her mouth. "Now you won't be yelling."

As he picked her up again, she grabbed for the chair, but he shoved it away. It toppled off the edge of the porch.

The next thing she knew, he had her in front of him on a horse. Her eyes filled with tears, not only because she was frightened, but because of the pains shooting up and down her leg.

Twenty-five

Grace looked up at Lance. "Thank you for walking me home."

He chuckled. "Thanks for walking you home, or for volunteering to carry these bags for you."

She giggled. "That, too."

He grew serious. "Grace, do you think going to Clay's ranch is the right thing for Wilma to do?"

"I hope so. I do know that ever since we were in school, she has had a secret wish to become a teacher."

"Then I'm like you. I hope this works out for her."

"I'm sure..." she stopped. Her heart began to beat fast when she saw the wheelchair half on and half off the porch. "Wilma's chair...."

Lance dropped the bags and darted toward the porch. Setting the chair upright, he looked around.

Grace joined him. "I'll check the house."

"She won't be there."

"How do you know?"

He grabbed a swatch of cloth caught on the porch post and handed it to her. "There was a scuffle here."

Holding the baby in one arm, Grace took the cloth with her free hand. "That's from the dress she had on."

"I was afraid of that."

She began to cry. "Who could have done this, Lance?"

Kathrine let out a cry.

"I'll try to find out. Take the baby in and get her settled. I'll see if I can pick up some tracks."

"I'll go get Bryce."

"Please, Grace. Take care of Kathrine and let me handle this."

She sighed and nodded. "Come on, sweetheart. Let's go get you fed. Then Mommy will see if she can help Daddy."

~ * ~

Wilma felt as if she were going to pass out if they didn't stop soon. She'd cried until she could cry no more. But it hadn't done any good. She was still in pain. The most severe pain she could ever remember having since the fall.

She tried to think of something besides her pain. Why were these fools doing this to her? They hadn't even covered their faces, so of course she recognized them as the two drifters who periodically came into the store.

The only trouble they had given her was the day the one called Merve had attacked Thomas. The other thing she could remember was the times Merve had tried in his crude way to flirt with her. Maybe she should have taken his actions more seriously.

The horse stopped and Merve jumped off. He began pulling Wilma down. "Here we are, missy. Now let's see how much fun we can have."

As her feet hit the ground, he let her go and she fell. She cried out but with the gag, only a muddled sound came out.

"Damn it, woman. Can't you stand up?"

"I don't think she can, Merve."

Merve reached down and jerked the gag off her mouth. "Can't you get up by yourself?"

She rubbed her sore mouth and tears streamed down her cheeks. "No, you fool. Can't you see my leg is hurt?"

"Don't you call me a fool!" Merve started to slap her.

Woody grabbed his arm. "Don't hit her, Merve. She looks like she's in pain."

Merve turned away and said as he stalked off, "Then you help her up. I'm gonna get some wood to make a fire. I want some coffee."

Even in her pain, the thought crossed Wilma's mind that a fire would be a good thing. When someone came to look for her, the smoke would help them find her location. That was the last thing she thought before she passed out.

~ * ~

Merve returned with an arm full of dry limbs. He dropped them and turned to his partner. "Are you shore we ain't on that crazy man's land, Woody?"

"I'm shore."

"Good. I jest think he might of meant it when he said he'd kill us if we ever came back on his land without the crazy woman."

"I told you we might ought of tried to get her out of jail before we grabbed this one."

"Nah. We got the one I wanted."

"But what if'en he decides to kill us like he said he'd do if'en we don git his sister?

Merve ignored him as a frown crossed his forehead. "Why's my woman lying down?"

"She was in pain, so I got the blanket and told her to rest a bit. I think she passed out."

"Well, damn. I had plans to..."

Woody interrupted. "I know what you planned, Merve. But the poor woman was hurtin' and needed to rest."

Merve shook his head and mumbled, "I need some coffee." He said something else, but it was indistinguishable.

Woody ignored him as he began building the fire.

~ * ~

Nelda handed Grace a cup of tea. "I'm glad Lance insisted you come here while he's gone, Grace."

"I thought I'd be safe at home, but he wouldn't hear of it. He said you can never tell what outlaws will do and he wouldn't take a chance on them coming back to the house."

"He only wanted to protect you and Kathrine. He loves you, you know."

Grace grinned. "I know, and in case you wonder, I love him, too."

"I never doubted that."

"Now, that's enough about my brother and me. How are you feeling?"

"Believe it or not, I'm doing better." She laughed. "There for a while, I thought I wasn't going to make it, but in the last couple of weeks, I'm feeling more like my old self."

"What does Doc say?"

"He says I'm fine and the baby could arrive at any time in the next couple of weeks. Of course, Spencer won't leave me alone."

"I noticed Kathy was with you when I got here."

"I'm glad she was able to go help Spencer in the store. I hear they're busy today." She sipped her tea. "Now tell me what happened to Wilma."

"Oh, Nelda. I wish I knew. I came to the mercantile to get some of her clothes and when I got home, her wheelchair was half on and half off the porch and she was gone."

"I'm sure you were frightened."

"Oh, yes. Lance had gone with me, so he went into his sheriff mode and began searching. All I know is that while he was looking around, Clay showed up and I'm sure Bryce joined them. I don't know if anyone else joined the posse, but they've gone to see if they can find Wilma."

Nelda didn't say anything, and Grace glanced at her. The teacup in her hand was shaking.

"What's wrong, Nelda?"

"I don't know." She managed to set the cup on the table and stand. When she did, a puddle of water appeared on the floor and ran out from under her dress.

Grace jumped up. "Sit back down, Nelda. I think you're about to have your baby. I'm going to get Spencer."

"I...no..."

"Don't argue. Kathrine is asleep and she'll be fine. Now, sit down and try to relax. I'll be right back."

Before Nelda could protest, Grace was out the door.

Twenty-six

A rider came across the pasture and headed toward the posse. They stopped their horses. "I know that horse. It's Jed Wainwright," Lance said.

Jed reined up beside them. "What's going on?"

"Somebody kidnapped Wilma Lawson and we're on the trail. Want to come along?"

"Sure. I'm headed in the same direction. I saw some smoke in the distance and thought I'd better check it out."

"Was it on your land?" Lance asked.

"It looked like it was on one of the north pastures."

Clay butted in. "You know, the men who took the kids built a fire. Maybe the ones who took Wilma aren't any smarter."

Lance nodded. "That's right. Let's head in that direction."

Within a short time, they began to glimpse the smoke as it curled upward. Jed motioned for the group to stop. "Since this is part of my ranch, why don't I go ahead and ask them why they're here?"

"Makes sense." Lance glanced around and the others nodded. "When we get close, we'll take cover and wait."

"I'll let you know what's happening. But if you hear shots, don't wait. Come on in."

"Don't worry. We will."

As they moved ahead, the smoke smell became distinct. The posse slowed and Jed rode ahead of them. It wasn't long until the campfire smell was so strong, he knew he had to be close. He moved his hand to the top of his holstered pistol and rode forward.

Making no attempt to slip up quietly, he rode his horse close. The bearded man jumped up and grabbed his rifle. "Wait a minute," Jed said. "You don't intend to use that gun, do you?"

"Depends on what you want."

"Saw your fire and came to see what you were up to on my ranch." He saw Wilma lying on a blanket away from the fire. He wondered if she was asleep or if she was sick.

Merve frowned. "This your ranch?"

"It is."

"I can't believe a man like you would have such a big ranch."

"What do you mean, a man like me?"

Merve waved the rifle. "Well, fellow. It's purty plain you're part Injun. Didn't know breeds would even work on a ranch, and I know they ain't smart enough to own one."

"Well, I do. I'm Jed Wainwright and my ranch is the Circle Two." Jed raised an eyebrow as the other man got to his feet.

"Better listen to him, Merve. I heard about that there Circle Two. A Injun by that name does own it."

"How do you know, Woody?"

"Heard some hands in the saloon talkin' about working there."

Jed changed the subject. "What's the matter with that woman?" He nodded toward Wilma and made sure they didn't know he recognized her.

Woody looked confused, but Merve said, "That's my wife. She fell and hurt her leg."

"Maybe you should take her to the doctor."

"Nah. I give her some tonic. She'll be fine. You want some coffee?"

"No thanks. I need to get back to work. Be sure you put that fire out before you move on. It's not that far from one of the grazing fields and I don't want the grass to catch fire."

"We'll make sure it's out," Woody said.

"You do that." As Jed turned his horse, he added. "You might want to rethink the idea of taking your wife to the doctor."

"She'll be all right. She's tough."

Jed nodded and rode away. As soon as he was out of sight, he gigged his horse and hurried to where the posse waited.

Before he could say anything, Clay blurted, "Did you see Wilma? Is she all right?"

"Yes, I saw her. She was asleep on a blanket and didn't wake up while I was there."

"How do you think we should do this, Jed?" Lance asked.

"There's only two of them, so I think I should go back. I'll tell them I wanted to make sure the fire is out. You can come in right behind me and I'm sure you can arrest them before they know what happened."

Jed was right. The two outlaws were so confused, they ran into each other trying to get away. Bryce cuffed them while Jed made sure the fire was out, Lance rounded up their horses, and Clay hurried to take care of Wilma.

Taking her in his arms, he said, "Wilma. It's Clay. Can you wake up?"

Her eyes fluttered. "Oh, Clay. Help me." She reached for him but was unable to get her arms up high enough to put around his neck.

"It's all right, Wilma. I'm here and I'll take care of you." His heart raced as he eased her back to the blanket.

The corners of her mouth lifted but she didn't open her eyes again.

Lance walked up. "Is Wilma all right?"

"No, but I don't know what's wrong. She's semi-conscious and I don't know if it's something they've done to her or what."

Lance knelt beside them. "She looks pretty out of it. They could've given her something. In fact..."

"What is it?"

"Look at that mess on the collar of her dress. It's kind of sticky. I don't think Wilma would wear a dress with a dirty collar."

"You're right about that." He got to his feet.

"Where are you going?"

"I'm going to find out what they gave her."

"Wait…" Lance's protest was too late.

Clay had crossed the campsite and had Woody by the lapels of his vest. "You've got thirty seconds to tell me what you gave Miss Lawson."

"I didn't give her nothing."

"You've got fifteen seconds left."

Fright filled Woody's eyes. "What are you going to do to me?"

"I used to work for the government, and I've been taught ways to make a man talk that will make your skin crawl."

"What do you mean?"

Woody was about to cry, and Clay added. "Did you know I know how to castrate a man without leaving any blood or any sign of what I did?" Clay then reached down and pulled a wicked looking knife from his boot.

"All right! All right!" Woody said through tears. "Merve makes a concoction that will put you to sleep. She kept crying and wouldn't let him have nothing to do with her, so he held her down and poured it down her throat."

Clay let him go and grabbed Merve. "What's in your concoction?"

"I ain't telling you nothing."

"Oh, no?" Without another word, Clay flipped his knife around and made a six-inch slice down the front of Merve's pants.

Merve screamed. "I'll tell you. Don't castrate me."

In a matter of minutes, Clay not only knew the ingredients in Merve's drink, but he found out the cure was to make Wilma throw up. As soon as he had this information, he ran back to her and took her in his arms.

"I hate to run my finger down your throat, sweetheart, but it's the only way. You've got to get that mess out of your stomach."

~ * ~

When Grace ran into the mercantile, she saw Spencer was busy waiting on the mayor's wife. But she didn't hesitate to interrupt. "Spencer, Nelda's about to have the baby. You need to get the doctor."

Spencer, who was usually calm in any circumstances, handed Luella back her money, jerked off his apron and muttered, "I've got to get to my wife."

"No, Spencer," Grace said. "I'll stay with Nelda. You go get the doctor."

He was halfway to the door. "I've got to get to my wife."

Grace grabbed his arm. "Go get the doctor. Nelda needs him now."

Esther Wagner came from the section where she'd been looking at material. "Let him go home, Grace. I'll go get Sheldon." She hurried out the door.

As Spencer ran out the door behind her, Luella Baldwin shook her head and laughed. "Men get so excited when a baby decides it's time to make its appearance. You'd think they were then the ones giving birth."

Kathy Chalfant walked up. "What can I do?"

"Why don't you take care of the store until the doctor makes Spencer come back?" Grace said.

She looked pensive.

"What's the matter?"

"I haven't worked alone. Usually Wilma or Spencer is here with me. I don't think I'd be comfortable alone."

"I'm sorry I can't stay with you. I left my baby asleep at Nelda's house. I have to go get her."

"Why don't you close the store?" Luella suggested. "That way you can go see if you can calm your brother down."

"I think I will. Somebody needs to be with him."

Luella nodded. "I'll leave my purchases here and go with you. Somebody needs to make coffee and make sure everything goes as it should."

"Then, let's hurry. I'm afraid Kathrine will wake up and I know Spencer won't know what to do with her."

~ * ~

When they finished serving the meal to the prisoners, Bryce followed Lance back into the jail office. "After hearing Merve and Woody talk about it, I gotta ask you something."

"Sure."

"Do you think the government really taught Hunter how to castrate a man without leaving any scars?"

Lance chuckled. "I'm more inclined to believe the government taught him how to interrogate a criminal even if he has to make up lies to do it."

Bryce looked a little sheepish. "I admit he sounded so serious when he described the procedure, he almost had me believing him."

"He did sound as if he could do it, but think about it, Bryce. Whenever you cut into a person's skin, they're going to bleed, no matter how careful you are."

"That's true."

Lance dropped into his chair. "Now, why don't you go on home, check on Lettie and eat your supper? I'll wait here until you get back, but take your time."

"Think you can put up with the outlaws until I get back?"

"I don't see why not. Matilda Hurley has the same effect on them as Clay had. Did you notice how they cowered in their cell?"

"I did." Bryce grabbed his hat. "I'm a little afraid of her myself."

"I must admit, she's something to be leery of."

The door opened. Lance grinned and jumped up to meet them. "Look who has come to visit her daddy."

Grace stepped into the office and relinquished the baby to him. "Here you go, Lance." She turned and said, "Hello, Bryce."

"Good to see you, Grace." He grinned at her. "Your husband doesn't think much of his daughter, does he?"

"He's going to make her rotten if he doesn't quit spoiling her."

"My daughter will not be spoiled. She just wants a little attention from her daddy." He nodded to Bryce. "Just you wait until your baby gets here. I bet you'll be worse than I am."

"I don't know about that." Grace shook her head. "They don't come any worse than you, Lance Gentry."

He shook his head. "Now tell me, how do I rate you two showing up? I thought you were going to wait at Nelda's until I finish up."

She grinned. "There's too much going on at Nelda's."

"What do you mean?"

"Little Miss or Mr. Barrington decided to make an appearance and Spencer is just like you were. He thinks Nelda is going to die. His sister is trying to calm him down. Doc and Esther are trying to get him out of the bedroom and Luella Baldwin is hopping around telling everyone what to do."

Lance laughed. "I see why you wanted to get out of there."

"I wouldn't have mind staying, but Kathrine was restless, and I didn't think we were needed. Besides, I thought we'd check back by there after supper."

"Sounds like a good plan to me."

Bryce said, "I better get home and tell Lettie what's going on."

Lance looked down at Kathrine. "I guess you'll be the next to have one of these."

Bryce looked at the baby. "She sure is cute, but I'm not going to hang around here and watch my boss make a fool of himself over his daughter."

"Tell Lettie I said hello, Bryce. I know she's getting anxious."

"We both are, and I'll tell her you asked about her." He turned and headed out the door. "I'll be back in a little while, Lance."

Lance nodded and looked at his wife. "I'm always glad to see you, but I need to tell you about Wilma."

"Clay dropped by on his way home and said Doc insisted on keeping Wilma overnight at his place. He wanted to make sure she had no lingering effects of the stuff the outlaws made her drink."

"I'm glad Doc did that. I thought she was going to insist on going out to the ranch with Clay."

"According to Clay, she did try, but he sided with the doctor. He said he didn't want her to come until he was sure she was going to be fine."

"Good for him." He grinned at her. "Now, again. Why are..."

She interrupted. "We are here because I needed to come."

"You needed to come?"

"Yes." Her eyes misted. "Not only was I upset because of what happened to Wilma, but I'm concerned about Nelda. I just couldn't go home and stay alone. I kept thinking about what could have happened to Kathrine if we'd been home when those men kidnapped Wilma. I also hope Nelda will do as well as I did when I gave birth." She sighed. "Besides, I wanted to see my husband because I knew he would give me a hug and. tell me everything was going to be all right."

He stood, reached for her, and folded his arms around her. "Come here, darling."

She locked her arms around his waist. "Oh, Lance. Being in your arms makes me feel better already."

"I love you, Grace. You and Kathrine are the most important people in the world to me. There's nothing in the world I wouldn't do for you, if it's within my power."

Before she could answer, the door opened, and Juliette Cramer came in. She glanced at them. "Sorry to interrupt, but I want to see Miss Hurley."

Twenty-seven

Lance handed Kathrine to Grace and nodded at Juliette. "I need to tell you that we arrested two outlaws and they're in the other cell.

"Oh." She glanced at Grace. "Does that mean I can't see her?"

"No. I just felt you should know they're here."

She glanced at Grace. "Will you be here when I come out?"

Grace raised an eyebrow. "I'm not sure. Why?"

"In that case, before I go in to see Miss Hurley, may I see your baby?"

Surprised, Grace muttered, "Of course."

She moved beside Grace's chair and looked down at the baby. There was an almost smile when she muttered, "I don't know much about babies, but I think she's cute."

"Thank you."

Juliette shrugged, then turned to Lance. "I'm ready to go see Miss Hurley now."

When he opened the door and Juliette followed him into the cell area, there were whistles and catcalls. "Simmer down," Lance said. "She's not here to see you."

"You better shut up," a loud female voice bellowed. "If you don't, I'm going to cast a spell on you."

Silence followed.

In a moment, Lance came back into the office, closing the door behind him. Shaking his head, he moved beside his wife.

"She acted strange, Lance. She usually has something snide to say to me. But she didn't this time."

"She's acted strange ever since she came to see the Hurley woman a few days ago."

"Well, at least she wasn't asking you to leave me and come away with her."

He winked at her. "As if that would ever happen."

She looked down at her Kathrine. "Even if you were tempted to leave me, I don't think you'd ever consider leaving your daughter."

He shook his head and dropped into his chair. "I'd never leave either of my girls. Now, let's talk about something else until Bryce gets back. Then we'll walk home together."

~ * ~

Sheldon and Esther entered the bedroom without knocking. Spencer jumped up from the chair beside Nelda's bed. His eyes were misty. "Thank God, you got here, Doc. What took you so long?"

"Wilma had been abducted by an outlaw and I had to see to her."

"What happened?" Nelda whispered.

"He gave her something that made her sick. But she's fine now. It's time you concentrated on getting your baby into this world."

Nelda nodded and let out a little scream.

Spencer looked as if he were going to panic. "You've got to do something. I'm afraid she's dying."

Sheldon chuckled. "She's not dying, Spencer. Now move aside and let me take a look."

"You've got to save her, Doc. I can't stand the thought of losing Nelda."

"I don't think you'll be losing Nelda, Spencer. Now, like I said... move aside."

"What do you mean, you don't think? She's groaned and hollered ever since I got here, and all the time she's telling me she'll be fine."

Between breaths, Nelda said, "Tell him to calm down, Doc. I'll be all right."

"You heard her, Spencer. Now, move out of the way."

"Please, darling. I love you dearly, but I need Sheldon right now."

Esther moved beside him. "Come along, Spencer. Your sister is over there wringing her hands. You need to take her to the parlor to have a cup of coffee, while we help your son or daughter into the world."

"Grace is with her."

"Grace left. Her baby woke up and was fussy, so she took her home."

"But Nelda might need me."

"Be truthful with me. How many babies have you birthed?"

"None, of course."

"Well, Sheldon and I have brought many into the world."

"But..."

"Stop arguing with me, Spencer. You're delaying my helping your wife."

"All right, but you'll let me know..."

"Absolutely. Now, go give your wife a kiss, then get out of here."

When he was out of the room, Nelda looked at Sheldon. "I'm sorry. He's always been stubborn."

"Don't worry about it, Nelda." Esther patted her arm. "He's acting the same way most husbands act. No matter how strong and smart they are, they become lost little boys when the woman they love is about to give birth."

Sheldon chuckled and winked at Esther. "Believe it or not, when our little Eli came along, I acted the same way."

"He did, Nelda. If it hadn't been for Luella Baldwin and our daughter, Benita, I would probably have had to deliver our son myself."

Between her moans, Nelda laughed and nodded at him. "Glad to know Spencer is the typical father."

Sheldon smiled at her, "Now, let's see how long it takes to get this little Barrington into the world."

Four hours later, Jesse Spencer Barrington made his arrival known by yelling loud enough that his father heard him all the way in the parlor.

~ * ~

Clay came through the back door and hung his hat on the peg. "I'm home, Alice."

"I see you are. But I don't see Miss Wilma. You didn't leave her outside, did you?"

"No."

Before he could explain further, David ran into the kitchen. "Where's the woman you went to get?" he asked. "We were waitin' in the parlor so we could meet her."

"Let's all go back to the parlor and I'll tell everyone at the same time." He turned toward her and said, "You, too, Alice. Also get Phoebe."

"Phoebe's in there. Mary wanted to sit in her lap."

When they entered, Sarah raised an eyebrow and asked, "Did Miss Wilma change her mind about coming?"

"She's still coming, but she couldn't make it today."

"Why? Didn't she want to—"

Clay interrupted. "Don't say it, Thomas. You being an Indian didn't have a thing to do with it. Miss Wilma was hurt and had to spend the night at the doctor's office."

"Oh my. What happened?" Alice asked as she sat beside Sara on the settee. Clay took a seat in the empty chair beside the one Phoebe sat in with Mary in her lap. In an instant, Mary jumped down and came running to him with her arms outstretched. He took her into his lap and said, "An outlaw decided to kidnap Wilma, and I had to help the sheriff track him down and rescue her."

"Was it the big woman who grabbed Mary?" Luke asked.

"No. This was a man." He was trying to be patient with their many interruptions. "When we caught up with him, we learned he had made

Wilma drink something that made her sick. I took her to the doctor, and he wanted her to stay there for the night."

"Is she going to die?" David gave him a serious look.

"No, David. She's going to be fine, though it might take her a few days to get well."

"Well, whenever she's ready to come here, we're ready for her." Sarah said. "Me and Miss Phoebe got the downstairs bedroom ready for her since you said she was in a wheelchair."

"The doctor said I could go get her tomorrow if I promised I wouldn't let her overextend herself for a week or so."

Phoebe spoke for the first time. "You can count on me to help her all I can. I'm sure Alice feels the same way, don't you, sister?"

"You know I do." Alice shook her head. "I just don't understand why people in this town keep grabbing those who don't belong to them. I never dreamed there were so many mean people in the area."

"There's mean people everywhere, Alice." Clay glanced down at Mary. "I think my little darling is getting sleepy. In fact, why don't all of you get ready for bed?"

"Are you going to bed, Mr. Clay?"

"I'll go soon. But first, I'm going to see if you guys left any food from supper. I haven't eaten and I'm getting hungry."

"My goodness." Alice jumped up. "Phoebe, get these kids upstairs and I'll make sure Mr. Clay gets something to eat."

Twenty-eight

Clay walked into the mercantile and saw the nervous man behind the counter. He couldn't help smiling at the new father. "Hello, Spencer."

"Hello, Clay."

"I'm a little surprised to see you working today."

"I didn't want to. I even thought of closing the store, but Nelda insisted I stay open. Kathy wanted to take care of her and the baby, so I came in."

"How's Nelda and the baby?"

"Doing fine." He smiled. "How can I help you?"

"I wanted to see if I could set up an account for the ranch."

"I don't see why not."

"Good." Clay stuck out his hand. "Before we get started, I believe congratulations are in order. A boy, right?"

Spencer continued to grin and took Clay's outstretched hand. "I appreciate it and yes, I have a son. Name's Jesse Spencer Barrington."

"Good name."

"I would have been happy if the Spencer part had been something else, but Nelda insisted. Jesse is after my grandfather. He was a special man to me."

"Then it was good you honored him by giving your son his name."

"I thought so." He looked around the floor, and added, "Since you're the only customer now, why don't you look around and I'll go get the paper I need you to sign out of the desk in the back? It's a simple one, but I have all my customers sign it to open an account."

"Sure." Clay ambled over to the tool barrel.

In a matter of minutes, Spencer returned. "Nelda keeps the desk back there in such good order, it didn't take me long to get it. Come read it over and sign it on the front page, then initial the back and I'll sign and initial that you've read it."

Clay returned to the counter. "I don't have to read it, Spencer. I trust you. Just show me where to sign."

"It won't take you long and I prefer you know what you're signing."

"If you insist." Clay read the paper, then said, "Sounds fair to me."

Spencer handed him the pen and uncovered the inkwell on the counter.

After signing and initialing the page, he handed it back to Spencer to do the same.

When he did, there was a moment of silence as both men stared at each other. Then a smile spread across both their faces. "I can't believe this," Spencer muttered.

"You're MB," Clay muttered.

Spencer frowned. "I put MB instead of SB, didn't I?"

"You did."

"Must be from force of habit. Can you forget I signed it that way?"

Clay lifted an eyebrow and nodded. "I think that might be good."

"Just one thing."

"What's that?"

"It was great working with you, though I had no idea who CH was until I saw it written here the same way you always signed your notes."

"Same here. I kept hearing her talk about the major. I never dreamed I'd meet him someday."

"I'm sure the princess never knew my given name."

The bell jangled and Gertrude Ellsworth walked in. "Hello, gentlemen."

Clay tipped his hat and Spencer said, "Hello, Mrs. Ellsworth. How can I help you today?"

"I don't need a thing. I just dropped in to congratulate you and to see if it would be all right if I visited Nelda and that new son of yours."

"I'm sure Nelda would be delighted to see you." He glanced back at Clay. "Is there anything else you need today?"

"Not today. I'll see you later." On the way out the door, he again tipped his hat to Gertrude. "It was nice seeing you again, Mrs. Ellsworth."

As Clay climbed in the buckboard, he was still stunned. He never dreamed he'd ever run into one of the men who was in the team to protect the princess until they caught the men trying to overthrow her government and take over her throne. Now, not only had he met the head of the secret government ring, he was going to be one of the people he'd be dealing with in town. His other thought was, did Spencer know about his prison term and would he tell anyone in Settlers Ridge about it?

Shaking his head, he pushed the thought aside. It was time to collect Wilma and head to the ranch. He could think about his past later.

~ * ~

Though she didn't think she needed to go to bed when they reached the ranch, Clay had insisted. Now, here she lay, looking around at this lovely bedroom with its pink and green curtains and the matching spread. Before she could complete her inventory, a knock sounded on the door.

"Come in."

The door opened and Alice appeared with a tray. "I brought you a bite to eat."

"I could have come into the kitchen."

"No, Miss Wilma. Mr. Clay told me to make you stay in bed, and what he says is to be listened to in this house."

A head appeared around the door. "Can we come in?" Sarah asked.

"Why don't you—"

Wilma interrupted. "Please do."

Sarah entered the room leading Mary. In her hand she had a bouquet of wildflowers. Mary had a few flowers clutched in her little hand.

"We picked you some flowers." Sarah gave her a shy smile and handed her the bouquet.

"Oh, how sweet." She took the flowers from each of them. "No wonder you're Clay's two favorite girls."

They both grinned. "Do you want us to go get a vase to put them in?"

"Yes, please. That way I can set them on the bedside table and enjoy them."

After the girls left, Alice said, "It was nice of you to be so gracious to them, Miss Wilma. Those girls are just now beginning to realize there are nice people in the world."

"I hope they will soon learn I care about them and I want them to like me."

"I think they like you already." She moved to the bed. "Let me put pillows behind your back so you can sit up to eat, before it gets cold."

By the time Wilma had the tray on her knees, the girls returned with the flowers. "We couldn't find a vase. I hope this glass will be all right."

"I think they look beautiful in that glass." She took the flowers and put them on the tray. "I want them here so I can look at them while I eat. I'll put them on the table later. Thank you again for picking them for me."

"You're welcome," Sarah said.

Mary grinned.

"Come along, girls. Let's leave so Miss Wilma can eat her dinner before it gets cold." Alice put her hand on Sarah's back. "You can come back and visit with her later."

"I'd love for you to come back. So please come soon."

"We will."

At the door, Mary turned, grinned, and waved goodbye.

It was all Wilma could do to keep smiling and not show the tears that wanted to fill her eyes. She knew she was going to love these children.

~ * ~

Clay reined his horse up, ground hitched it and dismounted where the boys and the new hand, Red Castlebaum, had finished repairing a fence. "Sorry I'm so late in joining you. It took me longer to get things arranged in town than I thought it would. But it looks like you've done a good job."

"It weren't no problem," Red said. "I've enjoyed working with these fellows. They're right smart guys."

Clay nodded. "I kind of think so, too."

Both boys smiled but said nothing.

Red said, "Since we're finishing up here, we thought we'd head back to the ranch and work on the chicken coop."

"That's a good idea, since we need to add more chickens to the flock. Miss Alice says we need more eggs."

Luke turned and looked at him. "Did you bring Miss Wilma back home with you, Mr. Clay?"

"I sure did."

Red said, "The boys told me she was coming to work on your ranch as the schoolteacher, and about how those outlaws kidnapped her. I hope she has recovered."

"She's mending fine, but the doctor said after the ordeal she went through, she needed to take it easy for a few days before she started to work. I insisted she take a nap when we got back."

"Knowing how Miss Wilma didn't let anybody tell her what to do when she worked in the mercantile, I bet she wasn't too keen on that."

Clay grinned. "She wasn't. Luckily, I had Alice on my side. I'm sure she had Wilma in the bed by the time I got saddled up and headed out here."

Thomas chuckled. "Nobody on the ranch argues with Miss Alice. Not even Mr. Clay."

Clay nodded. "He's right."

Red lifted an eyebrow. "But I thought you were the boss."

"I suppose you could say that's my title, but I like to eat, and Alice is an excellent cook. I'm afraid she'd not feed me if I buck her."

"I've got to admit what she served me today was mighty good."

"I'm sure it'll be just as good tonight." Clay turned back to his horse. "Let's get on back and get our work done. Then we can all enjoy the supper Miss Alice serves us tonight."

Nodding, they all climbed on their horses and headed to the ranch.

Twenty-nine

Few people knew Gertrude Ellsworth had a habit of going into the church during the afternoon. If asked, she would have said she did that because she felt it renewed her spirit to sit in the quiet and reflect on her life and her faith. On Thursday, while Margo was in the baby's room rocking her to sleep and Eli was holed up in his study working on his sermon, she eased out of the house and walked the short distance to the church. Opening the door and slipping inside, the last thing she had expected to see was a woman with her head bowed sitting in a pew near the front.

At first, she thought she would turn back and leave the woman alone. But something about the scene stopped her. There seemed to be something about the still figure that made Gertrude think she needed comforting.

Before she could change her mind, she cleared her throat and moved forward as Juliette Cramer turned around and looked in her direction. The girl muttered, "I guess I should go."

Gertrude reached the pew and smiled. She could see Juliette had been crying, but she didn't mention it. "Please don't let me interrupt you, dear. I only came to sit in the quietness and think about things. I'm pretty sure the church is big enough for both of us. I'll sit on the other side where I won't bother you."

Juliette gave her a small smile. "You don't have to do that. You may sit beside me if you like."

"I would like that." Gertrude slipped into the pew.

Several minutes passed in silence. Juliette broke it. "With the exception of my mother and father, nobody in Settlers Ridge likes me." She sighed and added, "And sometimes I wonder about them."

"Why would you think such a thing, dear?"

She didn't answer and another few minutes passed. Then she said, "When I started school, I was a shy young girl who was so afraid of making a mistake I hardly ever spoke. This lasted into my teens. It became so pronounced my parents decided a boarding school might help me overcome my unreasonable shyness. When I was sixteen, they sent me to St. Louis."

She took a deep breath. "In St. Louis, this small-town girl was introduced to a way of life I never knew existed. My beautifully dressed classmates were mostly from moneyed families who lived in lavish homes and had servants. Though I was still shy, I decided I wanted that kind of life for myself. No matter what it took, I decided my life goals were to become a lady just like them and live the good life with a handsome man who would love me and make sure I was looked up to as he would be. Then everyone would envy me the way I envied my classmates."

When she paused, without speaking Gertrude reached over, took her hand, and gave it a squeeze.

With a slight smile, Juliette went on. "When I came home from school last spring, I thought I was the kind of person everyone would envy and would look up to. I based my ideas on how to achieve my goals on a theory Professor Smyth had introduced us to. Only recently have I learned I had a warped idea of how the theory worked. Now I realize what a mess I've made of not only my life, but my parents' lives, too, and there's nothing I can do about it."

"My dear Juliette. You're right about one thing. You don't have the power to change a thing you have done in the past. Even God Himself can't change whatever has already taken place. But there is nothing in this world that can stop you from changing what you do in the future. That is, if you want to change it."

Juliette stared at her. "Do you really believe that?"

"With all my heart."

"Do you think God would listen if I prayed about it?"

"I've always found prayer helps." She patted Juliette's hand.

With tears in her eyes, Juliette whispered, "Will you stay with me while I pray?"

"As long as you want me to stay, my dear."

~ * ~

After supper, Clay went to his office and recorded the supplies he'd bought at Barrington's. He glanced at the other entries he'd put in the book and decided everything was in order. Shoving the book in the bottom drawer of his desk, he stood and went to the window.

The sun had almost disappeared, but it was still light, and from this view he could see most of the back yard. The barn, the corral, and the bunkhouse were all to the left. To the right were the chicken coop, the vegetable garden, and the wash house. He knew beyond that was the outhouse, though it was out of sight because of the small grove of trees.

Sarah appeared out of the trees, leading Mary. He knew she was getting the little girl ready to go to bed. For her age, Sarah was a responsible young girl. But was it fair for her to always have the responsibility of little Mary?

In fact, was it fair that all the children in his care had so much responsibility? They all worked hard without complaining, and what did they get out of it? To his way of seeing, all they got was a place to live where they weren't picked on or abused.

And what about him? He wasn't a rancher, so why had he taken on the responsibility of this ranch and these children? Weren't there more responsible people out there who could do a better job? He hadn't even been sure he wanted to settle down in Settlers Ridge when he'd come this way to see his sister. His plan had been to see Grace, see if a relationship with her could be rekindled and then to find a job more to his liking.

He'd even considered applying to be a U.S. Marshal. A job like that would take him all over the west. He'd be able to use the skills he'd learned working for the government. He'd also meet a lot of beautiful women and the idea of having different friends in different towns had often crossed his mind.

But it hadn't turned out that way. Here he was with five kids, two old women and one hired hand on a ranch and he wondered why he felt trapped.

A knock interrupted his thoughts. He crossed the room and opened the door. "Yes, Phoebe?"

"Miss Wilma wanted me to ask you if you'd come see her before you turned in, Mr. Clay."

"Thank you. I'll be right down."

She turned down the hall and he closed the door. And a smile crossed his face. How could he have left Wilma out of the group who were gathered here and were trying to make a home on this ranch? If he thought she would become a permanent resident, it might all be worth it.

Giving Phoebe time to get to her room, he opened the door and headed downstairs. He only hoped Wilma hadn't sent for him to tell him she'd changed her mind about staying there and teaching the children.

He didn't have time to worry about it long. He was at her door. He took a deep breath and knocked.

"Come in."

Stepping inside, he wasn't prepared to see her looking so beautiful. She sat up in bed and smiled at him. Her lips were soft and rosy. Her hair was pulled back and tied with a blue ribbon and the gown she wore had the same color of ribbon around the neck. He bit his lip, and hoped she had no way of knowing how he wanted to reach out and take that ribbon out of her hair and watch it cascade down her back and shoulders. He stopped his mind from thinking about the ribbon holding together the neck of her gown.

"You wanted to see me," he blurted.

"I did. Please have a seat."

His mind was saying, *I don't need to have a seat. I need to find out what you want, then I need to get out of here.* But he didn't voice it. He dropped in the rocking chair a few feet from her bed, and managed to mutter, "What's on your mind, Wilma?"

"I was afraid you'd go out to work on the range in the morning and I'd miss you, so I decided I needed to show you what I've done tonight."

"Oh."

She reached for the paper on the table beside the bed and handed it to him. "I made a list of the things I'll need to start teaching. I wanted to see if it's all right with you if I purchase them."

"Of course it's all right. I want you to get whatever you need."

"I thought if I had some of them now, I could start teaching a few simple things to the younger children."

He raised an eyebrow. "From your sick bed?"

"That's another thing I want to discuss with you. I know you brought my wheelchair with us and I plan to get out of this bed in the morning and use it."

"I'm not sure you're able, Wilma."

"Yes, I am. If I wanted to stay in bed, I wouldn't have left the doctor's office. I only went to bed when we got here because I promised I would. I didn't promise to stay there, though."

He glanced at the list she'd given him. "Am I right in saying you want me to go to town and get these supplies right away?"

"That would be nice."

A knock sounded on the door, then it opened. Alice looked in. "I thought I heard voices in here."

"I asked Clay to come down so I could give him the list of things I need to begin teaching."

"She wants me to go get them tomorrow, so if you need any supplies, let me know. That way I won't have to make two trips."

"I'll make you a list." She eyed them. "Would you like some coffee while you're talking?"

"You know I'll never turn down coffee, Miss Alice." He glanced at Wilma.

"How about you?"

"I don't think I want anything."

"Then, I'll have my coffee on the porch, Miss Alice. You wouldn't happen to have any more of that cherry cobbler you made for supper, would you?"

"Yes, I do. I figured you'd want more, so I made an extra-large one."

"Then, if Wilma's through giving me instructions, I'll go with you to the kitchen. I want to make sure you put a big helping in the bowl."

"I'll say goodnight, Clay. Thank you for coming in and for agreeing to buy the supplies for me."

"You're welcome." He stood. "I'll see you tomorrow."

Alice turned down the hall and he followed her. In the kitchen, he chuckled and winked at her. "You're a slick one, Miss Alice."

She frowned. "Whatever do you mean?"

"Don't try to play innocent with me, woman. I know you came into Wilma's room to make sure I got out of there."

"Why, Mr. Clay. Why would you say such a thing?"

"You know good and well why." He chuckled. "Put another spoon full of pie in the bowl."

"Well, we do have impressionable youngsters in this house."

"I understand that. I also understand I'm an honorable man. You don't have to worry about me taking advantage of Wilma."

"I know that. I also know she's a beautiful woman and she's single. I just want to make sure if you do get things in your head, you go buy a wedding ring." She nodded at him. "Here's your pie. Now let me get your coffee so you can go on out on the porch and relax. I'm sure we understand each other."

As he sat on the porch eating his cobbler, drinking his coffee, and watching the darkness close in, he couldn't help laughing to himself.

Miss Alice hadn't known it, but she didn't have to warn him about Wilma. He'd known from the first time he saw her that if anything ever happened between Wilma Lawson and any man, a wedding ring would be involved.

Thirty

Clay was on the way to town when he saw a hunched-over man ahead of him, dragging a beat-up saddle and stumbling along. Remembering what happened the last time he encountered a stranded group, had he been on his horse he might have turned across the field and headed in the other direction. But he was driving a wagon and it would be impossible to leave the road.

Pulling up beside the man, he was shocked to see the bloody clothes and battered face. He wondered how the man was still on his feet. "Man, what happened to you?"

The man looked at Clay through swollen but suspicious eyes. "Had some trouble."

"I see that. Where's your horse."

"They decided I didn't need a horse."

"How many attacked you?"

"What difference does it make? Nothing you can do about it."

Clay held back his anger. "I can't do anything about the attackers, but I can give you a lift if you're headed to Settlers Ridge."

"You'd do that?"

"Throw your saddle in the back and climb in."

The man hesitated for only a moment. Then without saying another word, he put the saddle in the wagon and pulled himself up to the bench.

Clay could tell the fellow was in pain but was trying to hide it. He didn't say anything because he could tell that not only the man's body had been beaten and bruised, but his pride had been as well.

They traveled for a short way in silence, then the man said, "They came at me from behind, lassoed me and jerked me to the ground. There were four or five of them, I think. Didn't really have time to count."

"I know it's a stupid question, but do you have any idea why they attacked you in such a vicious manner?"

"I think it started out as a robbery. Then they got a look at me and decided to rid the world of another breed."

"So they thought you were dead or dying when they left?"

"There for a while, I thought so, too."

"I'll take you to see Doctor Sheldon Wagner when we get to town. Then you need to see Sheriff Lance Gentry."

"Those men took my money. I can't pay the doctor and I'm sure the sheriff won't give a damn what happened to me."

"The doctor won't refuse to help you because of no money, and I assure you the sheriff cares. He doesn't stand for this sort of thing happening. I know because he's my brother-in-law."

When the man said nothing, Clay added, "By the way, my name's Clay Hunter."

For a minute he said nothing, then he muttered, "John White Feathers Durant."

Instinctively, Clay knew the man was having a hard time talking, so he curbed his questions. "Why don't you relax until we get to town? It shouldn't be much longer."

They pulled to a stop in front of Sheldon's office half an hour later. "I'm not sure..."

Clay wrapped the reins around the brake stick and jumped from the wagon. "Let's see if the doc is in."

"I don't need an escort."

"I know that. I have business with him. Come on."

As soon as they stepped in the office, Esther took John's arm. "You look like you need to lie down. Come with me."

"Ma'am. I'm not sure..."

"Well, I'm sure. Now come along. Sheldon is in the examining room, so you won't have to wait." She looked back at Clay. "I'll be back in a minute."

She returned shortly. "What can you tell me about the man you brought in?"

"I came upon him on my way to town. Seeing what shape he was in, I brought him here. He said his name was John White Feathers Durant and some men jumped him, robbed him of his money and his horse."

Esther shook her head. "So you played Good Samaritan again."

He shrugged. "What else could I have done?"

"Not a thing. You're a good man, Clay Hunter."

He wondered what she'd think of him if he told her he was an outlaw. Not wanting to go to that subject, he said, "Wilma is determined to start teaching right away. I'm not sure she should start so quickly and wanted to ask Sheldon what he thought about it."

"I'll ask him when he finishes. Are you going to wait here until he's through with your friend?"

Again, he wanted to correct her. John White Feathers Durant was not his friend. But he let it go. "I'm going to the mercantile. I'll come back when I finish up there."

"That'll be fine."

Clay thanked her and left the office.

~ * ~

Clay couldn't believe what he'd done. It had just seemed the right thing to do at the time. Now he wasn't too sure. After he'd left the doctor's office, he'd gone to the mercantile, purchased the school supplies that were in stock and had Spencer order the rest of them.

Then he made a quick stop to see Lance and tell him about

finding the man on the road. Back at the doctor's office, he found John. White Feathers Durant was going to recover with rest, but he had refused to spend the night in the doctor's office. Clay did convince the man to go to see the sheriff.

After getting a description of the bandits, Lance asked, "I'll see what I can find out about those men. Where can I get in touch with you?"

John looked as if he didn't know what to say, so on impulse Clay had blurted, "He'll be at the ranch."

Lance lifted an eyebrow. "Your ranch?"

Clay let out a little chuckle. "I don't think any other rancher would appreciate me sending a new hand to them."

"Then if and when I find the outlaws, I'll come talk to you there."

A surprised John only nodded.

Now here they were in the wagon headed to the ranch. Clay wondered if he'd lost his mind. He didn't know this man or much about him. Yet, he was taking him home to the two elderly women, a crippled Wilma and five innocent children. This could turn out to be a disaster. What was he thinking?

They talked very little on the way out of town, and Clay was surprised when John asked, "Why did you do it?"

Though he knew what John was talking about, he asked, "Do what?"

"Tell the sheriff I'd be at your place. Then keep your word and take me home with you."

"I always try to keep my word."

John looked over at him. "Then you're the first white man I've ever met that does."

Clay ignored the remark and asked, "Where you headed when I found you, John?"

"I've been working on a ranch in Colorado. Though I'd been there for over four years, for some reason the owner decided he didn't want any of my kind working there any longer. He paid me off and told me to get out of the country if I wanted to continue to live. I don't know why I believed him, but I decided to head north. I'd gotten this far without incident, and you know what happened from there."

"You sound awfully educated to be a ranch hand, John.'

A slight smile showed at the corner of his lips. "My pa was a teacher. He made sure I got a good education. He said since I was of mixed heritage, it would serve me well."

"Where are your folks?"

"Ma died when I was six years old. Some sort of fever. Pa raised me and things were fine until he happened to be in an Albuquerque bank at the wrong time. Robbers came in and started shooting at everyone in there. Pa didn't make it out. I was sixteen at the time."

"You're a long way from Albuquerque."

"As long as Pa was alive, the town seemed to accept me as the headmaster's son. After Pa died, I found out what they really felt about me. I decided I'd go elsewhere. That was seven years ago."

Clay calculated the figures in his head and realized the man was twenty-three years old. There were other questions he had, but he decided he'd ask them later. He changed the subject.

"Let me tell you about my place." He wondered when he'd decided the ranch belonged to him, but he couldn't take the time to figure it out now. He went on and explained about the children, the women, and the hired hand. He ended with, "You may find you have things in common with Thomas. He's mixed breed and he hasn't had it so easy either."

"And you took him in?" John blurted.

"Of course. What was I supposed to do? Put him out on the street?"

"Some men would."

"Well, I'm not one of those men. I have my own code of ethics."

Though he mumbled it, Clay heard him say, "I'm beginning to believe that."

~ * ~

When they reached the ranch, Clay pulled the wagon close to the house. "The bunkhouse is the building just beyond the corral. Go pick yourself a bunk while I take these supplies in."

"You don't want me to help?"

"No. You need to lie down. You look tuckered out, and the doctor said you should take it easy for a couple of days. I'll expect you to start helping out after you're better."

John looked at him with a question in his eyes. "Are you saying you're hiring me to work here?"

"It depends."

"On what?"

"You said you worked on a ranch and I can use another hand. What was your main job where you worked?"

"I did most anything. Mucking out stalls, mending fences, rounding up cattle and breaking horses. Stuff like that."

Clay nodded. "I've seen some wild horses around and we could use more stock on the ranch."

For the first time since he'd met John, the man smiled. "That's the job I like best."

"Good. We'll talk later. Now, go get some rest. I'll introduce you to our other hand, Red Castlebaum, when you get up. I'll also let you meet Miss Alice. She's supposed to be my housekeeper, but to be honest, she runs the household."

John nodded and muttered, "Thanks."

Hoping he'd made the right decision, Clay turned to get an armload of school supplies when Luke walked up.

"You need any help, Mr. Clay?"

"I sure do. I didn't realize how much stuff I'd bought."

Luke filled his arms, too. "What is all this?"

"School supplies."

Luke's eyebrow went up. "Looks like Miss Lawson intends for us to do a lot of work."

"She probably does. Some women can be demanding, you know."

Luke laughed. "Like Miss Alice?"

"That's a perfect example."

They went into the house and down the hall to the extra room Wilma intended to use as her classroom. Putting the supplies down, they turned when a squeaky sound drew their attention.

Wilma wheeled into the room. "I'm excited to see all this. I didn't realize you'd buy so much."

"I got everything on your list that didn't have to be ordered."

She moved to the table where he'd put an armload of books. "I can't wait to get the children started on these."

"I'll go get another load, Mr. Clay."

Wilma's eyes opened wide. "There's more?"

"Yes, ma'am." Luke scurried out of the room.

Clay felt a little awkward as he watched her excitement. Not sure what to say, he finally came out with, "If I missed anything, let me know and I'll get it the next time I go to town."

"After seeing all this, I'm sure you didn't miss a thing. But I didn't mean for you to buy it all at once. It must have been awfully expensive."

"I wanted you to have what you needed."

"You're a good man, Clay Hunter."

"I see you're back," Alice said as she came into the room.

"Yes, ma'am."

"Who was that fellow you had with you? I haven't seen him around here before."

Clay didn't ask how she knew he brought someone home with him. He simply explained about his meeting John.

"I guess that means you have another mouth to feed, Miss Alice."

Alice grunted. "I better go see if I've got enough cooked."

Wilma looked up at him with a big smile. "Like I said, you're a good man, Clay Hunter."

He was glad Luke returned with the supplies at that moment and he didn't have to answer.

Thirty-one

The next morning, Wilma went to the room she'd dubbed as 'the school' and placed a slate and chalk in each of the five chairs. Though Alice and Phoebe both told her there was no need to bother teaching Mary anything since she couldn't talk, Wilma insisted she have a place in the room, too.

She explained her reasoning. "It doesn't matter that she can't talk. She'll know if she's left out and I don't want any of the children to feel that way."

Clay walked into the room. "Looks like you're anxious to get started."

"I am." She moved her chair so she could look at him. "I thought I might start with David and Mary this morning while Sarah is doing her chores. Then I can work with the older children. Sarah's time is more flexible than the boys'. When would be a good time for Luke and Thomas to come in for lessons?"

"Midmorning until midafternoon would be good. They can get their barn work done and then come to school. Red and I can cover everything else until John is able to put in full hours."

She nodded. "That sounds good."

"Then why don't I go get the kids and you can work with them?"

"Thank you, Clay."

In a matter of minutes, he returned with Mary in his arms.

An excited David rushed into the room in front of them. "Mr. Clay said we could be first to come to school, Miss Wilma."

"That's right." She smiled at him.

"Goody. I want to learn to read and to write and maybe add up some numbers and then I can—"

She interrupted. "It's great to see your enthusiasm, David. I promise I'll teach you all those things, but we'll have to take them one at a time. Why don't you take one of the chairs beside the window? Mary can sit beside you."

Mary didn't look too sure as she clung to Clay's neck. He chucked her under her chin. "You want to go to school with David, don't you, little darling?

She gave him a slow nod.

"Then you go over there and sit in that chair beside David." He bent and sat set her on the floor.

She stood there for a few seconds, then she toddled to the chair.

Wilma smiled at them. "I'm happy to have my first two pupils on their first day of school."

"What's a pupil?" David asked.

"The children who come to school are called pupils." She picked up the slate on her makeshift desk. "Now, let's wave good-by to Mr. Clay and we'll start our first lesson."

David and Mary both waved.

Clay waved back and turned to leave the room. "I'll see you two when your school day is over."

"Why don't we start with counting? I have a stack of books here on my desk. Let's count and see how many there are." She held up a book. "This is one." Adding another to her hand, she said, "Now we have two."

Clay closed the door and went down the hall.

~ * ~

Sarah came into the kitchen with a basket of vegetables over her arm. "I decided to gather the ripe vegetables before it gets too hot, Miss Alice."

"Smart girl."

"Where is everyone?"

"Miss Wilma has the two little ones in school and the boys are finishing up their outside work. I have no idea where the men are. You know it's impossible to keep up with them."

Sarah frowned. "You mean Mary is in school?"

"We told Miss Wilma there weren't no need to let her go to school, but she insisted she be there with David."

"I guess when she sees Mary can't learn, she'll let her play while David is studying." She sat the basket on the table. "There were a lot of beans to be picked. Would you like for me to string and break them for dinner?"

"That would be helpful."

Phoebe came into the room. "I've finished the rooms. Do you need my help cooking?"

"Sarah's helping me. Why don't you go peep in the school room and see if Mary is behaving herself? Miss Wilma shouldn't have kept her in school. I guess she's one of those women who has to see for herself."

"If Mary's acting up, I'll go in and get her."

In a matter of minutes, Phoebe returned. "I peeped in like you said and was surprised at what I saw."

"What did you see, Miss Phoebe?"

"That little Mary is sitting right there watching and listening to every word Miss Wilma is saying, just like David's doing."

Alice shook her head. "Then I guess it's all right if she goes to school, too."

There was the sound of horses entering the backyard area. Glancing out the window, Phoebe's voice shook when she said, "I don't know those people. Where's Mr. Clay?"

"He's probably working on the range with the rest of the men." Alice moved to the window and glanced out. "I don't know those men either, Phoebe. Calm yourself and I'll go see what they want. You stay in here, too, Sarah."

One of the men yelled, "Hello, the house."

Alice stepped out on the back porch. "What can I do for you today, mister?"

The skinny man moved his horse closer to the porch. "Howdy, ma'am. I'm a lawman and this here's my posse. We're looking for a rough outlaw we was taking to jail. He was hurt, but he must have somehow got loose and wandered off while we were asleep last night."

Alice remembered what the sheriff in Settlers Ridge looked like and this wasn't him. She didn't believe a word this man was saying, but she didn't want him to know that. "Why in the world would you think your prisoner was here?"

"You're the closest ranch from where we camped last night, and since he was kind of out of his head, we thought he might have got mixed up and come here. We didn't think he was strong enough to go anywhere, but like I said, he got gone while we was asleep."

"As far as I know, nobody hurt came here. You might check with the men. They're around somewhere."

The man on the horse looked around. "I just thought we'd check. You might better keep your doors locked when the men are not here. We don't want him hurtin' nobody."

Alice saw Luke and Thomas come to the barn door and she pretended to wave away a fly. She hoped they caught on and wouldn't come outside. "Is that fellow dangerous?"

"Yes, ma'am. He's a half-breed. If you've ever had any dealings with their kind, you know what I mean."

Alice knew she didn't trust him or anything he said. All she wanted to do was get rid of him before Thomas took a notion to show up. "I'll do that."

It was then she saw Luke start out the barn door. Thinking fast, she yelled, "Luke, Mr. Clay wanted you and Thomas to check those loose boards in the loft before you come in for your lessons. Get back in there and do it. I don't want him fussing at me because you didn't do what he asked."

"Is that your kid?" The man glared at her.

"No, sir. I don't have any children. He's Mr. Clay's son. I'm their housekeeper."

"I see." He looked around again. "If the man shows up, he calls himself White Feathers. You might want to get this man you call Clay to tie him up. Like I said, he's a dangerous criminal. We won't bother your boss right now since he's probably on the range, but we'll check back later today to make sure everything is all right. We need to catch that crook."

Alice nodded, but said nothing as the five men rode off. She waited until they were out of sight and she called, "Hurry up and come here, boys."

Thomas came out of the barn. "What's going on, Miss Alice?"

"Where's Luke?"

"He's looking for loose boards."

"Tell him to stop and hurry in. I have something I need him to do."

"Can I do it?"

"No, Thomas. I need you in the house. Get Luke and I'll explain everything."

Luke came wandering up. "I couldn't find any loose boards."

"There aren't any." When he looked puzzled, Alice said, "I was trying to keep you boys in the barn until those men left."

"Why?"

"I think that gang of men were outlaws. What I want you to do, Luke, is saddle a horse and go get Mr. Clay. I think he said they'd be working in the south pasture. I'd fire a distress shot, but I'm afraid those men would hear the signal and come back."

Luke frowned. "What in the world is going on?"

"I'll explain everything when you get back." She turned toward the door. "Let's hurry inside, Thomas."

Both boys had confused looks on their faces, but they didn't argue with Miss Alice. Mr. Clay had made it clear that when he was away, she was in charge.

Thirty-two

Clay rushed into the house behind Luke. Alice was at the stove stirring something in a pot. Thomas sat at the table nibbling on what looked like the last of a cookie. Nobody else was around and Clay wondered what in the world the danger had been.

"What's going on, Alice?"

"We had some visitors a while ago and I'll tell you all about it as soon as these boys go to their room and make sure everything is done in there."

"It is, Miss Alice," Luke said.

"Go make sure."

He looked at Clay as if asking if he had to obey.

"Listen to Miss Alice, guys. Remember, she does the cooking and we all want to eat, don't we?"

They looked as if they wanted to argue. Instead, they headed toward the stairs and their room.

"They're gone. What happened?"

"There was a group of five men. I knew right away they weren't who they claimed to be."

"And who was that?"

She put her big wooden spoon aside. "They told me they were lawmen and they were looking for an outlaw who had run away from them during the night. Said the escapee was a fellow by the name of White Feathers. I didn't believe a word they said about White Feathers being an escapee, but I think I made them believe me when I told them no strangers had shown up at our place."

"Looks like you handled it. Why send for me?"

"Because they said they'd come back, and I believe they will. But that's not the worst of it."

Clay was about to become frustrated, but he knew Alice had her own way of telling something and he knew he couldn't rush her. If he did, she'd walk away and not tell him all of the story. "What is the worst part?"

"The leader said the escapee was a no-good Indian, though he said Injun. He told me all Indians were bad and for me to keep the doors locked. I figured they were looking for the man you rescued yesterday."

"You're probably right."

She picked up her spoon again. "I figured Thomas wouldn't be safe if they saw him, so I had him come inside and sent Luke to get you. I was afraid they'd come back if I signaled you with the gun. But I wanted you here. I didn't want us women to be here alone with the children when they come back, and as I said, I believe they will come."

A squeaky noise came from down the hall and they all looked around as Wilma, followed by David and Mary, rolled her wheelchair into the kitchen.

Seeing Clay, Mary ran around Wilma and held her arms up to him.

He picked her up and winked at her. "Has my little darling been to school?"

She nodded.

David rushed up to him. "It was fun, Mr. Clay. I can count to ten and I'm learning my ABCs. I want to go back tomorrow."

"That sounds great, David. I'm proud of you." He looked over the boy's head and smiled at Wilma. "The teacher didn't have to spank you, did she?"

David gave him an incredulous look. "No. She wouldn't do that. She's a good teacher."

Clay chuckled and looked at Wilma. "So, it went well?"

"Very well. My two students were attentive, and I'm pleased with the progress we made today."

"I bet I'll be able to read a book soon, Mr. Clay."

"That will be wonderful." He set Mary down. "Why don't you two go find Miss Phoebe? I bet she'd like to hear about your first day of school."

"All right. Come on, Mary."

Clay turned to the women. "I think you should tell Wilma what's going on, Miss Alice. I'm going to make sure John is still out."

"Out?" Both women said.

"When we were getting ready to go this morning, he insisted on helping us. I knew he was determined to go, and I was just as determined he'd rest today, so I told him if he'd take the tonic I had, he could go." He grinned. "I might not should have done it, but I gave him a big dose of laudanum. I figured it'd keep him asleep until we came in for the mid-day meal."

"It must have worked, because I didn't know he was still in the bunkhouse."

"I'm going to check on him. You tell Wilma about the visitors while I'm gone." He turned and went out the door.

Alice nodded and looked at Wilma. "Let me get you a cup of tea and then I'll tell you."

Wilma rolled up to the table and as soon as Alice handed her the tea, she launched into her story.

~ * ~

Later that afternoon, the older children were with Wilma for their lessons. Mary was taking a nap and David was playing under the tree in the backyard where he could be seen from the barn, the bunkhouse, and the corral, as well as from the kitchen window. Clay had no doubt

Alice and Phoebe were keeping a sharp eye on the boy. Probably taking turns standing at the window watching.

After thinking of what Alice had told him about the men who had come to the ranch, Clay almost knew they were the men who had attacked John and thought they had left him for dead. Now, for some reason, they decided he must have survived and had wandered to their ranch.

Since this was basically what had happened, Clay decided not to go back out on the range. The fact that Alice was sure they would return also played a part in his decision.

Now that John was awake from his laudanum-induced sleep, Clay assigned him to work in the tack room. He told him the job of taking care of the saddles and other equipment needed doing and there hadn't been time to do it.

As he stood in the barn door watching David, a faint sound drifted to his ears. Knowing it was the hoofbeats of approaching horses, he hurried to the tree where David was playing. On his way, he waved toward the kitchen window.

"David, I need you to go to the house right now."

David looked confused. "Why, Mr. Clay?"

Alice rushed up. "I figure you want me to take David inside."

Clay nodded. "Go with Miss Alice, David. She needs you inside."

"Why?"

"Don't argue with Mr. Clay, David." She put out her hand. "Hurry."

David looked confused, but it was as if he knew something was about to happen. Without argument, he took Alice's hand and followed her inside.

Clay hurried back to the barn and went into the tack room. "John, I think your attackers might be on the way here looking for you and I want you to stay in the barn out of sight."

John jumped up. "I can't ask you to fight my fight, Mr. Hunter."

"I told you to call me Clay. I need another hand on this ranch and I expect you to be the one to catch and break horses for us when the other work is done. You won't be worth a damn to me if you're dead."

John stared at him. "Are you serious?"

"I am. Now consider this your first order. Stay in here and keep out of sight. I'll handle those men."

"But, Mr. Clay..."

"Don't disobey your first order, John. I don't want to fire you before you get started."

"Yes, sir. If you insist."

"I do." Clay went out the door, then paused. Making a quick decision, he grabbed the board and slid it across the door so it couldn't be opened from the inside. That way if the men got in the barn, they wouldn't think there was anyone in the tack room.

The horses came into the yard and Clay went out the barn door. He immediately recognized the leader by the way Alice had described him. Even in the saddle, he could tell the man was taller than the others. He was also one of the skinniest men Clay had ever seen.

"How can I help you fellows?"

Skinny said, "We were here earlier, and your housekeeper said you'd be home later. Thought we'd check back by and see if you'd run into the escaped outlaw we were looking for."

"Can't say as I have. My hand and I have been on the range most of the day. Fact is, he's still out there."

"How long has he worked for you?"

"Almost from the beginning."

"Wouldn't happen to be part Injun, would he?"

"Don't think so. He's the town blacksmith's brother and I've never heard anyone say anything about them being Indian."

Skinny frowned. "Think he could've come and hid out here while you were on the range?"

"I don't see how. Alice keeps an eye out when I'm not here. You're welcome to look around if your deputies stay mounted. I can't have everyone messing around the place."

The skinny man nodded, turned to his men, and said, "Relax. I'm going with Mr..."

"Clay Hunter," Clay said.

"I'm going with Mr. Hunter to look around a bit. Stay mounted and I'll be back shortly." He got off his horse. "Shall we start with the barn?"

Clay nodded and followed him inside.

He took a quick look around, climbed halfway up the ladder and looked in the loft, then turned toward the door. He paused when he saw the board across a door. "What's in there?"

"That's the tack room."

"Why do you have it locked?"

"Learned the hard way that we should do that. Had an animal get in there and he had him a good time chewing on a saddle and ripping a couple of bridles apart. Always keep it locked when nobody needs to get in there."

Skinny nodded. "Good idea."

Their next stop was the bunkhouse. Skinny looked in the door and frowned. "I thought you said you just had one man."

"That's right."

"Then why's there two used bunks in here?"

Clay thought fast. "My nephew sleeps out here sometimes. You know how teenage boys act sometimes."

"Where's that boy?"

"He and his sister are having their lessons right now."

The man eyed Clay. "I want to see him. The girl, too."

"I don't care if you are a lawman, I think you've bothered me long enough. I suggest you take your men and leave."

Skinny put his hand on his gun. "Lawmen have to be sure, Mr. Hunter."

Knowing there was no way he would stand a chance against all of them, Clay said, "All right. I'll have Miss Alice send them out on the porch. Will that satisfy you?"

"It will."

"Stay here. I'll tell her." He went to the back door but didn't go inside. In a low voice, he explained what needed doing and Alice nodded.

He turned back to the yard. "They'll come on the porch, but I don't want you talking to them. They've been through a lot and it would upset them."

Sarah and Luke appeared on the porch and the men looked disappointed. Skinny said, "I guess you were telling the truth."

"Of course I was." He turned to the children. "Go on back to your classes. I'll explain later why you had to come out."

They nodded and left the porch.

Clay turned to the men. "Now, I suggest you get off my ranch. Whoever you're looking for is not here, so you need to look elsewhere and leave us be."

At that moment, Red rode up.

"Who's that?"

"My one and only hand."

Red dismounted. "What's going on, boss?"

One of the men said, "He ain't no Injun. Let's go, Skinny."

Without another word, they turned their horses and rode away.

Clay chuckled.

"What's funny, boss?"

"The fact that I was calling the leader of that gang Skinny in my mind. Turns out that's his name."

There was a banging inside the barn.

"What's that?"

Clay laughed out loud. "Come with me. I'll explain everything when I let John out of the tack room."

Thirty-three

Lance looked up when the door opened. "Hello, Red."

"Sheriff." Red stepped inside. "Mr. Clay sent me to tell you what's going on at the ranch. He didn't come himself because he thought the women and children would be afraid."

Lance frowned. "What in the world has happened?"

Red told him about the attack on John and then how Skinny and the other outlaws came to the house twice to try to find the man.

"I've heard of this man called Skinny. He has three men and they're making a name for themselves, mostly by robbing stagecoaches and killing Indians. I didn't know he'd come to our area, though."

"There were five men with him at the ranch."

"I suppose his gang has grown. I'll get three or four men to join the posse. With the deputy and me, that should be enough to handle it."

"Then I better get what Miss Alice wanted at the general store and hurry back. Mr. Clay might need my help if they decide to come to the ranch again."

"Tell Clay I'm rounding up a posse, and I'll be out there as soon as I get them together. I have a feeling Skinny's gang isn't the type to give up as long as he believes the Indian he attacked is in the area."

"I'll tell him." He went out the door.

Lance's mind began making plans. First, he'd get Morris Fenton to watch the jail, since he'd need the deputy to go with him. Next, he'd put the word out he was looking for men. And last, he'd have to tell Grace he wouldn't be able to get home for supper, even if the Barringtons were coming.

On the other hand, maybe he should tell her first because he knew she was going to give him an argument. It would take a little while to make her understand.

Better still, he'd go to the mercantile and tell Spencer.

Fifteen minutes later, he was glad he'd gone to Barrington's Mercantile first. Spencer had insisted he would leave the store in Kathy Chalfant's hands and join the posse.

~ * ~

Wilma looked around as Alice came into her room. "I thought you might need some help getting into bed, Miss Wilma."

"Thank you, Miss Alice. I think I can do it alone." Wilma bit her lip. "Has Clay come back yet?"

"No, ma'am. I'm sure he'll be home as soon as he can."

"It's after nine. Is he often this late?"

"Not usually."

"I know he went after those outlaws. I just hope nothing bad has happened to him."

"May I ask you something, Miss Wilma?"

"Of course."

"I don't know any delicate way to ask this, so I'm going to come right out with it. What's the situation between you and Mr. Clay?"

Wilma frowned. *What in the world gave Alice Baker the idea there was something between Clay and me? I hope and pray I'm not obvious about the feelings I'm beginning to have about him.*

Taking a breath, Wilma said, "I don't know what you're talking about, Miss Alice. Clay asked me to come teach the children because we're friends. Is that what you mean?"

"I admit, I have no idea what Mr. Clay's life was like until I met him here with the children a few weeks ago. As I understand it, Lucy chose him to take her place and he promised her to do so. I only know he's been wonderful with them and they need him. I expect him to continue to be their guardian until they're grown, and I hope nothing in his life before will interfere with that goal."

It dawned on Wilma that Alice knew little to nothing about Clay. Should she tell her? Maybe she'd give the woman hints and see if she asked any questions. "Miss Alice, I knew Clay when we were young, but I hardly know him as a man. I hadn't seen him in years."

Alice frowned. "Are you telling me he didn't grow up here?"

"Though he was born in Settlers Ridge, Clay has been away for a while. His parents are deceased, and he has one sister, Grace, who just happens to be married to the sheriff, Lance Gentry."

"Maybe you should tell me more about him, Miss Wilma."

Wilma shook her head. "I think you should talk to him."

"Why can't you tell me?"

"I'm not one who likes to gossip about a person."

"That's admirable, but you must understand I need to know so I can be assured the children are in good hands."

"As you said, Miss Lucy chose him to take her place. I'm sure she felt he was the right choice."

"I know that, but..."

The sound of a door opening and someone entering the house interrupted. Alice stood and headed out of the room. "That's probably him. I need to see if he's had anything to eat."

Wilma followed.

Both women gasped when they saw the bruised and bloody man standing in the kitchen.

"Oh my goodness, Clay. You're hurt. Please sit down."

"I'll be fine, Wilma."

"Listen to her. You can barely stand." Alice moved to the table and pulled out a chair. "Sit! I'll get some water. I need to clean the blood off your face."

Wilma rolled her chair up beside his. "Who did this to you, Clay?"

"We caught up with the outlaws and they didn't want to be arrested. If you think I look bad, you should see the other guys."

"Who else was hurt?"

"We all got a few bruises, including Skinny and his gang." He chuckled. "The ones who came out the best were Jed Wainwright and his hand, Ward Keller."

"Why didn't they get beat up?"

"They didn't leave town with the posse. But when Jed heard we were tracking the man, he and Keller followed us. The sheriff, the deputy and me thought we would be able to handle them and we were about to get them under control when Jed and Ward rode up. Skinny took one look at Jed and went berserk. He started screaming, 'Forget the posse. Get the breed. Kill him.' About that time, Jed whipped out a knife and said loud enough for everyone to hear, 'You men take care of the others. I've decided to scalp this one first. That scared the men we were trying to subdue so bad they quit fighting us and stared at Jed and Skinny."

"Too bad they didn't get there before you got in this mess." Alice put the pan of water and a bottle of medicine on the table. "Now, sit still. I'm going to wash your face and fix your wounds."

"I'll let you wash it all you want to, if you'll let me have a cup of coffee, Miss Alice."

"I reckon I can do that." She smothered a grin as she moved to the stove and poured him a cup of coffee. "I bet you didn't eat anything either."

"No, I didn't."

"Then after I get your face cleaned, you go change your shirt and wash up a bit, then maybe I'll warm you up some supper."

"She really loves me, Wilma. She just likes to play like she doesn't."

"Hush up and sit still." She washed his face, then applied the ointment.

He jerked backward. "Ouch. That hurts."

Alice punched his shoulder. "Stop complaining and go get some clean clothes. You can tell us what happened when you come back to eat."

He finished his coffee and without a word, stood and left the kitchen.

Alice picked up the dirty water. "I swear. That man has got to start taking care of himself. He's going to worry me to death."

Wilma laughed.

Alice looked at her. "What's the matter with you?"

"I just realized something."

"What?"

"Clay is right. You do care for him, and you don't want him or anyone else to know how much."

Alice stared at her. She looked like she might deny her feelings, but in a minute she said, "You're smart, Miss Wilma Lawson. So, I'll make a deal with you. You don't tell Clay I care about him and I'll do you the same favor."

"Why, Miss Alice. I...uh..." she paused and after a minute she nodded and whispered, "Then I guess the two of us will have to worry about him together."

Alice gave Wilma one of the rare smiles she bestowed on a person.

~ * ~

Clay was surprised when he opened his door and saw a boy sitting in the hall outside. "What are you doing here, Thomas?"

Thomas stood quickly. "I didn't mean to disturb you."

"You didn't bother me. But shouldn't you be asleep?"

"I wanted to be sure you were all right."

"I'm fine."

"You don't look fine, Mr. Clay."

"I had a little fight. He got in some good licks, but I won. He's on his way to jail or he may already be there by now."

"When he gets out, will he come back?"

"It'll be a long time before he gets out, that is, if they don't hang him."

"What if they don't?"

"Thomas, come in my office a minute." Clay held the door open. Taking a seat in one of the chairs in front of his desk, he pointed at the other one. "Have a seat and tell me what's on your mind."

"I told you. I wanted to make sure you were all right."

"And what else?"

"What do you mean?"

"Thomas, you would've gone to sleep as soon as I got home if you were only interested in me. There's something else."

"I know you went after the man who beat up John. I also know you hid me because you thought they'd hurt me if they saw I was Indian. So, I figured if you were going to fight for me, I wanted to be here in case you needed me when you got back."

"I might be a little sore for a day or so, but I'm sure I'll be fine."

"Why'd you do it, Mr. Clay?"

Clay didn't have to ask him what he meant. "I had to, Thomas. I'd do it for any of you."

"But I'm the one who is hated."

"By some people, I guess you are. But not by me. You're one of the family, and as I said, I'd fight for any of you because you're all the same to me. I wish you'd accept that, Thomas."

"I do, but it's hard for me to believe you care."

"Good. I'm glad you're trying, and one day I know you'll realize what you kids mean to me." Clay stood and put his hand on Thomas's shoulder. "Now, you need to get back to bed. We have a lot of work to do tomorrow and I'm not sure if I'm going to be worth much. You may have to do an extra job."

"I'll be glad to do it." He jumped up.

Clay was shocked when Thomas gave him a quick hug around the waist and then ran out of the room. At that moment, he realized taking care of these children was no temporary job. He was in it for the long run. Now all he had to do was figure out how to make sure this place became a real home. Not only for the children, but for him as well.

Thirty-four

Juliette came into the kitchen. "Can I help you cook supper, Mama?"

Marjorie looked around in disbelief. Was this her daughter? Not only had she called her mama, she was acting strange. "I guess you could set the table, if you want to," she muttered, because she couldn't think of anything else to say.

Juliette moved to the cabinet. "I have been so wrong about things."

"What are you talking about, Juliette?"

"You know what, Mama. I came back from school all mixed up. Now, I wish I had been more like I used to be." She turned around with the plates in her hand and tears in her eyes. "I'm sorry I've been so horrible to you, Mama. I don't blame you if you hate me."

Marjorie put the spoon aside she was using to stir the stew and moved to her daughter. "You're my daughter, Juliette. I might disapprove of what you do at times, but I could never hate you."

"Oh, Mama." She put the plates on the table and fell into her mother's open arms. Sobbing, she managed to say, "I'm so sorry. Please forgive me."

"Of course, I do, darling. Let's go to the parlor where you can relax and calm down."

For almost half an hour Juliette cried. Then her mother cried. Soon they talked and talked and talked.

Neither noticed the passing of time until the front door opened and Hal came into the room with a frown on his face. "What's burning?"

"Oh, my goodness! The stew!" Marjorie jumped up and ran to the kitchen.

Confused, Hal looked at Juliette. "Why are you crying, Juliette?"

She gave him a smile through her puffy eyes, got to her feet and flung her arms around his neck. "Please forgive me, Daddy."

Awkwardly, he patted her back. "What have you done now, daughter?"

"Oh, Daddy. I understand why you think I've done something bad. But believe me, you're wrong this time. I just want you to forgive me for the awful way I've treated you and Mama since I've been home from school."

Before he could answer, Marjorie called from the kitchen, "Hal, come help me. I've got to get this out of the house before it catches fire."

He and Juliette broke apart and ran to Marjorie's aid. Hal moved to the stove, grabbed a towel and picked up the pot of burned stew. "Open the back door!"

Juliette did and he ran out and tossed the pot in the backyard. He turned to Marjorie. "What in the world happened here?"

"I'm sorry, dear. Juliette and I were having a discussion and I wasn't paying any attention to the stew."

"No, Father. Don't blame Mama. It was my fault. I'll help Mother fix something else if you're hungry. It shouldn't take us too long."

"What's going on here? I can't believe you're volunteering to help your mother cook."

"It's kind of hard to explain, but most miracles are."

He frowned.

"We have our old Juliette back, Hal."

"I don't understand."

"Hal, since supper is ruined, why don't you take us to Olsens for supper? Juliette and I will explain everything then."

"But my eyes are all red and swollen."

"You can put some powder on them. I'm so happy, I want to celebrate."

Juliette smiled. "If it makes you that happy, Mama, I don't care if my eyes are all puffy. Let's get our bonnets and go. If anyone asks, I'll tell them I was a naughty girl and Daddy gave me a spanking— which I've deserved even if I am a grown woman."

Hal was still too confused to argue. Within a few minutes, the family climbed into his buggy for the ride to Olsen's Hotel.

~ * ~

"A man came to talk to Mr. Clay, Miss Alice," Luke said as he and Thomas came into the kitchen.

"He said to tell you not to hold up supper," Thomas added.

She frowned. "Who was the man?"

"I don't know, do you, Luke?"

"No. All I know is that the sheriff sent him to see Mr. Clay."

"Must have something to do with those outlaws." She set a bowl on the table. "I wonder if I should set a plate for him."

Neither boy answered, and she glanced at them. "One of you go tell Sarah and Phoebe to bring the kids and we'll go ahead and get settled. Maybe he'll finish with the man in time to join us, and if the man comes in with him, I'll get him a plate then."

Thomas headed to the parlor.

"Can I help you, Miss Alice?"

"Yes, you may. You can pour glasses of milk for your brothers and sisters."

He finished as the group came through the door and took their seats.

"Where's Mr. Clay?" David asked.

"He'll be here in a little while." Alice nodded at him. "Now, if everyone will bow their heads, we'll say our blessing, then we'll eat."

They were in the middle of the meal when the door opened and Clay walked in. He headed to his chair at the head of the table where Alice had designated as his spot. "Sorry I'm late, folks."

"Didn't your friend want to eat supper with us?"

"No, Miss Alice. He brought me a message from the sheriff and said he had to hurry back to town."

As serving bowls were passed to him, and he began filling his plate, he added, "Miss Alice, we all need to go to town tomorrow."

"You and me or all of us?"

"He said they request you, Miss Phoebe and me to be there. Since I don't want to leave Miss Wilma alone with the children, I think we should take them with us."

"Are you including me?" Wilma asked.

"Do you think you can make the trip?"

"I don't see why not. I'm fine now."

"I was going to see if my sister would watch Mary and David, but they don't know her very well. Since they like you, I think they'd be more comfortable if you were there with them."

"Then I'll definitely go."

"Will we be staying with your sister, too, Mr. Clay?" Sarah asked.

"If you want to. But I think you're all three old enough to go with us."

"What's going on, Mr. Clay?" Alice asked.

He glanced at Mary because he didn't want her to understand what was happening. "The circuit judge will be in town for a trial."

"Why do you have to go?" David asked.

"They just want us there."

"Oh." He grinned. "I bet it's for—"

Clay's voice was sharper than he meant it to be when he interrupted. "That's enough, David."

For a moment David looked confused. "What did I say?"

"I'm sorry I was sharp, but I don't think this is something we should be saying aloud."

David frowned, then it seemed to dawn on him, and he muttered, "I'm sorry. I didn't think."

Clay grinned at him. "That's all right. We all speak too quickly at times."

Alice spoke up. "There's been enough talk and not enough eating. Let's get at it so we can clean up this kitchen. We all need to go to bed early since we have to get up and go to town tomorrow."

Phoebe spoke for the first time. "Miss Alice made a peach pie for dessert. I bet she'll let the first one through eating have the biggest piece."

They all began eating with gusto.

~ * ~

Clay, Alice, and Phoebe entered the makeshift courthouse accompanied by Hal Cramer. They took a seat at the table at the front of the room.

Phoebe looked around, then leaned over to Clay and whispered, "There are a lot of people here. Are you sure this is where we should be?"

"Yes, Miss Phoebe."

She shook her head. "This is the first time in my whole life I've ever been in a saloon. I hope nobody gets drunk and starts fighting."

"They won't, Miss Baker. The trial is held here because it's the biggest building in town to hold court," Hal explained. "As you can see, they've covered up the liquor and moved the gambling equipment to the side. Nobody will be allowed to drink."

Alice said. "Relax, Phoebe. We're here to see that woman who grabbed little Mary gets what's coming to her. Not worry about where we are."

She frowned again. "Why are there so many people here?"

"People are always curious when there's a trial in town." Hal smiled at her. "Since Big Matilda is on trial, there are more people here than usual. Listen to your sister and try to relax."

Clay looked around and saw the jury lined up on the right side of the room. He then glanced at Sarah, Luke and Thomas seated behind them. He was glad Mrs. Cramer and her daughter had saved a seat with them.

He knew they were nervous and nodded at them. They seemed to relax a little as they gave him tentative smiles.

At that moment, a door to the side opened and an overweight man with a handlebar mustache came through it. Clay figured he was Judge Herbert Wallburg. The judge was followed by a smaller man. The judge took a seat behind the raised table in the front of the room and the smaller man stood beside the table.

Almost immediately, the sheriff and the deputy escorted a handcuffed Matilda into the room and sat her at the table opposite theirs. They sat on either side of her.

Matilda looked around the room and her eyes landed on Clay. She seemed to be trying to intimidate him with her eyes. When he only stared back at her, she jerked her head around and ignored him.

Judge Wallburg rapped his gavel and the trial was underway.

"Miss Matilda Hurley, you are charged with kidnapping a child. How do you plead?"

"I ain't kidnapped nobody. I took the girl to make her talk. These folks ought to be grateful, 'cause they shore can't do it. But I can."

The judge said, "Put down that Miss Hurley claims to be innocent." He then turned to Hal Cramer. "State your case."

Hal stood. "Your honor, Little Mary Hunter is a mute, and has been all her short life. The doctors say there is nothing they can do because her voice box is damaged beyond repair." He took a breath. "Miss Matilda Hurley broke into the home where the child lives. Knocked Miss Baker down, grabbed the child and took her to her cabin in the mountains."

The judge nodded. "Call your first witness, Mr. Cramer."

"I call Miss Alice Baker."

Alice gave her testimony, then stepped down.

He then called Miss Phoebe.

Though Phoebe was frightened, she spoke clearly and told how Matilda had knocked her down and had gone out the door with a frightened Mary.

"I had to do somethin'," Matilda yelled. "They wouldn't let me have the little girl."

The judge rapped his gavel and warned her to be quiet.

After Alice was excused, Clay and Lance testified about arresting Matilda.

It was then time for Big Matilda to tell her story.

"I have magic powers," she said. "I don't care what the doctors say, I can make the girl talk. I can also cast a spell on ever-body in this room, and I intend to do it if'en you don't stop this foolish trial and give me the girl so's I can show you I can do it."

The judge rapped his gavel. "I've heard enough. Take your seat."

She glared at him. "I'll put a curse on you right now."

"You'll have to get in line. The prisons are full of people who want to put a curse on me. Now, step down." He then charged the jury and sent them out of the room. His words left no doubt on how he expected them to vote.

In ten minutes, they returned, and the foreman announced they found Matilda Hurley not only guilty of kidnapping, but of assaulting the sheriff.

Judge Wallburg looked down at Matilda. "Miss Matilda Hurley, you have been found guilty of kidnapping, which is a heinous crime. I sentence you to sixteen years in prison. The sheriff will turn you over to the prison wagon, which I understand will be by later this afternoon." He then pounded his gavel. "Court adjourned."

Matilda screamed. "You fools! You will all have trouble in your homes tonight. Your houses will burn, or your wife will poison you, or snakes will get in your bed…"

"Shut her up and get her out of here!" the judge yelled.

Clay turned to the children behind him. "Let's get out of here, too. I'm ready to head for my sister's house."

Thirty-five

Before they could get out, the little man with the judge came running up. "Mr. Hunter, the judge would like to speak with you for a moment."

Clay glanced at the women and the children. "Wait for me outside." They nodded.

He turned to Hal. "I have no idea what he has on his mind, but maybe you should come with me."

When they worked their way to the front of the room, the judge was standing in front of his makeshift bench. "Thank you for speaking with me."

"What do you need, Judge Wallburg?"

"I wanted to check on the little boy you have been caring for. My niece was wondering if you had found him a real home."

Clay began to feel defensive. He looked the judge in the eye. "He has a home with me, sir."

"I understand you are taking care of him at this time. But don't you think he'd be better off with a real family instead of a single man and two older women? My niece and her husband can give him a loving home."

"David is a happy child and he wants to stay with his brothers and sisters."

The judge frowned. "It's my understanding that he has no blood kin, so how can you say they're brothers and sisters?"

"They've been together for a while and *they* consider themselves brothers and sisters."

"But the fact is they are of no blood kin. Therefore, the boy should have the opportunity to be in a home where he might have real siblings one day."

Hal Cramer broke into the conversation. "Mr. Hunter and I have discussed the situation, Your Honor. The children want to stay together. Mr. Hunter is pursuing his adoption of all five of them."

The judge frowned again. "What would a single man do with five children? As a judge, I would never approve of him adopting the children."

"So, it doesn't matter that the children love him and want to stay in the home he's providing for them?"

"I will say that I admire Mr. Hunter for taking on the responsibility of these orphans. But I feel his duty should come to an end when it's in the best interest of the child. To my way of thinking, their interest is best served when they're in a loving home with two parents, not with a single man and two older women."

Clay wanted to argue with the man, but he knew it wouldn't do any good. Instead, he blurted, "I have plans to marry, then my wife and I will continue to pursue the adoption of all the children."

As soon as the words were out of his mouth, he saw the shock on the faces of Hal and the judge. But their shock was not as much as his own for having said what he had.

"Then I guess there's nothing else to say." The judge turned and left the room by the door he had come through.

Hal glared at Clay. "Who are you planning on marrying?"

"When I figure that out, I'll let you know." He chuckled. "Now I better get outside and gather up the rest of the family. Thanks for all your help, Hal."

Before Hal had time to answer, Clay hurried out of the courtroom. He climbed in the wagon where the others had been waiting for him.

~ * ~

"Ma, Pa's coming back." Beetle shouted as he ran into the backyard where his mama was taking the wash off the line.

She dropped the sheet she'd folded into the basket, turned and took the baby out of the makeshift crib under the cottonwood tree. "Let's go see what your papa has to say."

Beetle nodded and headed back toward the front of the cabin. He waved frantically and his father waved back.

Virgie Mae took a seat on the big rock that served as a step into the cabin and waited. "I wonder why Matilda's not with him."

Beetle dropped to the ground beside her. "Maybe the sheriff wouldn't let her come back."

"I guess we'll see in a minute."

Virgie Mae walked up to them. "Well, unless she pulls somethin' 'tween now and evening, I guess it's all over."

"What do you mean?"

"The jury found her guilty of kidnapping and the judge give her sixteen years in prison."

"Sixteen years? Didn't she fight them?"

"She shore did. Kept sayin' how she would make the little girl talk and they should be thankful for that."

"What'd they say?"

"She had done a crime and it didn't matter for what reason, she had to pay for doin' it."

"Sixteen years is a long time. Are you shore you heard 'em right?"

"Yes, I heard 'em right." He smiled. "I was glad they was going to send her away."

"What are we gonna do now, Ezra?"

"I been thinking 'bout that on the way home. I decided that'll give us plenty of time to leave here and settle somewhere she'll never find us."

"Are you telling the truth?"

"I shore am. We'll go so far away that when she gets out of jail she'll never find us."

"Are you shore...?"

"Yeah, Vergie Mae, I is very shore."

"What if she can cast a spell on us from prison?"

"It won't work."

"How do you know?"

"She tried to cast a spell on the judge and the people in the court room, but it didn't work. She must have to be close enough to look people in the eye."

"How'd you know?"

"I waited around until they opened up the saloon and nothing out of the ordinary happened. She said she'd get them all, but they ignored her, and they all seem to be fine."

"Will they keep her in jail in Settlers Ridge for sixteen years?"

He shook his head. "They said the prison wagon would be around later today. They'll take her to a prison somewhere away from here."

Tears came into Virgie Mae's eyes. "I can't hardly believe we'll be free of Big Matilda."

"As soon as I make sure she's gone, we'll start planning to get out of here. I been thinkin' 'bout Colorado."

"That's a long way off. Does we have the money?"

"Not now, but I know she's got the money she's took from us and other people, too. I'll go to her cabin and find it. She ain't gonna need it for a long time and we shore can use it."

"I don't know, Ezra. Don't do nothing that'll make her mad at us."

"Don't worry." He looked at Beetle. "It'll feel good to be able to play without worryin' about your Aunt Matilda yelling at ya, won't it?"

Beetle grinned. "It shore will, Pa. I can't wait to leave here."

Virgie Mae stood. "I'll finish gittin' the dry clothes in, then we'll eat. I bet you're hungry."

"I am a little."

"Then wash up and I'll be in the house in a minute."

He nodded as she took the baby and went back to the clothesline.

~ * ~

Wilma pushed the door open and rolled her chair out on the front porch. "May I join you?"

Clay smiled. "You must have read my mind. I was thinking of coming in and asking you to join me."

"I took the liberty of asking Alice to bring you a cup of coffee and tea for me when I told her I was coming out to check on you. I hope you don't mind."

"I'm glad you did. My cup is empty."

Alice appeared with the drinks. "Now, don't stay out here too long, you two. You need your rest so you can work tomorrow, since we missed working today."

"We won't be long." Clay smiled at her. "Thanks for the coffee."

"You know you're welcome. Now, good night."

"Good night, Miss Alice."

Wilma waited until she was sure Alice had left, then she said, "Clay, we all noticed how quiet you've been since the trial. Did something happen you didn't expect?"

"It did, and I'm trying to figure out what to do about it."

"Miss Alice said the judge talked to you privately after the trial. Did that have anything to do with it?"

"It has everything to do with it, Wilma."

She frowned. "Is there anything I can do to help?"

"The only way you could help would be if you would marry me."

Wilma was so stunned she almost dropped her tea. "What?"

"I'm sorry, Wilma. I shouldn't have said that. I'm just frustrated." He sighed. "The judge reminded me that his niece and her husband want to adopt David. I had talked with Hal Cramer about it and thought she'd given up, but she hasn't, and I need to come up with a reason to keep her from getting him."

"Did you tell him the children didn't need to be separated?"

"I did. I even told him that we'd discussed the fact some people wanted to adopt some of them, and they voted they wanted to stay together. I didn't tell him this, but I promised the children I'd do everything in my power to see that they stayed together." He shook his head. "When Hal said some people were worried about them getting an education, I hired you to teach them. I even told him I'd adopt them myself if he thought that would help."

"I'm sure it would."

"Not according to the judge. He said since I didn't have a wife, I didn't stand a chance of adopting them."

"So what are you going to do?"

"I don't know, Wilma." He chuckled. "You wouldn't happen to know a woman who'd like to marry a stranger and adopt five children ranging from age four to twelve, would you?"

"I might." She didn't know why she said it, but it was out before she could stop herself.

Clay stared at her a moment, then smiled. "Yeah. I bet she's just my type. Kind of bossy, carries a gun like a man, has warts on her nose, is fifty years old, doesn't like kids and has a bum leg."

"You must be magic. You described her perfectly."

"I know it's a foolish notion. But I'm serious. If I found the right woman, I'm not against getting married, though I hadn't planned on such a thing this soon after my return to town." He shook his head again. "Of course, I hadn't planned on having five kids under my care, either."

"Life has a way of changing things on its own, when we least expect it."

"That's for sure." He smiled at her. "A year ago, I bet you never dreamed you'd not be working in the mercantile but be a schoolteacher for five orphans."

"You're right. But I did dream of one day being a schoolteacher. I thought I was too old to start doing anything like that."

"Old? I bet you're not even twenty."

"I'm twenty-one, not that you need to know that fact, Clay Hunter."

"Well, I'm twenty-eight. Not that you need to know that either." He drained his coffee cup. "Thank you for listening to me, Wilma. I feel a little better by talking about my dilemma."

"I know I didn't help you solve anything, but sometimes it helps to talk it out. Who knows? Something could work out yet."

"You're right." he grinned at her. "You could introduce me to the woman you have in mind as my future wife."

"Maybe you've already met her, Mr. Hunter." Wilma rolled her chair toward the door, knowing Clay was gazing at her.

"Wait a minute," he stood. "What do you mean, I may have met her?"

"I'll tell you this much. When you were listing what you thought she might look like, you got one thing right."

"What was that?"

"She has a bum leg." Without giving him time to answer, she rolled her chair inside and hurried down the hall to her room.

Thirty-six

"Miss Wilma, what in the world do you mean by hobbling in here to eat dinner without your chair?"

"I have to start walking around again sometime. I can't spend the rest of my life in that wheelchair."

"She stood up some in school," David said.

"She did, did she?"

"Yes, ma'am."

"David," Wilma said. "I know you and Mary are hungry. Let's go over there and wash your hands at the sink. The others will be in to eat shortly."

"Why do I have to wash here in the kitchen with Mary? Why can't I go wash with the others out there?"

"I guess because you've been going to school this morning and they've been working outside."

He frowned but said nothing else.

They washed their hands and were drying them when the others came through the door and the youngsters started taking their seats around the table. Clay stood back and frowned. "Why are you not in your chair, Wilma Lawson?"

"I'm fine."

"You don't look fine to me. Sit down before you fall down."

She gave him a hard look. "So, you're ordering me to sit down?"

He glanced at all the eyes that had turned toward him. "No, Miss Wilma. I'm asking you to please sit down. I don't want you to fall and reinjure yourself."

"Thank you for being concerned about me." She smiled at him and hobbled to a chair. She didn't want him to lose face in front of the children and the hired hand, so she added, "I'm sorry I was snappy. I will admit, my leg does hurt a little and I didn't want to admit I probably should have used my chair."

He took his seat. "One of us will go get it for you after we finish. We don't want you to feel so poorly that you can't teach your afternoon classes."

"Thank you, Mr. Clay. You're very thoughtful."

Alice spoke up. "I fried chicken, so there are four chicken legs. One for Mary, one for David and one for Mr. Clay. I guess you'll have to decide yourselves who gets the fourth one."

"Miss Wilma should get it," David said.

"Why do you think she should have it, David?"

"'Cause she's special, like Mr. Clay."

Everyone laughed, and Alice said, "I agree, David. Miss Wilma is special. Now, let's say our blessing and we'll pass the food around."

~ * ~

The hands had finished eating and left the kitchen. The rest were finishing their dessert when the sound of an arriving buggy filtered through the window. Clay wondered who would visit this time of the day. Before he could comment, Alice stood.

"I'll see who it is." She headed to the front door.

In a minute, she returned. "It's a man wearing a fancy suit and a derby hat. Maybe you should go to the door, Mr. Clay."

As Clay stepped outside, he recognized Hal Cramer. "Hello there."

"Hello, Clay." He wrapped his reins around the brake and climbed down.

"What brings you out this way, Hal?"

"I've got something important to discuss with you and it couldn't wait until you were back in town."

"Come inside. It's too hot to have a discussion out here."

Hal followed him into the house.

"We just finished dinner. Would you like something to drink?"

"I wouldn't mind."

"Good. Miss Alice made an awfully good cherry cobbler for dessert. How about a bowl?"

"That sounds even better. Marjorie makes me one every now and then because she knows it's my favorite."

"Good. Come on in the kitchen."

"Hello, Mr. Cramer," Wilma said when he came into the room.

He nodded and removed his hat. "Miss Lawson."

Clay introduced him first to Alice and Phoebe, then the children. After greetings, Clay said, "I offered Mr. Cramer some of your delicious cherry cobbler, Miss Alice. He has something to discuss with me and I thought we'd do it over the pie and coffee."

Phoebe stood. "I'll put Mary down for her nap, then David and I will be upstairs if you need us."

Before they left the room, Mary ran to Clay and threw her arms around his neck.

"It's fine, little darling. You go with Miss Phoebe and I'll come see you when Mr. Cramer and I finish our business."

She kissed his cheek, nodded and climbed down, then reached for Phoebe's hand.

David moved to Clay and touched his shoulder. "I'll help her take care of Mary, Mr. Clay. Don't worry."

"Thank you, David. I knew I could count on you."

Wilma started to stand. "The other children and I will go to the classroom and start our lessons, if you'll excuse us."

"Don't get up, Miss Wilma," Thomas said. "Mr. Clay didn't want you to try to walk, so I'll go get your chair."

She didn't argue. "Thank you, Thomas."

Soon only Clay and Hal were left in the kitchen with Alice. She looked at them. "Since I need to clean up in here, why don't you take Mr. Cramer to your office to talk, Mr. Clay? It'll be more private for you there and I'll get the pie and coffee up there to you."

"Thank you, Miss Alice." He turned to Hal. "Follow me."

As they started up the winding stairway, Hal said, "I don't understand, Clay. With that beautiful dining room we just passed, why were you all eating in the kitchen?"

"We eat dinner there because we come in from work dirty and sometimes smelly. We only wash our hands because we know after we eat we have to go back out to work. It's different at night. Miss Alice insists we clean up better and put on a clean shirt if necessary. Then we have supper in the dining room."

"It looks like Miss Alice has the place running smoothly."

"Just like a well-greased wagon wheel. I don't think I could do it without her." He opened the door to his office. "Come in and have a seat."

Alice came with the pie and coffee, served them, then left.

From his seat behind the desk, Clay said, "What's the important message you had for me, Hal?

Hal reached into his pocket and pulled out a paper. "I got this wire this morning and knew you had to see it today."

Clay took the wire and read it quickly. His heart lurched, and he knew Hal was right. This couldn't be ignored. "So the judge's niece says she's coming to Settlers Ridge to pick up David this Saturday."

"According to Judge Wallburg, she wants to get here before he leaves so he can finalize the adoption for her."

Clay pushed his pie aside. "What can I do to stop it, Hal?"

"If you were serious about getting married. I suggest you do it right away. It seems to be the only way."

"You sound like you think I should keep the children."

"I didn't think so when I first met you, but I've changed my mind."

"Why?"

"I thought you may have wanted to get your hands on this ranch and the kids were a way to do it. Then I started watching you."

"What do you mean?"

"It was a lot of little things, then the deal with Big Matilda happened. I knew you must care when you went after her. The clincher was when the little girl ran to you tonight. I saw how much she loved you. I also saw how David spoke to you with admiration in his eyes for you, too. I've always been told you can trust somebody a child and a dog trust. There was no dog around, but the trust those children have for you is undeniable. It was not only in their actions, but it was in their eyes. Whether you know it or not, the way you feel about them is in your eyes, too."

Clay sighed. "You're right, Hal. I'm crazy about all five of them. I promised them I'd do anything I could to keep them from being separated. It hurts to know they'll think I lied, but I can't think of anything I can do to stop this from happening."

"What about getting married?"

"To whom?"

"Think about it, Clay. You're a smart man. Come up with something like giving some woman fifty dollars to marry you until you adopt the children, then if the marriage doesn't work out, divorce her."

Clay frowned. "I don't know..."

"As I said, think about it." Hal finished his pie and stood. "I'll get back to the office and fill out those adoption papers to send to a judge, just in case you get it all figured out."

After seeing Cramer to the door, Clay went back to his office. He had some serious thinking to do and that was the best place to do it.

~ * ~

Juliette and her mother were looking at the material in the mercantile when the bell jangled and a tall cowboy walked in. "Do you know that man, Mother?" Juliette whispered.

"It's Virgil Danforth," Marjorie whispered back.

"Do you know him?"

"Not well. I do know he came here to find his half-brother and they have a ranch south of town. Why do you ask, Juliette?"

"He was eating at the hotel when Daddy took us for supper the other night. He was at the cafè when we ate lunch there today and now he's in here. It's as if he's following us."

"Hello, Virgil," Spencer called out. "How can I help you?"

"I need some tobacco for my pipe."

"Sure. Got it right here at the counter."

Juliette picked up the bolt of fabric with the little white and yellow flowers on a green background. "This is what I want. I'll take it to the counter to be cut."

Marjorie took the bolt of black with little white dots and followed her.

At the counter, Spencer said, "So you decided, ladies?"

"We did."

"Have you met Mrs. Cramer and her daughter, Virgil?"

"I've seen them about town, but we haven't been formally introduced."

"Then, let me remedy that."

"So, your husband is the lawyer here in town. I've seen his shingle."

"Yes. We've been here since he finished law school all those years ago."

"I think that's wonderful. I always dreamed of being a lawyer in a nice town like Settlers Ridge."

Juliette lifted an eyebrow. "To be a lawyer you have to study the law."

He smiled at her. "I understand that, Miss Juliette. As a matter of fact, I had finished law school when I had to go west in search of my brother."

She was puzzled. If this man was a lawyer, why was he living on a ranch? "But you're a rancher."

"My brother, Shawn, was too young to run a ranch alone. Therefore, I chose to put my career aside to help him. Now that he's matured some, I've been thinking of going back into practicing law, at least part-time."

"If you do, I'm sure my husband would be happy to talk with you. Since the town has grown so much, he's overworked and could use some help."

"Then I'll make an appointment to talk with him soon." He handed Spencer money for his tobacco. "It was nice meeting you, ladies. Hopefully, I'll see you again."

Juliette didn't voice it, but as she watched him walk out the door, she couldn't help hoping he was right. Then the thought crossed her mind that it would be ironic if she ended up with a small-town lawyer, just like her parents had always hoped she'd do. Shaking the thought away, she said, "Please cut me a dress length of this material, Spencer."

Thirty-seven

Midnight had come and gone, and Clay was still in his office. He'd managed to go back to work after Hal Cramer left, but he couldn't get the blasted wire off his mind. Why did the judge's niece think she'd be a better parent then he was? He didn't have to think long before he knew the answer: she had a husband and he didn't have a wife. She could give David a real family and all he could give him was the fact that he was a part of their motley family.

Family. When did he start thinking of the group as a family? He didn't have an answer for that. The fact had crept up on him and had lodged in his mind without him even thinking it through.

It had been hard to get through supper, but somehow, he managed. He did excuse himself early and had gone to his section of the house. He knew if he would be able to come up with an answer for his dilemma, it would be here in this room.

Tonight, he'd run so many scenarios in his mind he couldn't distinguish them. He'd thought of everything from hiring someone to marry him to packing up the kids and running away. But he knew he could never do any of those things. None of them would be fair to the children. Above everything, he wanted to be fair to them.

He knew he needed to talk to somebody who could help him clear his mind. The first person who came to mind was Wilma. He wondered if she was asleep. Then he answered his own thought. *Of course, she's asleep. It's the middle of the night.* He should be asleep, too. But he wasn't. He wasn't even sleepy.

He got up from his desk and poured himself a shot of whiskey. Clay wasn't much of a drinker, but tonight he felt he needed the jolt the alcohol would give him.

Downing it, he set the glass aside and stared at it for a minute. It was a fancy heavy glass and he wondered how many times Mr. Anderson had been seated at this desk trying to work out a problem.

He closed his eyes for a minute and a thought drifted across his mind. *You know the answer to your problem, Clay Hunter, so why are you avoiding facing it? It's simple. You have to get married and you must do it this week.*

But who am I going to get to marry me? You know that, too, you fool. You don't have to go looking for some stranger. You know who you want and from the little hints she gave you, she wants you, too.

Didn't she say you'd met the woman who would marry you? Didn't she say the woman had a bum leg?

He jumped up from his chair. Aloud, he muttered, "How could I have been so dense? Before I talk myself out of it, I'm going to ask her right now."

He was down the stairs and half-way through the parlor when he stubbed his toe on one of the tables, making it almost fall over. He grabbed it, but not in time. One of the trinkets on it fell to the floor with a crash. He cursed and wondered why he hadn't brought a lamp with him. Then he decided he'd gone too far to turn back and get one. He was going down the hall to Wilma's room before it crossed his mind that he would probably scare her if he didn't slow down.

At her door, he knocked. There was no sound from inside.

He pushed it open. "Wilma, it's Clay," he said in a whisper.

She didn't answer.

He said her name again. This time a little louder.

She stirred. "What's the matter, Clay?"

"I need to talk to you."

"Why?"

"It's important, Wilma. May I come in?"

"Of course."

In the dimness, he saw her sit up.

"What time is it?"

"I'm not sure. It's somewhere around midnight."

"What in the world is wrong?" She started to get out of bed.

"I promise. Everything here is fine. I just have to tell you something."

She fell back against the pillows. "Then tell me."

"I want us to go to town tomorrow and get married."

"What?" Her voice sounded startled.

"I wish I had time to court and woo you, but I don't. We need to get married right away so we can save our family."

"Clay, I don..."

"Please don't say no, Wilma. The judge's niece is coming this weekend to take David away. Since I have to get married, I don't want to marry some stranger that I have no feelings for. I think the world of you, Wilma. I may already be in love with you. If not now, I know I will be soon. I don't want to be tied to any woman but you."

"All right, Clay."

"I know we can have a happy life together. If you feel anything at all for me, please say...what did you say?"

"I said, all right. I will marry..."

The door burst open and Alice entered carrying a lamp. "Clay Hunter! What are you doing in Miss Wilma's room this time of night?" She sat the lamp on the bureau, crossed her arms and glared at him.

"I needed to talk to her."

"That's a likely story, since it's this time of night."

"He's telling the truth, Miss Alice. I'm as shocked as you are, but I think things will be fine. Clay just asked me to marry him and I said yes."

Confusion covered her face. "You mean...he actually...you said yes..."

"She said yes, Alice!" He turned to her, grabbed her in his arms and whirled her around. "I'm going to get married and it's going to be to Wilma. Isn't that wonderful?"

"For heaven's sake, Clay Hunter. Put me down."

"I'm sorry, Miss Alice. I'm just excited. I can't believe she's going to marry me, and I can't help being excited about it."

"That's all well and good. But do we have to celebrate it in the middle of the night?"

Wilma laughed. "She's right. If we're going to get married tomorrow, maybe we should get some sleep."

"You're right." He moved to the bed and took her outstretched out hand. "Thank you for saying yes. I promise you won't regret it."

"I don't think I will either."

He leaned down and kissed her on the lips.

"Now, stop that," Alice said. "There'll be time for that later."

"You're right. There'll be lots of time later. But I need one more kiss from my fiancée." He leaned down and kissed her again.

Alice took hold of his arm. "Do I need to escort you to your room?"

"No, ma'am. I'm going." He managed to lean down and steal one more kiss. He then turned and Alice shooed him out the door.

She looked at a smiling Wilma. "I knew this would eventually happen. I just didn't know it'd happen in the middle of the night."

"I didn't think so either, Miss Alice. But I'm glad it did."

"I'm waiting in the hall for you to escort me to the staircase, Miss Alice."

"Good rest of the night, Miss Wilma." She picked up the lamp. "I'm coming. I want to make sure you hightail it up those stairs."

They went down the hall together and when they were out of earshot, he said, "I need to talk to you a minute, Miss Alice. I want you to know what's going on with us."

She gave him a puzzled look. "Do you need a cup of coffee to tell me?"

"That would be good."

"Then come on into the kitchen. We'll talk there."

~ * ~

In the morning, the children looked at Clay and Wilma with disbelief showing on their faces. Finally, Luke said, "What does this mean for us?"

Clay smiled at him. "It means we're going to be a real family."

"I thought when we voted to stay together that made us a real family."

"It did, Sarah."

"Then, why do you have to get married to make us a family?" Thomas asked.

Clay looked frustrated, so Wilma reached over and touched his hand. "May I say something?"

He nodded.

"I think you should be told the truth. The judge doesn't like the fact that Clay isn't married and thinks you'll be better off in homes where there is a mother and father. So, to make sure you all stay together, Clay and I want to get married and show him there are a mother and father in the home where you belong. We want to adopt all five of you and then there will be no way anyone can ever try to take one of you away again."

Sarah was the first to smile. "Does that mean you really want to adopt us so we can all stay together?"

"Yes, Sarah. That's exactly what we mean."

She looked at the others. "Do you realize that means we have real parents? We'll grow up here with them acting as our mother and father. Nobody will ever mistreat us again."

"Does this mean my name will become Thomas Hunter?"

Clay nodded. "If you want it to be Hunter, it will be. In fact, it would please me if all of you want your last name to be Hunter."

David turned his head to the side. "When I'm David Hunter, can I call you Daddy Clay?"

"You most certainly can, David."

Mary jumped up from her seat beside Sarah, ran to the settee where Clay and Wilma sat. She kissed Wilma's cheek, then turned and threw her arms around Clay's neck and kissed him several times.

"It looks like our little sister approves," Sarah said. "And so do I. Yes, I want my name to be Sarah Hunter."

In a minute, the room burst into chatter as they each tried out their new last name. Clay looked over at Wilma, and she would have sworn she saw love in his eyes. She gave him back the same look.

Two hours later, the house was abuzz. Clay and the boys had helped John do the morning work around the barn and feed the animals. Clay had sent Red to Settlers Ridge to ask Grace and Lance to bring the preacher to the ranch house as close to ten o'clock as possible. Phoebe and Alice had started cooking and baking. Sarah and Mary were in Wilma's room helping her get ready.

"I wish I had a new dress to get married in, but there just isn't time to make one, or even to buy one."

"I think you look beautiful, Miss Wilma. That blue brings out your eyes. Besides, I bet Mr. Clay won't care what you're wearing."

"Thank you, honey." She smiled at Sarah. "You make me feel better about what I'm wearing."

"Would you like for me to put your hair up? I'm pretty good at that."

"I'd love for you to." Wilma took a seat on the stool in front of the bureau.

"I'm so nervous I probably would make a mess of it."

Sarah smiled. "I doubt that."

Mary moved beside the stool and looked up at Wilma. She had a smile on her face.

Wilma reached down and touched her cheek. "We need to find some flowers so you can be my flower girl. Would you like that?"

Mary nodded.

"I know where there's a big patch of pretty wildflowers. When I get Miss Wilma's hair done, you and I will go pick some for her to carry when she gets married, Mary. Would you like to do that?"

Mary nodded again.

"We might be able to work some of the flowers into Miss Wilma's hair when we get back."

There was a knock on the door.

"Come in," Wilma called.

Grace came through the door carrying Kathrine in one arm and a huge bag in the other. "Could you help me a little?"

Sarah ran to her. "I'll help you, Miz Gentry."

"Good." She put Kathrine in Sarah's arms.

Wilma stood. "Oh, Grace. It's good to see you. I was afraid you wouldn't be able to come."

"Of course I'd come. You don't think I'd let my brother get married without me being here, do you?"

"I'm glad you said that with a smile on your lips." Wilma smiled back. "I hope you approve of my marrying him."

"I approve, though I am confused. I had no idea there were romantic feelings between you."

"It happened kind of fast."

"Well, you can tell me all about it later. The preacher is on his way, so let's get you dressed."

"I know it doesn't look like much, but I have on the best dress I own, Grace."

"I figured as much. What do you think I have in this bag?"

"Not a new dress."

"Nope. It's used, but I didn't think you'd had time to make one or even to buy one. Since you and I are about the same size, I brought my wedding dress for you to wear."

"I don't know what to say."

"You don't have to say anything. Now that Kathrine seems to like Sarah, let's get you ready before she realizes it's about time for her to eat."

"She's a beautiful baby, Miz Gentry. Do you mind if Mary and I play with her on the bed?"

"Of course not." Grace pulled the dress out of the bag. "Let's see how this is going to fit you."

The dress was a perfect fit. "Oh, Wilma. You look beautiful. All you need now is a bouquet."

"Sarah and Mary were going to pick some flowers for me whenever she finished combing my hair."

"That sounds good." She turned to Sarah. "Why don't you finish her hair, then go pick the flowers? I'll feed Kathrine while you're gone."

Sarah looked surprised. "You mean you don't mind if I fix her hair?"

"I don't mind at all. You're doing a better job than I can. Fixing hair has never been one of my talents." She moved to the bed and sat beside Mary. "She's smiling at you, Mary. I think she likes you."

Mary grinned and nodded.

Grace touched her cheek. "You're a sweet little girl. No wonder Clay is so crazy about you."

Mary grinned wider, then reached out and patted Grace's hand.

It wasn't long until Sarah stood back. "How do you like it?"

"I love it," Wilma said. "You did a beautiful job."

"You sure did, Sarah."

"Thank both of you." She turned to Mary. "Let's go get the flowers for Miss Wilma."

When they had gone, Grace said, "Wilma, I'm baffled. I know you had feelings for Clay, but I never dreamed they were deep enough for marriage."

"I care a great deal for him, Grace."

"I understand that, but..."

"Please, Grace. Just accept the fact that Clay asked me to marry him and I said yes."

"But why such a rushed marriage?"

There was a knock on the door. "Come in," Wilma called.

Alice entered. "Oh my, don't you look pretty!"

"Thank you. Grace was kind enough to lend me her dress."

"That was nice of you." She smiled at Grace. "I just came to let you know Preacher Ellsworth and his mother have arrived."

"Sarah and Mary have gone to pick me a bouquet. I'll be down as soon as they get back."

"And when I finish feeding Kathrine," Grace interjected. "I don't want her squalling out during the ceremony because she's hungry. This little lady had a big set of lungs in her."

"I'm sure everyone will appreciate that. I'll inform them."

"Miss Alice."

"Yes, Miss Wilma?"

"Is Clay...I mean, have you seen him?"

"Don't worry. He's as nervous as you are." She walked over and patted Wilma's arm, then headed for the door. "You'll both be fine. Now, relax and enjoy this day. A girl only gets married once, you know."

"If she's lucky," Wilma muttered.

The girls returned with an armful of flowers. Sarah chose a few blue and yellow ones to put in Wilma's hair. They tied the rest with a yellow ribbon for her to carry.

Then Sarah said, "The boys are coming to escort you to the parlor. Mary and I are going to go and stand with Mr. Clay and wait for you to get there. He wants all of us to be a part of the wedding."

"I think that's lovely." Grace stood. "Kathrine is through. She and I will go with the girls and get a front row seat."

As they went out the door, the boys came in. "Are you ready, Miss Wilma?" Luke asked.

She could tell he was nervous. "Yes, fellows. I'm ready. Let's go get this wedding started."

Thirty-eight

Alice and Phoebe had cooked a delicious dinner, including a wedding cake decorated with flowers. The hands had set tables up on the front lawn under the largest oak tree. The celebration lasted a couple of hours, then Clay and Wilma thanked everyone for coming. She changed clothes and when she was dressed, they loaded the five children in the family wagon and headed to town. They hoped Hal Cramer would be in his office when they got there.

Clay reached over and took Wilma's hand. Squeezing it, he said, "You've made me a happy man."

"I'm glad, because I'm a happy woman."

"I'm sorry I can't take you on a fancy honeymoon."

"I don't need to go on a fancy honeymoon, Clay. I just hope you'll never regret marrying me."

"There's something I need to tell you, Wilma. I should have told you before we got married. But to be honest, I was afraid you wouldn't marry me if you knew the whole truth."

She gave him a hard look. "You're not going to tell me that you're already married and have children with her, are you?"

He chuckled. "No, Wilma. I have no wife except you, and I have no children except the five here in this wagon."

"Then whatever it is, I can handle it. I just didn't want to have to fight some woman for you."

He laughed out loud. "Oh, Wilma. We're going to have a good life."

She smiled and moved closer to him and they didn't talk again until they pulled up in front of Hal Cramer's office.

"Children, I want you to wait here in the wagon until I make sure Mr. Cramer is here."

Mary ran toward the back and held up her arms.

He glanced at Wilma.

"I don't think it'd hurt to take her, Clay."

"Come on, little darling." He reached for her and glanced at the others.

"One of us will come and get the rest of you soon."

Inside the office, Clay encountered a man he hadn't met before. "Hello. I'd like to see Mr. Cramer, please."

"Virgil Danforth, what are you doing behind that desk?"

"Hello, Miss Wilma. I'm helping out here part time."

"As Clay said, we need to see Hal Cramer, please."

"Sure. I'll tell him you're here."

The rest of the children were brought inside, and they all gathered in Hal's office. "Now," he said from behind his desk. "I asked Virgil to be here because he's well versed in what we're up against. In fact, he has connections in St. Louis that can help us expedite the adoption."

"That's wonderful," Wilma said.

"There's one thing we need to get straight before I send these papers in."

"What's that, Hal?"

"I need to have a last name to put down for the children. I assumed it would probably be Hunter for the two smaller children, but the three older ones may want to retain their original names."

"Hunter will be Mary's name for sure," Clay said. He glanced at David. "How about you, son? Do you want your last name to be Hunter?"

"Yes, I do. I want to be your son."

Clay glanced at the others. Thomas spoke. "We talked it over on the way here and we all decided we'd like for our last name to be Hunter, too. I hope you don't mind."

"I don't mind at all, Thomas. In fact, this pleases me more than you can imagine. It's what I wanted, too, but I wanted you to make the decision."

"Then it's settled," Hal said. "I'll put Hunter down for all of you and we'll get the paperwork in the mail this afternoon."

Wilma frowned. "Won't it take longer than this weekend to process everything? I know the judge's niece will be here then."

"We won't worry about that, Miss...I mean, Miz Wilma," Virgil said. "I've already wired the bureau that takes care of adoptions. We can handle the entire thing by telegraph. The paper will just confirm it when they receive it."

"Thank you for everything, Hal. You, too, Mr. Danforth."

"Please call me Virgil. I'm pleased you let me help Hal handle your case. I feel sure everything is going to work out. In fact, we plan to get in touch with the judge just as soon as we send the wires. I'm sure he'll inform his niece there is no longer any way she could adopt...uh...any child in Settlers Ridge."

They all left the lawyer's office with happiness showing in their eyes.

~ * ~

As they started up the winding staircase, Clay glanced at Wilma. "How's your ankle holding out?"

"It's a little sore but it'll be fine."

"Want me to carry you upstairs?"

"No, Clay. I can walk."

"What if I want to carry you?"

"In that case..."

"Say no more." He swooped her up in his arms.

"I was kidding, Clay."

"Well, I'm not. I like carrying my wife."

When they entered his room, she muttered, "Wow. This place is fancy."

"I assume it was Anderson's room." He chuckled. "Now, it's ours."

Clay could tell she was nervous and, though he wanted nothing more than to take her in his arms and make love to her, he knew he should put her mind at ease before anything happened between them.

"Wilma, I told you there was something I needed to tell you about me before you commit completely to this marriage."

She frowned. "You sound so serious, Clay."

"It is serious." He took a deep breath. "Let's go sit on that fancy couch and I'll explain everything."

They seated themselves and he reached for her hand. "I know you know I left home when I was a young teenager. I had taken the last beating I intended to take from my drunken father. I hated to leave Mama and Grace, but I was afraid if I didn't get out, he'd kill me or I'd end up killing him."

"I didn't know it was that bad, Clay."

"It was pretty rough, but at least he didn't beat Grace like he did me. He did occasionally hit Mama, though. That's when I thought about killing him." He sighed. "I didn't intend to stay gone so long, but things didn't change here until the fire."

"Why didn't you come back then?"

"I'll get to that. When I first left here, I thought I'd go to Colorado. I'd heard about the gold mines there, but that didn't work out. I ended up taking any job I could find. I worked in saloons sweeping floors and on ranches mucking out stalls. Nothing brought in enough money for me to make a decent living. I was only surviving, and not very well at that. Ten years slipped by and nothing good had happened for me. Then I met Stud Reynolds. He was a two-bit gambler with big dreams. He talked a big game and like a fool I fell for it."

"I thought you worked for the government."

"I'll get to that, too." He smiled at her. "I joined Stud and a couple of other men who were down on their luck. It wasn't long until I was doing a little gambling. Occasionally I'd win, but most of the time I lost. I was soon in debt to Stud and that was when things went south for me."

"What do you mean?"

"Stud talked me into helping him and his friends rob a bank. I knew it wasn't right and I told him I didn't want to do it. It was then I learned what kind of man he was. He said if I didn't do as he asked, he'd kill me. I knew he meant what he said. So I went with the gang to this little town I don't even remember the name of now. It was somewhere in Dakota Territory.

"Well, things didn't go like they'd planned. I was stationed outside to have the horses ready when they came out. The thing was, the sheriff happened to go in the bank while they were sticking it up. Reynolds was shot and killed. One of his men was wounded and the other was arrested. Of course, they arrested me because when I saw what was happening, I tried to run. At the trial, I was sentenced the same as the other man. Twenty years in prison."

"Oh, Clay. I'm sorry."

"Don't be, Wilma. I deserved it." He smiled at her. "I was branded an outlaw, which I was. I served three years of my twenty-year term. Then one day the warden sent for me. I was offered a chance to get out of prison if I'd do a special job for the government. Of course, I jumped at the chance. That job lasted longer than I ever thought it would. I was only released from it the day before I headed back to Settlers Ridge." He gave her a small smile. "I think you know the rest of my story from there."

"I also know you came to town now and then because of the wildflowers Grace would find on your mother's grave. Why didn't you let your sister know you were here when you came?"

"I couldn't, Wilma. I was working for the government and I was under strict orders not to contact any of my family or friends. They always had the threat of prison hanging over my head and probably still do since I'm still under that order. It's possible it will be there for the rest of my life."

"So, you're telling me you've been an outlaw, as well as a respected government worker."

"Yes, Wilma, I am. I'm also telling you this because I didn't want anything about my life while I was away to be a secret to you." He took a deep breath. "I also wanted you to know before anything happened between us tonight, so if you don't want to be married to a former outlaw, you can get an annulment of this marriage."

"I appreciate you telling me about this, Clay. But it only proves to me what a wonderful man you are. Nobody, not your sister, or her family, or our children, or your hands or Alice or Phoebe or anyone else in or around Settlers Ridge, will ever know about this. Only you and I will know." Her voice fell to a whisper. "I think it's kind of exciting to be married to an outlaw."

Clay looked at her and despite anything he could do, his eyes misted. He knew at that moment he loved this woman more than any words could ever say. Reaching for her, he whispered, "Are you sure, my love?"

She turned her face to him. "I've never been surer of anything in my life, my husband."

He pulled her to him and began kissing her. "Oh, Wilma. I'm going to have a wonderful life with my beautiful wife."

She kissed him back and smiled as he stood, lifted her in his arms and headed to the bed. "And I'm in for a wonderful life with my outlaw."

Epilogue

After church, the first spring dinner on the grounds was taking place. The four women who had been friends since childhood sat under one of the oak trees with their babies snuggled in their laps or playing nearby.

Amelia Wainwright, big with her second child, watched her toddler son, Aaron, as he played with little Mary Hunter. The fact they couldn't talk to each other didn't matter. They had their own way of communicating.

Grace Gentry held baby Kathrine in her arms because she was a little fussy. She was having trouble getting a tooth to come through her gum.

Nelda Barrington held the newest baby of the group, Jesse, who was asleep.

Wilma, the last to marry, had started out with a ready family. She and her husband, Clay, had adopted five orphans and their youngest, Mary, was unable to speak. But that hadn't deterred Mary from making friends and playing with Aaron.

Wilma glanced around to check on her other children and saw Sarah with Benita Wagner. The girls were near the same age and had become good friends. She was happy for her. Benita's mother was married to Doctor Sheldon Wagner, who had adopted Esther's two children and they had taken his last name.

David, her youngest son, had joined a group of boys his age who had gotten together to play a game of ball.

Her two older boys, Luke and Thomas, were hanging out under another tree with Teddy Olsen, son of the hotel owners and Joel Wagner. Wilma had a sneaking suspicion they were all eyeing the twittering young girls who had gathered at the swings.

"Well, my friend," Amelia broke into Wilma's thoughts. "Life has turned out just like I wanted it to. We're all married and living in Settlers Ridge and we're raising our children to be friends. Isn't it wonderful?"

"It is, but at one time I was afraid it wouldn't work out."

"Why not, Grace?" Nelda asked.

"Well, when you married Spencer and moved to the military fort, I thought we'd lost you for sure."

Nelda laughed. "I thought I'd always be a military wife and look at me now. Running a general store with a former army major, and we're both happy doing it."

"We're all glad to have you back," Amelia said.

Nelda pointed her finger at Grace. "I'm glad to be back, but I have to admit, when I came home and found you getting ready to marry my brother, I almost fainted."

Grace laughed. "I almost fainted when he asked me to marry him, too."

"I was concerned when Wilma's folks sold their ranch and moved to Texas," Amelia said. "I thought we'd lost her for sure."

"I was concerned myself," Wilma said. "I'm so glad I was able to talk my father into letting me come back to Settlers Ridge."

"If he hadn't let you, I don't know who I would have ended up with as a sister-in-law." Grace laughed. "Speaking of surprises. Isn't it strange the way certain people end up with each other? I was taken aback when Juliette Cramer showed up at church with Virgil Danforth last winter."

"You're right." Wilma shook her head. "Her father told Clay they plan a summer wedding."

Nelda chuckled. "She's such a different woman when she comes into the store that I'm actually beginning to like her."

"She sure had a turnaround for some reason. Something made her stop trying to separate Lance and me."

Wilma laughed. "Maybe it was those stints in jail."

"Or maybe it was her spending time with Big Matilda."

They all laughed. Then Wilma asked, "Is Kathy still working out well at the store, Nelda?"

"She's great. But I think we may have to look for someone else to work there in the future."

Wilma frowned. "Why?"

"She's spending a lot of time with Ward Keller. Spencer and I talked about it and we both think they're getting pretty serious."

"Do you mind?" Amelia asked.

"Not at all. I think the world of her and want her to be happy. I even invited her to join us here, but she's over there with Ward and it looks like they're having a good time."

Preacher Ellsworth called for attention and asked that families get together. The people began moving around. Wilma smiled as Clay walked up beside her followed by the four older children. Mary saw him, dropped the toy she had and ran to him with her arms up. He lifted her into his arms as David slipped his hand into Wilma's. She smiled at the other children and her heart filled with gratitude. Not just for the family they'd created, but for the one they would be adding to.

She hadn't told Clay yet, but she was sure she would be presenting him with a sixth child by winter. There was no doubt in her mind he'd be thrilled with the news. If ever a man had been born on this earth to be a daddy, it was Clay Hunter. That thought made her heart swell with pride.

Meet Agnes Alexander

Agnes Alexander has published hundreds of short stories and articles and has had over 50 books published. In 2011, she decided to concentrate on writing what she most likes to read, Western Historical Romance. *Wilma's Outlaw* is her sixth western with Wings.

A life-long resident of North Carolina, she counts traveling as one of her passions. She has visited 48 of the 50 States and says Alaska and Hawaii are on her bucket list, but she says getting older has slowed her traveling somewhat. Of course, she loves to read, but tries to limit herself to one or two books a week. Besides traveling and reading, Agnes enjoys jewelry making, watching old movies, playing with her cat, Victoria, and spending time with her family.

She can be contacted at her website:
www.agnesalexander.com.

Other Works From The Pen Of Agnes Alexander

Valissa's Home – After her brother gambles away Heartsong, Valissa's home, she learns a giant of a cowboy now owns it and expects her to move out in three weeks.

Opal's Faith - Though her family has been forced to move to Arizona, Opal has faith her father, with the help of a hired hand, will make a home for them out of the rundown ranch.

Ulla's Courage - After losing her home and the mercantile, it takes courage for Ulla to give up her life in Independence and marry a stranger who is headed to Oregon with his two children.

Zelda's Guilt - Feeling guilty because an accident took her father's life and left her stepmother disabled, Zelda tries to care for her siblings and save their small ranch.

Nelda's Homecoming - Thinking her husband has a mistress, Nelda returns to her hometown planning to get a divorce, but she doesn't count on him being determined to stop her.

Letter to Our Readers

Enjoy this book?

You can make a difference

As an independent publisher, Wings ePress, Inc. does not have the financial clout of the large New York Publishers. We can't afford large magazine spreads or subway posters to tell people about our quality books.

But, we do have something much more effective and powerful than ads. We have a large base of loyal readers.

Honest Reviews help bring the attention of new readers to our books.

If you enjoyed this book, we would appreciate it if you would spend a few minutes posting a review on the site where you purchased this book or on the Wings ePress, Inc. webpages at: https://wingsepress.com/

Visit Our Website

For The Full Inventory
Of Quality Books:

Wings ePress.Inc
https://wingsepress.com/

Quality trade paperbacks and downloads
in multiple formats,
in genres ranging from light romantic comedy
to general fiction and horror.
Wings has something for every reader's taste.
Visit the website, then bookmark it.
We add new titles each month!

Wings ePress Inc.
3000 N. Rock Road
Newton, KS 67114

www.ingramcontent.com/pod-product-compliance
Lightning Source LLC
Chambersburg PA
CBHW070637100726
47907CB00007B/2013